How Deep Is Your Love?

Jade Royal

© **2018**
Published by *Miss Candice Presents*

OTHER WORKS BY JADE ROYAL

Love is Worth The Sacrifice
(Completed Series)
Two Halves of a Broken Heart

<u>CHAPTER ONE</u>

The excruciating pain that pierced through her body jolted her into awareness. Her eyes popped open from her deep slumber. She clutched at her stomach. Dread creeped into her heart before crashing into her soul. Charm Bradley had felt this pain before. Three times. To be exact. Her body began to tremble as she slowly sat up. The pain made her grimace but she pushed through and sat up completely. Tears welled in her eyes as she reached for the lamp next to the bed. The bedroom was washed in the soft light from the lamp. Fear clutched at her and she didn't want to look but she didn't have a choice. Slowly looking down, she let out a suffocated squeal. Blood coated her thighs and spots of blood clots were on the bed between her legs.

"Not again," She breathed. "Please not again." Her shoulders shook as she began to cry silently. Reaching for her cell phone, she wiped her runny nose. The bed was empty next to her and it was past 7 in the evening. She'd decided to take a nap in the first place because she felt feverish. She expected that her husband would have been home by now, but their house was completely quiet. Pressing the dial button on her cell she called her husband. It rang ten whole times before finally going to voicemail. Knowing she couldn't wait on her husband to finally call her back she hung up and called an ambulance. Maybe there was a chance she could save the pregnancy. Losing another baby, she didn't know what to do now. Her body was physically drained, and she was mentally and emotionally suffocated.

Clenching her teeth through the pain she called an ambulance. She couldn't even say the words she needed to say so the EMT's would understand what she needed. Her mind couldn't transport the words to her mouth to formulate complete sentences. But they didn't need to hear more. They were sending her help. Ending that call, Charm tried calling her husband again. It rang out before going to voicemail. This time she left a message.

"Hey Terrell, it's me. Something…something happened. I'm going to the hospital. I really-really need you." She left it at that and just ended the call. So there she lay in a pool of her own blood waiting for the ambulance to come.

****

"I'm sorry Charm," The doctor said entering her room. "You are miscarrying." Charm sat there stoically. Tears painted her face but that was the only thing that suggested she had emotions. She didn't talk or even look at the doctor. She should have known this would happen again. After the last three times why should this one be any different?

"When can I go home?" Charm asked finally. The doctor was silent for a moment forcing Charm to look at her.

"What's the problem?" Charm asked. After a miscarriage she got a checkup, some medicine then she was free to go. She did not want to stay here longer than necessary, wallowing in the fact that the baby her husband wanted so badly was gone. Again.

"Charm you haven't passed the baby completely. Seen as you were about 4 months along we have to dilate your cervix and remove the rest of the baby from your uterus." Charm just stared at her. She began to shake her head.

"This is difficult for you Charm. I can get that and I emphasize. But the baby has to be completely removed so you can remain healthy and go back to trying to have another baby."

"So what happens?" Charm asked. In all her miscarriages, this has never happened to her.

"I can either give you some pills to make your body expel the baby, or I can go in surgically. Even though the baby is small, the pills will make you feel like you're giving birth Charm. Surgically I can put you under then clean out your uterus and that would be it." Charm sunk down into the bed. She didn't know what to do. But feeling like she was giving birth when she truly wasn't would break her completely.

"Put me under," She whispered.

"Charm is there anyone we can call for you? You shouldn't be going through this alone." Charm looked at the doctor.

"You're right. I shouldn't." Charm didn't know what was worse. Having to go under to have her baby removed from her uterus, or the fact that she had to do it alone since her husband was missing.

"I just want to get this over with," Charm said. "So I can go home." The doctor grimaced and nodded.

Soon Charm was given a drug that put her to sleep immediately. Then as if only 15 minutes had passed, she woke up again staring at the ceiling. Her body was racked with pain and she could barely move. The doctor came into view.

"I know you're in pain," She said softly. "I put some painkiller in the IV. You should start feeling it soon."

"Can't I just have some medicine to take home? I want to go home." The doctor clasped her hands in front of her.

"Unfortunately Charm I want to keep you overnight. Tomorrow morning you can go home with medicine but tonight I want you here under watchful eyes so your body can start healing."

"What? You think I'm gonna hurt myself?" Charm asked hotly. The doctor didn't respond, but she rubbed Charm's arm.

"Get some sleep honey."

"I want to see my baby," Charm said suddenly. She could tell the doctor didn't think it was a good idea but she didn't say so.

"Show me," Charm demanded. "I want to see." The doctor left the room and came back ten minutes later with a kidney basin. Charm fought through her pain to sit up. But she crumbled back down immediately when she saw the fetus in clumps and bloody in the small basin. She fell onto her back and just wept silently. Even when she closed her eyes she would never be able to forget what her fetus looked like outside her body. But it wasn't like she was ever going to be able to see what a normal baby looked like. She was a woman that was denied the basic natural function of a woman's body. Charm turned over, hiding her face from the doctor as her silent tears soaked the pillow beneath her head.

CHAPTER TWO

Terrell Robinson finally cut his phone back on. He was finished with his last clients for the day and he was exhausted. After his wife called him three times that day, he didn't want to be bothered anymore so he cut his phone off. He loved Charm to death. She was practically heaven on earth. His fellow coworkers envied him for being able to have a beautiful woman like her. She waited hand and foot on him, and she was seemingly the perfect wife. But then no one was ever perfect were they? They were married for five years and for three of those years she couldn't get pregnant, and when she finally did, they always lost the pregnancy. So much for being the perfect wife. He wasn't falling out of love with her no, but he wanted a family. And if he couldn't have that with her, it did put a little strain on their relationship.

The moment his phone was back on, it was vibrating with message after message. He ignored them all and just put his phone in his pocket then gathered this things to leave the office. He worked for one of the best Real Estate companies in L.A, and he was one of their best agents. Lately, he'd been working later and later shifts, anything that would keep his mind off possibly losing another baby. This time Charm was four months pregnant and it was looking good. Leaving the office, he got into his car and drove off.

Being married for five years but knowing Charm for five years previously, he knew her little quirks and he knew her routine. So when he entered the house and it didn't smell like dinner, and paint he knew something was wrong. Because if there was two things Charm loved to do, it was cooking and her artwork. She would probably be painting all day and then when she knew he would be coming home, she would stop and prepare dinner. Now the house was dark and seemed empty.

"Charm!" He called. "Baby where are you?" He left his briefcase in the kitchen and went up to their bedroom. He froze in his tracks when he flipped on the light and saw the blood on the bed.

"Shit!" He punched the wall in his anger. Pulling his phone out from his pocket he finally looked at his messages. Almost three hours ago Charm left her message on his voicemail. He turned around and rushed through the house. He grabbed his keys and bolted out of the front door. In his rush he bumped into someone trying to ring their doorbell.

"Jason what the hell are you doing here at this time of night?" Terrell asked.

"I've been calling Charm and I can't get ahold of her. I came here to figure out what the hell is going on. Where is she?" Terrell sucked his teeth at the man Charm would never get rid of. She grew up with Jason and they were practically like brother and sister. Which meant, whether or not Terrell wanted to, he inherited Jason because he was a part of Charm's life.

"She's at the hospital," Terrell grunted.

"What?! Why aren't you there with her?!"

"Because unlike you Jason I have a job. So move out of my way." Terrell pushed the man out of the way and continued to his car. Jason didn't have to beg for a ride. He got in his car and sped away before Terrell could leave in his own car. He knew if Charm was in the hospital then something had went very badly.

Even though he left before Terrell, both men arrived at the hospital at the same time. With Terrell being her husband he had precedent in getting information on what happened to Charm. But the moment they were led to their room, Jason pushed Terrell out of the way and rushed into Charm's room.

"Oh my god Charm," Jason sat next to her on the bed. She turned over slightly and looked at him.

"How did you know I was here?" She asked hoarsely. Jason looked back at Terrell who was standing in the doorway. Charm immediately shook her head and turned away from him.

"Baby please don't shut me out," Terrell said entering the room. He sat on the other side of the bed and tried to touch her.

"Don't touch me Terrell," she snapped. "Because if you didn't want to be shut out you would have answered my calls."

"Baby I was working!" He exclaimed.

"Past 5pm?" she asked. "Think I'm some sort of idiot?"

"Please don't do that," He sighed. "I was honestly working."

"Good for you. I was just here alone getting my baby surgically removed from my body." Terrell reached forward and wiped the tears from her face.

"We can have another baby Charm," He said. But even he didn't believe they ever could.

"You don't believe that," She called him out. She was charming like her name suggested, but she was not afraid to say the truth or call someone out.

"We just have to keep trying," He said. "That's all. We can get medicine, or something that will help you keep the baby."

"Maybe it's not just her," Jason said. "What if your men ain't marching all that straight?"

"Jase," Charm said.

"Why are you even here right now?" Terrell snapped at him. "This is between me and my wife. Everything that happens with her, you're always around and in the business. Last time I checked, I married Charm Bradley. Not Charm Bradley and her gay best friend."

"You know these past few weeks if I wasn't so obviously gay people would start to think I was her husband since her real husband is never around."

"Who are you to tell me about how much time I spend with her? Case you haven't realized we live in a luxurious ass house that needs paying for! So-"

"That's all material stuff! What about the quality time you need to be spending with her?!"

Charm rubbed her eyes. There was never a moment where Jason and Terrell were around each other that they weren't arguing. She usually just ignored them and let them bicker until it was over but tonight she just couldn't take it.

"Shut up!" She snapped. She grabbed her stomach in pain. "I can't believe the both of you right now. I just had to have my baby surgically removed and I was all by myself and you two can't stop arguing for just this moment? You know what, I don't need this. In fact I don't want any company. Both of you, get out."

"I am not leaving," Terrell stated.

"Yes you are Terrell," Charm said. "You too Jason. Stay out in the waiting area if you want, but I need to get some rest. My body aches and my head is spinning."

"I'm sorry Charm," Jason said softly. He rubbed her arm before he got out of the bed and left the room. Terrell stayed for a minute and looked at his wife. He saw the beauty in her as he did every day, but what good would it do their marriage if they couldn't start a family?

"We can't keep going on like this Charm," He said to her. "Something has got to change." Charm took a deep breath.

"Something like what?"

"I don't know baby. But I can't keep seeing you in the hospital from losing babies. We'll figure something out." He leaned over and kissed her on the forehead before finally getting up and walking out of the room too.

CHAPTER THREE

Denzel Johnson waited for his girlfriend to come out of her home, in his car. She'd hinted that she wanted to go to the particular restaurant they were going to over and over again so Denzel finally took the hint and made reservations. It was never a place that he would go to on his own to begin with. It was upscale, fancy, and too uptight. All of which were not words one would use to describe Denzel. But on the other hand, the woman he'd been dating since high school loved these kind of places. When he thought about it, he and his girl were two opposite people. But back then, he didn't think about who she was or she was going to be. He just knew her as a beautiful girl that was caring and smart. So he went with it, and they haven't left each other since.

When her front door open, Denzel shook his head and rubbed his eyes. Out came Gabrielle wearing a long sparkly fitted dress. And here Denzel was, wearing a blazer, with black pants, and a red t-shirt. Nevertheless he got out of the car and went to open the passenger door for her. He should have known to expect her to come out looking luxurious. That's just the type of woman she had become. And Denzel couldn't have been any more different than her.

"Didn't know we were going to the Oscars," He said to her. She bat her fake lashes at him before slapping him on the chest with her clutch.

"Shut up," She scoffed. "You know, it'll do you good to actually dress up once every now and then. And besides you haven't taken me on a date in weeks. So what if I want to get dressed up?" Denzel didn't answer her. Oh, they'd been on plenty of dates, only his high class girlfriend thought dates had to require an expensive outing and fancy champagne and wine. So all the little things he did with her didn't count as dates.

"I'm a little offended," Denzel told her. "Because you act like I don't spend my time with you." She rolled her eyes and tried not to spaz out on him and their date had barely begun.

"You know what I mean Denzel," She sighed. He opened the passenger side door for her and she slid inside. While he walked around to the driver's side, Gabrielle quickly pulled her medication bottle from her clutch and pop a single pill into her mouth. As he got in the car she quickly hid the bottle back in her clutch.

When he was in the car, Gabrielle leaned over and kissed him on the mouth. It was sort little pecks because of her lipstick. He tried to slip his tongue in her mouth but she pulled back.

"I'm wearing lipstick, behave," She said. Denzel rolled his eyes.

"I've told you many times you don't actually need to wear lipstick, or makeup around me all the time. And I'd rather tongue my girl down that see her in pretty colored lipstick." Even though they've been together for so long, Gabrielle always wore makeup. Not that he didn't like makeup or didn't want her to wear it at all, he just thought her natural beauty said more about her.

"I'd listen you more you know. If you put a ring on it," She said. Then there was this. Denzel shook his head.

"You are something else," Denzel commented. Sighing, he pulled out from the curb and drove off to their destination. They were quiet on the ride there, but she kept messing around with the promise ring he'd given her in 11th grade. It meant something that she still kept it but lately she'd been going on and on about getting a new ring or something. Almost like she wanted an upgrade. Denzel knew how to take hints, so he'd gotten her another one that resembled the one she had now but was just a little bit bigger. Maybe once she had it she would stop fussing with him about it.

The restaurant was full of people all who looked like they belonged in a fancy place like this. Denzel just kept his head down as they were escorted to their table.

"So have you been looking for work?" Gabrielle asked him. "You haven't mentioned that you were after we had that talk."

"Besides from the normal no I haven't been able to find anything."

"Denzel, you can't afford certain things seeing artwork on the corner, alright?"

"Actually I can afford plenty," Denzel said. "I'm affording this expensive ass restaurant you wanted to go to so bad. So what you complaining for?"

"Taking me to places like this once a month doesn't count as you affording anything Denzel. I told you, you need to apply for a real job and start making good money."

"Was this date of yours to lecture me Gabrielle?" he asked. "Because if so we can just leave now. I don't even see why you're worried so much about my work. I get money teaching my art classes and having my art events. You on the other hand have no job period! I'm the one that takes care of you."

"You know what, forget it. Let's just have a nice dinner."

"That's what I thought." Denzel wanted to have a nice dinner but the toxic nature of their conversation bled into everything. He suddenly didn't feel like talking period, even about his artwork. And he barely wanted anything on the menu. The only thing he recognized was the chicken options, so he went with that. Gabrielle proceeded on as if they weren't just arguing. What got to him was the fact that she was least supportive when it came to his artwork. There wasn't anything else in this world that he wanted to do. He loved painting, he loved drawing, and lately he'd even taken up photography simply because he wanted to expand his knowledge in the arts. He got gigs wherever he could get them, and he hustled his ass off to sell his painting and to even get jobs painting murals and personal portraits for people. The money wasn't always steady, but it was always there. And Gabrielle didn't seem to realize that.

As they had dessert, Gabrielle kept messing with her ring again and talking about their high school days.

"You forgot didn't you?" she asked him.

"Forgot what?"

"It's our anniversary," She said. Denzel gave her a look.

"No it's not Gabby. We started dating in October. It's only April. We have a couple of months to go."

"No Denzel. In April of our tenth grade year was when we met. It was October of our 11th grade year that we started dating. So it's the anniversary of when we met. How could you forget?"

"Forget? I don't forget meeting you Gabby but I didn't think we were keeping an anniversary for that." She shook her head and began twiddling the ring around her finger.

"And I suppose you didn't realize I wanted a ring," She said.

"Oh no, I noticed you wanted a ring."

"Really?!" She asked, hope filling her. Her eyes turned watery as he reached into the pocket of his blazer.

"Here," He said pulling out the small ring box. "You kept saying you wanted a newer one so I got you a similar promise ring." Her excitement dropped like a bomb. She slammed her hand down on the table.

"A promise ring?" She asked.

"Yeah! You were fussing about that one and I thought it was weird you wanted another once since we're kind of too old for that."

"I don't want your goddamn promise ring Denzel!" She shouted. A few of the people around them began looking over at them.

"Lower your voice," Denzel said.

"No! I'm not gonna lower my damn voice! You thought I wanted another promise ring? How immature can you be?! We've been together since 11th grade Denzel! All our friends are buying houses, moving in together and getting married and you're gonna give me another promise ring like we're teenagers?!"

"So then what do you want from me Gabrielle?! You kept saying you wanted a new ring!"

"You blasted idiot! I wanted you to propose to me Denzel!" Denzel's eyes bugged out.

"Propose to you? Gabrielle are you serious? You won't even sleep over my place or not wear makeup around me, but you want to be my wife?"

"You live in a one bedroom studio loft Denzel. And you want me to sleep over there? My entire closet wouldn't even be able to fit inside your bedroom. What you need is to buy a house and marry me so I can think about eventually having a family with you." Denzel couldn't believe what he was hearing. Was she serious?

"I'm not gonna propose to you Gabrielle," He said. "Maybe in a couple years we'll see how I feel about it, but right now I don't think marriage is our best bet."

"I thought you loved me," She said. Denzel didn't have an answer for her. He had very strong feelings for Gabrielle, there was no doubt about it. But love her? He didn't know that he did. At least not like he used to. And he wasn't going to put up a front just so he didn't look bad in front of people.

"I can't marry you right now," he said finally. "And that's just the god honest truth." With tears on her face she peeled off her promise ring and tossed the new one at him.

"Keep your little promise rings," she huffed.

"Gabrielle, wait." But she didn't listen. She grabbed up her things and stormed out of the restaurant. Denzel followed after her, but the moment she got outside she was hailing a cab and didn't waste time getting into it. Shaking his head, Denzel went to pay for their dinner before leaving the place himself. He couldn't believe what just happened.

CHAPTER FOUR

"She wanted you to propose?!" Denzel nodded his head at one of his best friends from high school. Like Gabrielle, he'd known Brianna for a while. They weren't attracted to each other not one bit, but the both of them shared a love for art that made them close.

"You know how I feel about Gabby but marry her? I'm not ready to be married period!"

"That's because you got commitment issues," Brianna snorted.

"Says Ms. Single every 2 months," He stated. She rolled her eyes at him as they packed up their art supplied to head downtown.

"Listen, it's not about me. This is about you. Honestly Denz, you've only been with one woman since high school. Which meant since you were 17 and all throughout college, and even now, you've been having sex with the same woman. You've never cheated, and you've never stopped caring for her. So don't you think your conscience is trying to tell you something if you don't have one inkling inside you that screams Gabrielle should be your wife?"

"Maybe I'm not ready to be anyone's husband. I want to be financially stable before I even commit to that. You know we do what we have to do to pay the bills Brie, but things change when it's not just you anymore. Either way I don't even think it matters now. She hasn't returned any of my calls so I guess that's her way of breaking up with me."

"Please," Brianna scoffed.

"What?"

"She may be mad at you right now but she ain't going nowhere."

"And why do you say that?"

"That girl has been bragging since high school why she won't ever let you go. Apparently it ain't just paint strokes you're good at." Denzel shook his head.

"I know we're just friends, but if you want me to lay down the hammer on you Brie, I will. I can put our friendship aside and take care of your needs. Simply because I care that much for you." Brianna cut her eyes at him and threw an empty canvas at him.

"Even if I liked chocolate men with dreads, you're still the last chocolate dread headed man I would ever think about sleeping with. I may be a woman, but I've got morals. Now, enough of this relationship talk. I'm starting to feel like Oprah."

"At least Oprah would be gracing my pockets with some money," He retorted.

"Shut up mop head," She snapped. "Come on. We're wasting daylight. I wanna see the new gallery opening then we should inquire about them purchasing our paintings. Maybe we can even do a little something nearby?" As part of when they went out to paint, sometimes Brianna caught people's attention by playing her electric violin while Denzel painted. Surprisingly enough, when people heard music and flocked around them and then saw what Denzel was painting in real time, people liked to stay to watch. They never did it for money, but people often left them tips. But doing something like this in front of a gallery might get the attention of the right people.

"I'm ready," Denzel said, grabbing his bags full of his things. He carried Brianna's violin case for her and they left his loft to head downtown.

****

"Are you sure you're okay?" Jason asked Charm for the tenth time.

"Besides my nerves, I am very much okay. I wish you would stop asking me if I'm okay though. It's a little annoying." Jason didn't want to keep bringing it up but he still worried about her. A month had passed since her miscarriage and for a week or two she was in a sort of funk. She stayed home, barely painted and didn't talk to anyone. But then after then she seemed to have a complete transformation. She popped up at the gallery and started working again. Jason didn't believe she was as fully recuperated as she let on and that's why he kept having to ask her if she was okay..

"I just think-"

"I know what you think Jase. But please believe me; being here, and working this is what I need alright? It makes me feel so much more relief than just staying at home thinking about what happened before. So please, be my bestie and not an annoying little twit." Jason gasped.

"Oh no honey you didn't call me a twit!" He gasped. Charm smiled at him. Being openly gay, Jason was basically her brother. The day they met, he was being bullied for his sexual preference and Charm wasn't just going to sit by and let it happen. And so it happened, she gained a brother but also a psycho friend who was there for her no matter what.

"Behave yourself. Look people are coming in." Her art gallery was newly opening and each weekend brought her a new flow of audiences. But trying to run an art gallery and an art business was taxing on her. Maybe it was the reason she kept miscarrying. She was trying to succeed in too many different places. She was working herself to the bone. But having people in to look at her work gave her this sense of release, it was almost orgasmic and she couldn't fight wanting to feel that all the time. So she busted her ass knowing that in the end she'd be able to feel some sort of satisfaction.

"Oh. My. God." Charm gave Jason a look as his mouth fell. He stopped sipping his Cappuccino and turned to face Charm.

"Tall, chocolate, and dreaded just came in through the doors," He said to her.

"Where? I don't see-" Charm swallowed her words when she spotted the man Jason was going goo-goo eyes over. Yes, he was tall. Very, very chocolate. And his dreads, they were neatly twisted and pulled back from his face. They were dark except for the tips that were colored golden. He was wearing black pants, with a white V-neck t-shirt that fit him smugly with black loafers and he was wearing suspenders. If it made any sense, he looked like one of those artsy kind of men even if he was wearing mostly black. There was just something in his styling.

"You should, you should go talk to him," Charm finally said. She blinked a few times and looked at Jason.

"You little smut, you were drooling just now!!"

"Jase, I am married, did you forget? And so what, I can look. It's the touching that's the problem. Go on over there and talk to him since you seem to have a crush on him." Jason turned around to look at him.

"Damn," He swooned. "He's sexy as hell. But too bad he's not for me."

"What do you mean?" Charm asked.

"Because someone just caught his attention. And I don't think that someone is me." Charm looked up and indeed tall and chocolate was staring straight at her. Even his eyes were chocolate.

"Oh my," Charm breathed finding herself not able to look away from him.

****

"Earth to Denzel," Briana said snapping her fingers in Denzel's face. He blinked and looked at her sharply.

"What?"

"I could ask you the same thing. What the hell you looking at so hard?" Denzel turned back to the woman he'd spotted across the room.

"Just…her," He said nodding over to the woman. Wearing a fitted yellow sundress, she was tall and ethereal but round in the bottom which Denzel appreciated. Her short hair stopped about neck length and was silky smooth. She wasn't wearing any makeup but the slight tinted gloss on her lips.

"Wow, she's something," Brianna said. "Gonna talk to her or just stand here looking crazy?"

"Shut up." He nudged Brianna out of the way and continued looking over the paintings. They were unlike anything he'd seen before. They were so real and pure.

"This artist is really, really good Denzel. We need to meet them."

"Tell me about it," Denzel sighed.

"Hey honey, are you two artists?" Denzel turned to look at the man who was standing next to the beautiful woman only a moment ago.

"Um yeah we are," Brianna spoke up immediately.

"We're having an open gallery event in a half hour. If you have your supplies you're welcome to set up a station at any open space and do your work live for anyone that visits the gallery."

"Really?" Denzel asked a little skeptical.

"Yes. In this gallery we are as laid back as they come. We're serious about art, but we also want to promote art through the entire community. This is a space for everyone to shine. So if I were you handsome I'd take advantage." Denzel looked at the man who winked at him.

"Thanks a lot," Denzel said. "I am actually very attracted to women though, so ummm,"

"Oh relax. If I was hitting on you I wouldn't be so casual about it. Love those shoes," He said to Brianna before turning and walking away.

"I like him," Brianna smiled. "Now at least we don't have to set up outside. We can do it in here. I'll start unloading the things from the car." When she rushed off, Denzel looked around the gallery again not stopping until he found that woman. She was talking to the same man that just approached Denzel. She laughed at something he said, and the vibrancy of it trembled through his own body. What Brianna told him earlier sparked in his head again. He never once had to urge to cheat on Gabrielle or even wanted to break up with her, or even found another woman attractive. This was the first time he could look at another woman and find himself battling the thought that she was just another woman and he already had someone in his life. And if Gabrielle was beside him right now, he'd be ashamed to say that he was attracted to a woman that wasn't her.

CHAPTER FIVE

"This was a good idea," Charm said looking at all the artists who were setting up stands and beginning to do their artwork. Since that started, the crowd began to thicken in the gallery. Charm loved having people out actually appreciating art. It was hard to do that in the age of technology but she was going to keep up her efforts. Now it seemed to be paying off. With Jason alongside her, she walked around the gallery viewing artwork that the artists were creating. Most of them knew who she was, but otherwise she was just another art muse. She liked to remain low key like that because she didn't want to appear better than anyone else that was here.

"Everyone is pretty good. I like the crowd coming in now to look at everything. Maybe we can get some of them to sign up for our paint classes or something."

"Our?" Jason asked. "I'm not the artist you are. And the classes will be awesome. But you can't do it all by yourself." Charm smiled at Jason.

"Sometimes I wonder why you're-"

"Is that a violin?" Jason asked cutting her off. Charm stopped talking and listened. True enough, the sound of a violin being played punctured the small chatter of the gallery. She noticed then that people were beginning to gravitate to one spot. Jason took her hand and began leading her to where everyone was going. They pushed through the crowd and got to the front. Charm's mouth fell open as she witnessed what was happening. Tall and chocolate from earlier had his canvas set up with his paintbrush in his mouth while he looked deeply at the woman he was with earlier. He'd taken his white shirt off and now he was only wearing a white wife beater with his suspender straps still around his shoulders. The woman with him was playing her violin artistically and he was looking at her as if he was deeply studying her. And after a minute of him just staring, Charm figured out why he was studying her so closely. When the violin beat picked up, tall and chocolate pulled his suspenders down and then he started getting to work. Seemingly as if the two of them were in sync, he began painting to the rhythm of the violin. The image that unfolded before everyone's eyes was that of the woman playing the instrument. Charm had never seen something quite like it. She was in awe at the whole presentation. She'd never seen art done like that and strangely it inspired her.

"Damn," Jason said to her. "He's real good."

"Yeah, he is," Charm commented.

"And he looks damn good in that wife beater. Shit." Charm nudged Jason with her elbow.

"Do you need a cold shower?" she asked him.

"No! I just wish I could get an hour with that man alone." He shook his head. "Charm you can't make this man leave here without talking to him."

"And say what? You're a great painter and my friend wants an hour alone with you, think you can handle it?" Jason rolled his eyes.

"Don't be catty alright? Don't you need a partner? You have me Charm but I can't draw or paint for shit. A man with his talents can help you host your paint nights and you can get some more gigs. Your goal is to have an art company Charm. And you can't do that alone."

"Oh I don't know. How would that even work out? He's going to expect steady income and-"

"He's an artist Charm. The last thing he expects is steady income." Charm waved Jason off while she thought about what he told her. She knew she could use the help, and she had to admit that working with a man as talented as him would do her own craft some good. But she just didn't know. Something was holding her back.

"Incredible," Jason said in awe when tall and chocolate finished his painting the same time the woman ended her song. The crowd clapped and eagerly went to get a closer look at his painting. Charm found herself moving forward to get a closer look to. It was only of her upper body, with her eyes closed and her violin at her neck. The way he was able to implement the colors that he did in such a manner that didn't take him days struck Charm. She got so lost in the painting she didn't even realize how close she was to it. She leaned forward and studied it closely. It was real. Not artificial and that's what was drawing her in so closely. Why hadn't she ever seen or heard of a painter as talented as him? There was always talk in the art world and she'd never come across anything like this.

"You're gonna talk to this man," Jason said in her ear. Charm jumped, so focused on the painting that everything else around her faded away.

"Alright fine," She huffed. "You won't stop bothering me if I don't anyway. And I really don't want to hear you complaining."

"Oh whatever. I'm gonna keep watch on him and make sure he doesn't leave before you get to speak to him. Because I know you'll do it on purpose and let him leave and play like you didn't see him leave or you forgot to stop him."

"I swear you're always on my back Jase. Maybe I should have married you instead of Terrell." He smiled at her.

"Even if I was straight you ain't my type," He shrugged. "You're too classy. I would like them round the way type of girls." Charm gasped and hit him playfully.

"I may be classy in the streets-"

"But a freak in the sheets, yeah, yeah I know." He waved her off. "But you ain't freakier than me," He grabbed a wine glass from one of the servers who were passing it around and walked off like he was on the runway or something.

"Drama queen," She called out after him.

****

"Wait don't pack up. Leave it here," Jason rushed over to tall and chocolate who was trying to pack his things up seen as the event was over. Other artists were on their way out and the crowd of people there to view their work was practically gone too. So far Charm had gotten 20 people to sign up for her paint and sip sessions and some of her art classes. But she did not even pay attention to the man whose painting she was so captivated by. But like Jason said, he wasn't going to let the man leave.

"Everyone else is leaving though," He said to Jason.

"Don't worry about it. We just want to talk to you." He raised his brow.

"Who's we?" He questioned. Right on time, Charm let the last person out of the gallery and closed the doors.

"Not really we, it's actually just her that needs to talk to you." Denzel was full on confused until he looked up and saw that woman from earlier walking towards them. He actually felt himself back up. Why did he have that feeling inside him that he couldn't face her? And when she approached, her coconut and vanilla scent wafted right to his nose, intoxicating him.

"Hi, sorry to keep you waiting. I just wanted to make sure everyone was gone before we spoke. But I know Jason here was fabulous company." Denzel heard the words coming out of her mouth and he knew she was talking to him, but he just couldn't form words.

"My name is Charm Bradley-Robinson. I just opened up this gallery. What's your name?" Denzel looked at her outstretched hand and did nothing. Her fingers were slender, with nails that were painted red and cut to perfection. Brianna elbowed him. He blinked but still didn't say anything. His brain was fuzzing out and not transmitting words to his mouth.

"My name is Brianna," Brianna spoke up for him. She gave him a look before sucking her teeth and turning to Charm. Charm turned to the woman and shook her hand instead.

"Loved the way you played the violin today that was really good."

"We do it as a way to catch people's attention enough so they can actually watch him paint. It's been working for us for a year." Charm looked back at the man.

"Are you two dating?" Charm asked.

"Absolutely not," Brianna said immediately. "Strictly best friends who will never have benefits trust me. He's kind of single so you can totally hit on him if you want," She smiled. Charm laughed.

"I'm married," Charm smiled. Denzel's gut bottomed out. He felt like he nearly died when she said the M word. Seriously? But of course, why would she be single? Wait, why did he care? Gabrielle was going to come back to him sooner or later. Even if Brianna called him single, he didn't feel as if he was.

"Are you going to tell us your name?" Charm asked him. "Or can me and Jason keep calling you tall and chocolate?" Everyone laughed. He even cracked a smile.

"Denzel," He final spoke. His deep voice filled Charm's body.

"Dear lord his name is Denzel," Jason breathed holding his heart. "Why? Why are you doing this to the world you-"

"Jason cool it," Charm said waving at him.

"I'm just saying. Hell. Tall and chocolate with a name like Denzel will do damage to these ladies out here. Or men."

"I told you," Denzel said. "Strictly women." He gave Jason a smirk.

"Don't smirk at me like that before I turn you! Charm talk to this man before I lose control up in here."

"Wait, is Charm really your name? Or just your artist name?"

Denzel asked.

"No that's my real name."

"It's gorgeous," He complimented. Charm cleared her throat.

"Tha-thanks," She smiled. She pushed her hair out of her face. "I'm sure you have somewhere else to be so I'll make this quick. I basically have an art company where I paint murals, portraits, host classes, and events. I even do work for parties, weddings, and all that kind of stuff. But it's just me. I want to gain more clientele and take on even more projects but I can't do that with just me. After seeing the way you work today Denzel I want to offer you a spot in my company."

"Seriously?" Denzel asked not quite believing how lucky he was to even be getting this offer. The art world was hard enough to be in and now this gorgeous woman was here offering him a chance to work with her? He couldn't believe it.

"Yes seriously. Now I'm not some big name in the art world so every day is going to be a grind and a hustle to get gigs. We keep getting gigs, we keep getting paid. Jason is the one that books the gigs for us and as you can see he's very mouthy and he will ensure we keep getting work. I just need a partner willing to go that extra mile I'm going to be an artist. The pay will be off commission really. Whatever we make doing any work we split it evenly and you're free to take on any solo work you're offered too. So what do you say? We can meet up tomorrow morning to go over all the details and whatnot And we can see if this is an offer you want to take and you can ask any questions you want and we'll get to know each other."

"This is amazing of you to offer me," He said. "But I couldn't take any job with you without Brianna. We've been a team for a while now. I couldn't just up and leave her like that." Brianna loved Denzel to death, and he was literally one in a million when it came to men and loyalty. He was the loyalist person she knew and he would go an extra mile for her no matter what it cost him. But at the same time he didn't look out for himself. And right now, this was the perfect opportunity for him to elevate his career. And yet still he was worrying about her.

"Forget about me Denzel! Are you crazy?! You need this kind of opening. I'll get my opportunity sooner or later. It's no big deal."

"Brie," Denzel said. Charm looked between the both of them. The commitment they had towards each other made Charm warm inside. She just loved to see that kind of relationship between two people. Charm had to admit she was impressed at his loyalty. A man that would pass up his own needs to see to it that someone else got the same chance was admirable.

"What else do you do?" Charm asked Brianna. "Only the violin?"

"I'm a painter as well. Though not as good as Denzel, that's why when he paints I just play the music."

"Do you have anything for me to look at?"

"No I didn't bring anything with me. We were coming so Denzel could paint, and maybe I would draw but I didn't bring any originals."

"Tell you what, no one is the perfect painter. But if you have the fundamentals there's nothing you can't learn. So if Denzel still wants to, we can still meet up tomorrow and you can bring some of your artwork." Denzel looked at Brianna with his brow raised.

"Don't look at me! Say hell yes!" Brianna said. Denzel smiled at Charm.

"Alright then I think we have a deal," Denzel said. Charm reached her hand out again.

"Don't leave me hanging this time," She smiled. Denzel took her delicate hand into his and shook it.

"Let's go to the office in back so I can give you my contact information," Charm said. She led the way towards the office but only Denzel followed. Brianna stayed back and looked at Jason. Jason looked her up and down.

"You sure you never rode that black stallion before?" Jason inquired. Brianna nearly choked on her own spit.

"I promise I haven't. He's not my type," She said. "Is Charm really married?"

"Yes. What kind of question is that?"

"Damn. That sucks for Denzel," She stated. "That's the first woman I've ever seen that man absolutely speechless in front of. The way he looked at her was different than any other time he looks at a woman."

"Charm does that to a lot of men. She's just one of those females where there's nothing to hate on, but you still just gotta hate on her because she's so damn perfect. Many men have been speechless around her. But she's faithful to her husband."

"That's why I said it sucks for Denzel," Brianna shrugged.

In the office, Charm handed Denzel her business card after writing her cell phone number on the back. He took it and immediately stored the number in his phone. He sent her a text so she could have his number also. While she went about saving the number in her phone, Denzel couldn't stop staring at her. She wasn't doing anything in particular that should have been attracting him. But just watching the way her hair swooped in her face as she looked down, and how she pushed it back behind her ear all captivated him.

"So you and Brianna go way back huh?" Charm asked. Denzel quickly snapped his eyes from her and acted as if he was staring somewhere else. But he knew that people didn't believe he and Brianna were just friends. They always assumed it was something else.

"No we haven't dated, we're not friends with benefits, we've never kissed or ever done anything sexual and we do not intend to be in a relationship. Period." Charm crossed her arms.

"I guess you've been asked a lot about your relationship with her?"

"It's hard for people to believe a male and a female can be just friends. Don't get me wrong, Brianna is a pretty ass girl but we just weren't meant to develop like that. She's like a sister to me."

"I can dig it. And if all four of us actually get to work together I feel like the dynamic will be amazing. I guess that's why I'm so eager to make this offer to the both of you."

"I'm looking forward to it," Denzel said. "Working for an actual company would be big for us." Charm smiled then began rummaging through her desk drawers. She found her wedding ring and slipped it onto her finger. She always took it off when she was in the gallery because she might end up painting and she didn't want it to get dirty. Now that she was through and was going to head home soon, she could put it back on. Denzel looked at the ring closely. She noticed him looking and it was like he wanted to say something but he just nodded at her.

"So tomorrow? Brunch hours?" Charm asked.

"Yeah, that's perfect."

"Great." She grabbed her bags and her keys before leading the way out of the office.

Back in the gallery, Brianna and Jason were chatting it up like they were long lost friends or something. It really did seem like the four of them would just click. She joined in on the conversation with them easily, and so did Denzel but every once in a while Charm would feel the back of her neck tingling and when she would look, Denzel's chocolate eyes would meet hers. Something so simply as eye connection turned into complexity where Charm and Denzel were concerned. And it just made her think. She thought about Terrell. When was the last time her husband looked at her the way Denzel did?

CHAPTER SIX

After seeing his wife mope around the house for two weeks then just jump back into work like they hadn't lost another baby made Terrell jump to his next decision. Charm was his wife and that was that, but she couldn't produce. And if they were going to have a family born of their creation things needs to change. They saw doctors, went to specialists, and even took medication. The last time he made love to his wife was on an ovulation day. There wasn't the sporadic love making that they used to do. Everything revolved around getting her pregnant. That was his focus too, but getting the same outcome over and over again was tiring. There was nothing else they could do so Terrell made his own decisions.

Without telling Charm, he'd met with a few people and set some arrangements. While she was parading around with her damn art company, Terrell was making the moves he needed to make. This was their chance at having a baby and even if Charm wasn't going to like the idea, she was just going to have to live with it. Maybe she could have a miscarriage and continue like everything was okay, but Terrell couldn't. And if she refused to accept the decision he'd made for the both of them, then he'd simply force her to accept it.

Finally after a whole month of phone calls, emails, brochures, and a healthy first payment, Terrell was finally getting the meeting he needed to put things in into motion. In their large kitchen, Terrell paced while constantly looking at his watch. Just as he was getting even more restless the doorbell rang. Terrell hurried to answer it.

"Charm! Get down here!" He shouted. He could hear her moving around upstairs but he had no idea what she was doing. It was a little after 11 in the morning. Terrell opened the door and smiled at the woman standing there. She looked just as her photos suggested and that's why Terrell had picked her out. She was a little shorter than Charm, but her dark brown skin was vibrant in the sun. Terrell knew immediately by just looking at her she was the one he wanted.

"Destiny right?" Terrell asked.

"And you're Terrell?" She questioned. He nodded and guided her into the kitchen. She smiled brightly at him as she looked around the kitchen.

"Have you had any breakfast? We have some biscuits."

"Sure I'll take some thanks." Terrell went into the oven and retrieved two biscuits. He set it in front of her with some orange juice and strawberry jam.

"Nice to actually meet you. The company has been doing most of the talking on both sides."

"They're real protective they wouldn't let me talk to you until I signed some papers and agreed to a whole bunch of stuff." Destiny smiled at him.

"Where's your wife?" she asked.

"Oh yeah. My wife." Terrell left the kitchen. Instead of shouting for her again, he took the steps two at a time and went up to their bedroom.

"You don't hear me calling you?" He asked. She was sitting at her vanity putting her short hair in a loose ponytail.

"Sorry what's up?"

"Come downstairs I want you to meet someone."

"I'm supposed to go meet with Jason, Denzel, and Brianna. Can this wait?"

"No it cannot wait-who the hell is Denzel?" Terrell crossed his arms and stared at her. She made a face at him.

"Just an artist relax." Charm stood and that's when he realized she was wearing her painting overalls that was littered with paint stains. He'd accepted the fact that his wife was never going to give up her painting and he didn't mind her paint ridden clothes. But when he was taking her out, or to his job, or when they had company like the woman downstairs, Terrell needed Charm to uphold a certain image. And Charm knew well he wanted her to look a certain way. If he was going to show his wife off to people then she had to look the part.

"Do you mind wearing something else right now?" he asked. Charm put her hands on her hips.

"Just who in the heck am I meeting anyways? You know I have to go to the gallery right?"

"Charm just do what I said," He snapped getting impatient. "Go put on one of your cute sundresses." Charm huffed out loud but still went to her closet to change her overalls.

"Meet me down in the kitchen when you're done." Like her husband asked, she put on a simple dress that was decent enough for whoever was downstairs. Which was weird to her. Terrell rarely ever had company over the house. He was more of a bring your wife to work and show her off type of man. Curiosity plagued her as she stayed barefoot and left the bedroom to head to the kitchen. As she got close she heard a woman's laughter.

"Don't say that, she's your wife," The woman laughed. Charm entered the kitchen, seeing a woman and her husband in full conversation. They hadn't noticed her for about 2 minutes. Charm cleared her throat. The woman turned and looked at her. She gave Charm a smile that didn't seem genuine.

"Finally, you're here," Terrell said walking over to where Charm stood. "Honey, this is Destiny. Destiny this is my wife Charm." The woman he was calling Destiny looked Charm up and down before tossing her another smile.

"Hi, nice to meet you," She said. But she didn't offer a handshake or even a wave. Instead she turned towards Terrell to speak to him.

"Wow Terrell your wife is stunning." Charm gave rolled her eyes but gave Destiny a smile. She noticed how Destiny was giving the compliment to Terrell instead of saying it directly to Charm as if she wasn't standing right there.

"So what's going on?" Charm asked. She hadn't said ten words to the woman but she was over the whole conversation already.

"Have a seat Charm," Terrell said taking her hand and trying to lead her to the island to sit down. But Charm pulled her hand away. No one ever got good news when they were told to sit down. And Charm didn't like it one bit.

"No thanks I'll stand." Her stomach was beginning to churn with worry and dread. She was queasy thinking about what her husband could possibly want to sit down and tell her.

"Terrell who is this woman?" Charm asked, forgetting her manners. She wasn't going to stand there being polite if Terrell had the audacity to introduce her to a woman he may be having an affair with. That wasn't going to go over well with Charm.

"Charm relax…"

"No I'm not going to relax. And I hope like hell you aren't going to have to audacity to bring this woman in here and tell me that you're having an affair with her!"

"Calm down!" Terrell snapped at her.

"Charm that's not what this is," Destiny spoke up. "This is the first time I've met Terrell." Charm crossed her arms and looked at Terrell.

"Explain," Charm demanded.

"Fine," he said tightly. "Before you left the hospital I told you something had to change. We want to have babies but your body just won't allow it." Embarrassment began leaking through her as he said that in front of another woman. The last thing Charm wanted people to know about her was that she couldn't have babies. She just completely felt like less of a woman. She turned to look at Terrell completely giving Destiny her back.

"So are we not going to continue trying? Maybe it'll work the next time," Charm said.

"Or maybe it won't," Terrell replied. "You can reproduce fine honey. That's not the problem. The problem is you just can't keep the baby to term. And if I'm real honest, I'm not gonna be happy if you force me to keep trying to conceive and then when we finally get you pregnant and you lose the baby yet again."

"Why are you saying this like it's my fault?" Charm asked. "I know it's my body but I don't have the answers you're looking for. It's not like I can physically do something that will prevent it from happening. But I won't just give up on trying to be a mother. Or giving you what you want." Terrell shook his head.

"You don't have to think about anymore answers Charm. Because I finally found one." He pointed at Destiny who smiled. Charm couldn't help the ugly expression that came to her face. She turned and looked back at Destiny.

"I'm still wondering who this woman is," Charm said.

"Well Charm, she's gonna be our surrogate." Charm's mouth fell open. She teetered on her feet as the news rocked her. Now she wished she was actually sitting down. She rubbed her temples to ease the headache that was slowly approaching.

"Wait, wait, wait. Surrogate?"

"Yes. I spoke with a company, everything is legit and I chose Destiny from all the candidates. I signed the papers and paid it's all a go. Now we just actually have to get the procedure done." Charm couldn't believe what she was hearing.

"When the heck did you do this? Doesn't these things take a long time to even start?"

"Well I was pretty firm about my intentions and I have

access to your medical records. So I was able to speak on your behalf and after I made that hefty first payment they weren't shy about speeding things along for me. They showed me all the candidates and I chose Destiny.

"I can't believe this," Charm said shaking her head.

"Well believe it Charm. Because it's going to be great. I didn't think this would ever be an option for us but it's perfect!" Charm gave her husband a look.

"The surrogacy is not what I can't believe Terrell! I can't believe you did all of this behind my back without asking me about it! Now you brought this woman in our home and I just simply have to accept that she's supposed to be our surrogate?"

"Charm I'm at the end of my ropes here. This is our only option."

"But-but Terrell the point of being pregnant is to actually be able to experience your baby growing inside of you. With a surrogate I won't be able to have that experience."

"Your body doesn't allow you to stay pregnant Charm. So it's either the surrogate, or it's nothing at all." This all felt like some sort of fairytale. Was he really doing this to her?

"Charm," Destiny spoke up. "I will ensure that you experience everything I'm experiencing when it comes to the baby. Terrell signed the agreement that I live with you while I'm pregnant so that way you miss nothing."

"To live here?" Charm looked sharply at her husband.

"That's the best option. She lives here we get to see the baby grow day in and day out."

"And what if I don't agree to this?" Charm asked. Terrell crossed his arms.

"Well then that's your choice Charm. But I'm telling you right now, I want to have kids with my wife." Charm knew what that meant. Either she agreed to this surrogate business or she would lose her husband. Even if she wanted to bear her own child she knew the possibilities of it happening would be rare.

"So what? My egg gets put inside you and fertilized by his sperm?" Charm asked Destiny.

"That is correct. I'm just the host body. This will be your baby." Charm sighed and rubbed her eyes.

"And when is this gonna happen?" She asked.

"In about a month. We have to run tests with the lab and I

want Destiny tested to make sure she's a good host for the baby which means no drugs or diseases. And some tests need to be done on you," Terrell answered.

"Okay," Charm whispered. "Guess we're going to have a surrogate."

"Glad you can see it my way baby." Terrell kissed her lightly on the lips. "I'm gonna help Destiny move into the guess room in about a week or so. That's okay with you right?"

"Surprised you even want to ask me," Charm said taking a shot at him, He was deciding everything else for her, why not just make every decision?

"Don't be like that," He said to her. "Do you want to be my wife Charm?"

"You know well I do," Charm snapped at him.

"Okay! So then stop acting like a spoiled brat. You can't get what you want when you can't even give me what I want. And it's either you're going to give a me what a wife is supposed to give her husband, or you simply just won't be my wife anymore. So you make that choice." Charm gazed into the hardened eyes of her husband. Ever since the second miscarriage he had that same hardness in his features as if he was tired of hearing her tell him that they'd lost another baby. Since then Charm had felt like she lost her husband, but she was always trying her best to keep him, to keep their marriage intact. But standing there she couldn't believe he'd just said something like that to her.

"I'll be at the gallery today," She said hoarsely trying not to appear weak in front of another woman. She'd cry in her car but not in front of Terrell and Destiny. Charm backed out of the kitchen.

"I guess I should say welcome to your new home Destiny," Charm shrugged. She gave Terrell a final look before finally leaving the kitchen and hurrying away so none of them could see her crying.

Destiny watched Charm leave. Yes, her new home was looking real good. She'd been at the surrogate company for a little bit but this was the first couple she'd ever worked for. And what was her luck that the couple who picked her happened to be well off? Destiny didn't know too much about Charm or Terrell but she knew a man with money when she saw one. And he didn't have just the money. He had the looks too. Destiny turned and looked at Terrell. He was about 6 foot tall with an almond like complexion. His hair was cut low and smooth with waves. His thin beard was trimmed perfectly to fit his face, where it wasn't too much hair, but it wasn't too little either. Destiny could see why Charm and Terrell were a couple. They were both incredibly good looking. But it was too bad Charm couldn't give the man a baby. But Destiny could. And for some wicked reason, Destiny didn't want to give the man a baby with Charm's eggs either.

"So the company didn't really go into details about you or Charm. And I know they didn't tell you much about me either. If you still have time we can get to know a little bit about each other. You don't want to remain strangers with the woman who's going to be carrying your baby do you?" Destiny asked. Terrell smiled at her.

"You're right. I don't mind talking at all. Let's go to the living room. And don't worry about Charm. She'll come around eventually. I know she wants a baby as much as I do. And this is the only way." Destiny smiled at him.

"I'm not too worried about her," Destiny said. "Most women would be a little hesitant about making these kinds of moves, but as her husband you did what was best. No fault in that." Destiny stood from around the island and took off her light jacket. She saw when Terrell's eyes raked against her chest. He tried to look away quickly but Destiny knew she had him. He just needed a slight push, and then she'd get more out of him than originally planned.

CHAPTER SEVEN

Charm rushed into the gallery. She was late. Not only had she cried on the way to the gallery, she had to spend ten extra minutes in her car constantly wiping her eyes and trying to get herself together. In her mirror she practiced her smile just to make sure she could pull off being okay.

But she was far from okay. She was sort of stuck in her head going over what happened repeatedly and what Terrell had said to her. Before she left her home she'd changed back into her overalls and tried quickly to leave the house. Only as she walked downstairs she saw her husband and their surrogate on the couch talking and sipping on lemonade. Right then in that moment she wanted to tell Destiny to just get out and never come back, but it was the look on Terrell's face that made her stop. The smile on his face was bright and he was speaking so openly as if for the first time he actually had someone to talk to. The notion that he was already getting comfortable with her sealed the deal that they were going to have this surrogate if she wanted it or not. And if she absolutely refused to have Destiny as their surrogate then she would lose her husband. Was it even right of her to deny his want for children knowing well her body couldn't carry a baby to term? But was it right of Terrell to even threaten her like that? That's not what married couples were supposed to do. They were supposed to support each other. No matter how tough the road got. And this just made Charm question he man she was married to.

It was all too much for her to think about but she wasn't going to stop him. Seeing Terrell smile like that she knew he was happy about their plan. And she wanted him to be happy. What kind of wife would she be if she didn't want her husband to be happy?

"So sorry I'm late," She hurried out trying to get her bearings.

"It's no biggie," Denzel spoke up. Charm stopped in her tracks and looked at him. He smiled warmly at her and for a moment she forgot that she'd just been bawling in her car. She sniffled and gave him her practiced smile.

"I'll carry that," He said taking her bags and her large canvas from out of her hands. "Nice overalls," He smiled. Charm felt the warmness of his smile and wished she could return the gesture.

"Thanks," She looked down at the overalls that her husband hated seeing her wearing, but Denzel had just complimented.

"I don't care how it makes me look I love painting in them," She told him. Denzel liked the denim overalls that she rolled up over her ankles to show off the converses she was wearing. Her yellow fitted t-shirt though it revealed nothing still made her look pretty.

Denzel carried her things further inside where Jason and Brianna were waiting. Charm hugged Jason and hugged Brianna in greeting too.

"So you have some work for me?" Charm asked Brianna.

"Yes. Here," Brianna showed Charm her sketchbook. Charm flipped through it while Brianna uncovered one of her larger paintings that was leaning up against the wall. After flipping through the sketchbook Charm looked at the portrait Brianna had painted.

"You're extremely talented. I don't see why all three well four if you include Jason though he's not a painter, can't work together. I drew up a contract last night. Be right back." Charm rushed off going to the office to finish the contract she had composed. She logged into her computer so she could download the file and print it out.

Denzel watched Charm rush off and close herself in the office. Brianna clapped him on the back.

"Looks like your sacrifice paid off," Brianna said. Denzel only nodded but he was still looking out after Charm. Brianna scoffed.

"Cut it out Denz. She's married. Don't do that it to yourself." Denzel waved her off.

"It's not about that," He said. "It's just something else."

"What?"

"She's just more distracted today than she was yesterday. I can practically see the wheels turning in her head. Like I don't know maybe something upset her. And she's been crying."

"Oh, I didn't notice," Brianna said. "Jason you know what's up with her?"

"Actually I don't. She hadn't told me anything happened. And knowing Charm she's going to put her work before anything and she's gonna pretend she's perfectly fine. I'm so glad she has other artists to work with now. She needs people to be close with." Denzel began to wonder hard at what could have Charm so distracted and unhappy. He only just met her but he felt like he should be concerned about the things that made her unhappy. But true to what Jason said, Charm came back out of the office with a smile on her face even though it didn't reach her eyes.

"Okay, I started on these last night I just had to add a few things. But if you two want to implement anything then feel free to say so." She handed both Brianna and Denzel a copy of the contract. While they looked it over she went to the large windows of the gallery and pulled down the large shades giving the four of them some privacy. With that done, she went into the storage closet and pulled out bean bags so they could sit down.

"I usually never have use for more than two of the bean bags," She smiled. "So nice to have people around now."

"The contract looks good," Brianna said. "I don't want to change anything. Do you Denzel?"

"No it does look good. Is this just your gallery?" he asked.

"No actually I use it as my studio too. It's big enough for me to do my paintings and it's already paid for so I didn't see why I had to get another place to serve as my studio while I can use this. You two are free to use the space for your paintings as well. The supply closet is filled with everything you'll need and there's a basement were I keep all my unfinished works. It's big enough for you two to store your paintings." Charm pulled out her phone deciding to send a text to Terrell just to check up on him. She was still unsettled about leaving him alone with Destiny.

"And you two have some catching up to do. We've already booked for the gallery to be open for viewing again in two weeks, plus we have a paint and sip session coming up this weekend on Saturday. So we need something for the participants to paint. What should we use?" Jason informed them.

"You're the boss Charm you choose," Brianna said. Charm didn't answer her. When they looked at her, it was clear that her eyes were distant and her head was probably ten thousand miles away from them. Jason cleared his throat.

"Charm," He said. Still she didn't answer her. Denzel reached forward and rubbed her arm. She jumped then, snapping out of her daze.

"Oh crap, I'm sorry," She said. "I just…got distracted." Charm was waiting for Terrell to answer back, but he was taking too long. She never clocked when her husband called or answered her texts, but knowing he was still with that surrogate, she starting thinking heavily about what they could possibly be doing. She'd never been like this before. Why all of a sudden were things different?

"We don't have to do this right now," Denzel said. "If you'd rather just relax to get your mind right we can do that."

"No, I told you two to come for business. Not to mind me and my distractions."

"Look," Brianna said. "We're your partners now. If you're down and out we're gonna help you out. I know I'm not gonna sit around and see you upset and I doubt that Denzel or Jason wouldn't help you out. We're artists which means we're always down to earth. You can tell us what's up." Charm looked at Jason who was nodding.

"Are you sure because I don't want to impose on you two. I just met you for Pete's sake."

"That's the best way to get advice. We're not yet biased," Brianna said.

"Trust us," Denzel said. He gave her a comforting smile. She was willing to tell them what was happening, but she didn't want to give all the details. Something about revealing she couldn't have babies with Denzel around made her uneasy. Truthfully she just felt like less of a woman.

"Okay well it's about my husband. He's invited a childhood friend of his to come stay with us for a while."

"Why would that have you so distracted?" Brianna asked.

"Because the childhood friend is a female," Charm said. Brianna immediately nodded. "I'm not one of those wives that look for a reason to be mad at their husbands or ridicule everything he does but for this it really took me off guard. We're married and well, the house we live in is ours. But he didn't ask me if I would mind that this woman was going to be living with us. He just took initiative and I feel like he should have come to me about it. What you guys think? I'm overreacting?"

"No he didn't," Jason gasped. "So she just showed up?"

"Yup, just like that. And all of a sudden I don't know my woman senses are tingling that something is off. But I literally have no choice."

"Why do you say you have no choice?" Denzel asked her.

"Because if I don't let this woman stay, he feels like it'll show that I don't trust him. And well, our marriage could be in trouble."

"Well do you trust him?"

"100 percent yes I do. I'm never suspicious about him doing anything because I wouldn't want him to be suspicious about anything I'm doing."

"So if you trust him Charm, and he's given you no reason to be suspicious then let it go. Yes, he should have told you the woman was coming to stay but since he didn't that was probably part of his motive to begin with. Maybe it's all a test to see how you'd handle it. And so far you're kind of failing." Charm's mouth fell open at his words. But then she realized he was speaking the truth. She was ultimately failing because she couldn't stop thinking about the bad things that would happen instead of thinking about the good that could happen.

"I guess I didn't see it that way," Charm said lowly.

"If he's doing this to make you prove you trust him then don't give him a reason to put your marriage in trouble. And if you're not suspicious and he willingly does something to jeopardize your marriage then honestly he's just dumb," Denzel said.

"Dumb?"

"Why would a man who has a woman like you in his life jeopardize losing you? Could only be because he's dumb."

"I don't know Denzel. When it comes to being a wife I'm not all that perfect."

"Bullshit, she's an amazing wife," Jason said. "And I agree with Denzel."

"Me too," Brianna added. "Just let this go, but always, always keep as eye out. It's not that you're looking for anything but at the same time you can't be oblivious to everything either." Even though it wasn't the complete story, Charm was feeling better. What if Terrell was so happy all of a sudden because of the possibilities that they could finally have a baby? Was it bad if he was excited? Charm shouldn't reprimand him for that, and he hasn't given her a reason to be doubtful of his intentions. So she was just going to let it go and hoped some good came out of this.

"Thanks for listening to me. It makes me feel a lot better," She smiled. Denzel looked at her and tilted his head to the side.

"What?" she laughed.

"I was just making sure you were being honest. Your smile is actually genuine now, so I believe you," He said.

"Oh and you can tell?" Charm asked.

"Yes I can tell."

"How?"

"I can just tell. Don't worry about it," He winked. Charm raised her brows and looked at him.

"Oh excuse me."

"So back to work now?" Jason asked. "You three need to decide what painting to use as the muse for the paint and sip session."

"And I was saying Charm you're the boss so you choose."

"Oh no, no, no," Charm spoke up. "I'm no one's boss. We're partners." She had an extra copy of the contract. "I signed the contract too so it binds me to working with you two as partners. We're artists. There are no bosses and big shots. Don't forget that."

"So then how do we decide what painting we chose?" Brianna asked.

"Why don't we just create something right now all three of us? Then we'll decide which to use for the session coming up and then we can use the other two in two other sessions. That way all of our works can be a muse," Denzel said.

"I like that idea," Jason clapped.

"You're not even in this part," Charm said.

"So what? I still like the idea," He pouted.

"Whatever," Charm smiled. "Okay we can do that Denzel. Let's get started, I'm dying to paint something anyway."

"Let's do it." Denzel stood first then he helped Brianna to her feet before turning to reach his hand out for Charm. She was taken aback by his gesture which seemed to offend him.

"My mama raised me to be a gentlemen you know," He said. Charm chuckled and took his outreached hand and let him help her up.

"And what about me?" Jason asked.

"If you don't get your ass up," Denzel laughed. Jason rolled his eyes and stood on his own.

"Damn just crush a man's dreams." Denzel shook his head.

"I'll get the canvases and the easels from the supply closet," Charm said.

"And I'll get you guys some drinks," Jason added.

"I have speakers to play some music," Brianna offered up.

"Then we're in business then," Charmed smiled. "I'll be right back let me get the stuff."

"Wait," Denzel stopped her. "I'll carry them out. You just relax your pretty self with Brianna." Charm felt herself blush.

"Oh-okay," She said. He smiled at her and continued into the supply closet to retrieve the easel's, canvases, and paints. Each time he brought out a different item Charm went over to help him, he would give her a stern look. When she reached for one of the easels he slapped her hand lightly.

"Baby girl I said I'll do it. Go on over with Brianna and just chill out."

"Baby girl?!" Charm gasped.

"Or I can just call you Charm. Whatever you want me to do," He said as he walked back into the supply closet. Charm walked away from him and went back over to Brianna.

"Don't worry," Brianna said. "He's not flirting with you. Denzel is just one of those unique ass men women only believe exists in their dreams. He's kind, he's sweet but he ain't a complete push over. Once you earn his trust there ain't shit he won't do for you."

"So why wouldn't you want that type of man as your man? I get you two are best friends but somewhere along the way you must have thought you two could be together?"

"In high school he was the popular one. He didn't play sports or nothing but when you're that good looking you have fans. I wasn't so popular and in a moment of weakness I was ready to do something just to fit in."

"Like what?"

"I wanted to be a cheerleader. So the girls on the squad told me I had to sleep with a football player to make the team. So they dressed me up in a stupid little slutty outfit and blindly I was going to do it. Denzel saw how I was dressed and he refused to let me do anything like that just to fit in. He had gym shorts and a t-shirt in his locker and he made me change into it to keep from embarrassing myself with what I was wearing. Everyone else, they just laughed and said how slutty I was. Denzel protected me from all of that. He punch dudes in the mouth that called me a slut and he told the girls off who was trying to get me to have sex with the football player in the first place. Long story short basically what I'm trying to say is the way Denzel protected me, I felt safe. I felt that if anything happened I could tell him and he'd have my back. And sure he was a good looking guy but that kind of safeness and closeness I felt with him isn't something I felt that I should be attracted to. I always just felt like he was my brother. And you can't be attracted to someone you consider family can you?" Brianna raised her brow when she asked that.

"No you can't," Charm answered.

"We started out feeling like family and that's the way it's been. Plus when he saw me draw we just had another connection that was unmistakable. We may not be blood but I'd do anything for that man. Just like he would do for me."

"Strangely that's how I feel about Jason," Charm said. "He's been in my life and not having him around would be hard. Even if he's annoying."

"I love you too!" Jason called out from where he was in the office.

"How can he hear us?" Brianna asked.

"He's a freak of nature," Charm laughed. Jason came from the office carrying four glasses and a bottle of Ciroc.

"You have any juice?" Brianna asked.

"Oh yes, I got some pineapple juice in the fridge so we can mix this ciroc with it. I'll be right back." Brianna shook her head.

"That's not why I was asking," She called out. Denzel came from the supply closet again his arms filled with paint. This time Charm left him alone as she watched him set up all three easels in the big space, then set up the canvases and gave them each sets of paint brushes and paint.

"Here's the juice! I'll pour for everyone," Jason said.

"I'll just take the juice," Denzel said grabbing the glass that only that the pineapple juice.

"Damn I know it's early but live a little," Jason stated. Denzel smiled at him.

"I don't drink," Denzel said. "If you don't mind."

"That's why I wanted the juice," Brianna spoke up.

"Why don't you drink?" Charm asked.

"My father was an alcoholic." That was all he needed to say. Everyone could understand his choice.

"Well then I'll have just some juice too," Charm sad just so he didn't feel left out.

"Ya'll can have juice. But my ass is drinking a little bit of this ciroc," Jason said.

"Pour me some of that good stuff too baby, shit," Brianna said.

"You know you don't have to drink juice," Denzel said when Brianna and Jason walked away.

"It's not a huge sacrifice," She said. "Baby boy," She added while winking and walking away.

"What kind of music you listen to Charm?" Brianna asked as she looked through her phone.

"I like all kinds of music," She answered.

"I'm putting on my Pandora." Charm didn't know what station she decided on but 'Ignition' by R. Kelly started playing. Charm watched the synchronization of how Denzel and Brianna started dancing while preparing their paints. It wasn't synchrony like choreography or something, but it was the synchrony to how they both starting singing and acting a fool to the music. With a smile on her face, Charm watched them hip bump each other and take turns singing the song. She could see it then what they meant by the fact that they were truly best friends. It was a reflection of her relationship with Jason.

"Are you just gonna watch his little cute booty or are you gonna paint?" Jason whispered to her.

"I am not watching his cute little booty," she scoffed.

"So then why you call it cute? Because you must have been looking at it. So you know it's cute." Charm gave Jason a look.

"Don't let me tell Terrell you tryna get me to look at another mans ass," She said.

"Always gotta bring Terrell goofy ass in the picture," He shook his head. "Go on and start painting." She smiled at him and went over to her blank canvas. The music went from R. Kelly to Ashanti but still the same Brianna and Denzel were feeling the music. They had both started on something meanwhile Charm's canvas was blank. For a moment, she closed her eyes and just felt the music. With everything going on with her, she related it to her painting and then she had an idea. Mixing her neutral colors she started painting a brown skin woman wrapped in ivory satin that covered her nude body except for the protruding of her round pregnant belly. She didn't want it to be obviously based on herself so she painted a mass of long dark curly hair on the woman to make her natural. Charm added little details like body jewelry, and those little imperfections like stretch marks on the stomach and a couple beauty spots.

The music played, and Charm continued to sip and paint her piece. It took the three of them about two hours to finish completely. Brianna was finished first of the three, then Denzel. It took Charm another ten minutes after they were done to finish her detailing on the kinky curls in the woman's hair.

"Okay I'm finally done," Charm said putting her paint brush down. "Let me see what you two got." When she turned around the both of them were standing behind her gawking at her painting.

"I say we do the first session with this painting," Brianna spoke up.

"Me too," Denzel whispered. "Damn, look at those details. I love it." He crossed his arms and leaned in close to the painting. It was hard for him not to reach out and touch it, but the paint was still wet so he had to restrain himself.

"Is that how you looked pregnant?" Brianna asked. "All regal and shit?"

"I um, I don't have kids," Charm said quietly.

"Oh sorry. It just looks like this is how you'd look pregnant. Right Denzel?" Denzel didn't answer her. He was too caught up in the painting. And besides if he started thinking about what she looked like pregnant he was going to start thinking about wanting to impregnate her. And that was not a good thing to think about.

"Yeah sure," He brushed off Brianna. Charm left from her painting and went to look at Brianna's. It was the image of a black girl with a big fuzzy ponytail with big round glasses reading a book. Charmed liked it. It too had details, like how she was sitting, the jeans she was wearing and the off the shoulder large sweater that gave her that comfy look.

"This looks real good," Charm commented. She moved onto Denzel's painting. Charm felt that his painting was even better than hers. It wasn't a full body painting like hers. It stopped just below the woman's shoulders. But the woman in the painting had her shoulder pressed to her cheek exuded a sort of sensuality that was sometimes hard to capture in paintings. She was wearing a bright green head wrap with her dreads painted coming out of the top of the head wrap stylistically. There were tribal marks on her face and her lips were painted a bright red.

"The both of you are some dope painters," Charm said. "Damn, we're gonna have some good paint and sip sessions!"

Charm backed up but didn't realize Denzel was right behind her until she felt his hard body against her back. He immediately moved away from her while looking uneasy.

"I'm sorry," She said quietly.

"It's no biggie baby girl," He said.

"You're really gonna keep call me that huh?"

"You really didn't tell me I couldn't," He countered.

"Don't think nothing of it," Brianna said. "Every girl is his baby girl. Like I told you before, he's sweet like that."

"Before? Wait ya'll were talking about me?" Denzel asked. Brianna waved him off, leaving him hanging with his question. Charm just snickered and kept her mouth shut too. She didn't want him to know she was inquiring anything about him to begin with.

Even with their paintings done, the four of them hung out at the gallery just talking and getting to know one another better. Already she could tell that Brianna was crazy yet cool type of friend. She kept it real, but she didn't have boundaries to anything she spoke about. And Denzel, he was the charming man that Brianna told her he was. There was this freeness about him. It was like he only saw the goodness in things in life and in people. That darkness in Charm that sprouted the first time she miscarried slowly began to dim in Denzel's presence. When someone was exuding that much positivity and lightness towards you, you almost were forced to take it in. And so she did. Because she didn't want to be a woman who was in constant pain over lost babies. Even when Terrell comforted her, she hardly felt the release she was feeling right now just sitting with Denzel and listening to him talk. Was that strange? She told herself it was just because he was an artist and they could just understand each other. Because if it was anything more than that then she shouldn't be the one suspicious at Terrell for having a woman live with them. He should be the one suspicious at her for deciding to partner with an artist she first started calling tall and chocolate.

CHAPTER EIGHT

"There's something I left out earlier when I was talking about Terrell and this woman moving in with us," Charm admitted to Jason. After spending hours at the gallery the four of them decided to split but Jason followed Charm home to have dinner with her. Instead of going inside, Charm had kept Jason out on their porch so she could tell him what the real deal was.

"What did you leave out? And I know your mind is still heavy on the baby. That's why you painted that pregnant lady today."

"Brianna was right. I do feel like I'd look like that woman I painted. Minus the large bouncy curls. But it was something I always imagined myself looking like while carrying a baby."

"So what's up honey?"

"That woman that's gonna be staying with us isn't a friend of Terrell's. In fact he just met her, and I just met her."

"So what the hell is she doing in your house in the first place?"

"She's gonna be our surrogate." Jason gasped and covered his mouth.

"No!" He exclaimed. "Are you serious?!"

"Completely serious."

"And what? You agreed to this? Charm if I know that you want to experience not just having a baby but carrying a baby, then Terrell must know this too! How could he even suggest a surrogate?! And why would you even agree to this?! You're not even 30 years old yet. In maybe 2 years where you are thirty you can talk about having a surrogate. I just think this is so premature to be doing this now."

"I don't think I really have a choice Jason. The doctors say my eggs are healthy yet I've never carried a baby past four months. Terrell claims he doesn't want to keep doing this to me, and that the miscarriages will keep happening. So basically I agree to the damn surrogate, or our marriage isn't going to work out because my body can't give him the babies he wants. And he made that perfectly clear. He specifically said that either I give him what a wife is supposed to give their husband or I just won't be his wife anymore." Jason shook his head. He'd told Charm from the moment she met Terrell, that he had a bad feeling about the man. But Terrell proved to be the perfect boyfriend. He treated Charm right and he cared for her and then he popped the question. Jason knew Charm wanted to be a wife and she wanted to start a family, but Terrell sometimes did shit, and said shit that made Jason question the type of man he was. He was clearly egotistical but Charm for some reason was just blind. What kind of man made that kind of threat to a woman who just had a miscarriage only a week ago? And then to bring a surrogate into their home not even thinking that Charm might need time to recuperate again before thinking about their baby issues. It was inconsiderate. Because it wasn't like Charm was purposely denying him a child.

"That's complete bullshit," Jason snapped fired up. "I'm not a fan of this. I'm gonna tell you right now. And I told you that Terrell be doing the type of shit that makes me question him. I just don't get it." Charm felt insecure for having to have a woman have her baby for her. Plus, whenever Jason was fired up over something it was serious business.

"Are you upset with me for agreeing to do this?" Charm asked.

"Yes! I am upset with you. You should have stood your ground to Terrell. And if he's threatening to divorce you because you're miscarrying then fuck him! I bet if you dared him to leave you he wouldn't! He's just scaring you into this. But this isn't all your fault and I don't blame you at all Charm. And I know the way you see it, it's hard to lose baby after baby. I just don't think you should give up."

"Well how can I not give up if Terrell will refuse to put his sperm in me so we can keep trying?! He's insisting on this and it will still be my egg and his sperm. Just another woman's body."

"Witchcraft. That's what that is."

"Jason!" Charm exclaimed. "Come on be serious!"

"I am being serious. The fact that you can put a woman's egg into another woman's body and fertilize it with the sperm of her choosing is witchcraft. It's not natural."

"Well it's as close to natural as I can be," Charm said. Jason hugged her tightly.

"Even if I don't agree you know I still got your back. We gonna get through this together."

"Thanks Jase."

"Come on I'm starving. What you gonna cook?" Charm shrugged her shoulders and turned to open her front door. She was pondering on what she needed to cook so Terrell had dinner, but that went out the window when she stepped into the house and could smell the fragrance of food.

"Looks like you won't be cooking nothing," Jason said. Charm took a deep breath and walked into the kitchen. There were pots and pans on the stove, and the place was a hot mess but no one was there. Hearing Terrell laugh, Charm following the sound into the living room. That's where she found them sitting down at the dining room table having dinner.

"Oh there you are!" Destiny perked up. "I'll get your plate set. And who is this handsome man with you?" she asked speaking of Jason.

"I don't swing that way," He said immediately.

"Don't mean you still can't be handsome." She walked off to the kitchen. Charm crossed her arms and looked at her husband.

"What part of 'I'm coming home, will be making dinner tonight, what do you want to eat?' didn't you understand when I texted it to you?" She asked Terrell.

"I didn't see the text until later and Destiny had already started cooking."

"So you couldn't text that to me?" Charm asked.

"I figured you were on your way anyway. I didn't think that would matter to you Charm."

"Another woman cooking in her house? Why wouldn't that matter to her?" Jason asked. Terrell only gave him a look. Destiny came back into the dining room with a bowl of Shrimp Alfredo.

"There's bread and wine on the table too." Destiny said. She put the plate down and motioned for Charm to sit down. But Charm stayed standing with her arms crossed looking down at the food.

"Shaking my head," Jason said out loud.

"I don't get it. What's the matter?" Destiny asked. "Don't you like shrimp Alfredo?"

"Actually no I don't," Charm said. "Maybe my husband didn't tell you, or he could have simply forgotten that his wife is allergic to shellfish."

"I didn't know she was going to make this!" He exclaimed. Charm couldn't believe the words coming out of his mouth. It was like she had the word 'stupid' written across her forehead.

"But your food is basically finished Terrell. Which means you were sitting here having dinner with her knowing damn well when I got home I wouldn't even know she was making you dinner in the first place or that it would be something I couldn't even join the both of you to eat! Are you that infatuated with her that you couldn't think to tell me these things Terrell?"

"Infatuated?!" He gasped. "Charm please don't do that. You know this is not why she's here! I'm sorry I spaced out and didn't say anything I don't know what I was thinking. Forget this whole dinner I'll make you something else to eat."

"Oh no it's fine. You stay here and enjoy the rest of your dinner with our surrogate. You should get to know the woman that's gonna be carrying our baby anyway right?"

"Charm I'm so sorry I didn't-"

"It's not your fault Destiny," Charm cut her off. She gave her husband a look before she took Jason's hand and led him upstairs to the master bedroom. She closed them in.

"Do you see why I was so distracted earlier?! Why I couldn't stop thinking about him here doing some shit with her?"

"Listen honey, Terrell has always been clueless sometimes. Like we told you earlier you just have to keep an eye out. Try to brush shit off and keep pushing. If you keep accusing him of something Charm, he's going to eventually do it. Like how I accuse him of being dumb, and here he is sitting eating shrimp when he knows you can't have it when you come in, so dumb. And again he's only thinking about himself." Charm sighed and flopped down on their bed.

"Look, I'm gonna go. You need to talk this out with Terrell, but call me if anything. And please eat something."

"I will. I just need to relax right now." Charm sat up in bed and gave Jason a tight hug before he left her for the night.

Once he was gone, she undressed then went to take a shower to further clear her mind. She pulled her short hair out of its ponytail and shook it out. When she emerged from her shower naked, Terrell was sitting in their bed with a bowl of pasta on her vanity.

"I made it fresh so you don't have to worry about anything." Charm looked at the bowl of pasta in Alfredo sauce with sweet peas and chicken breast.

"You made that?" she asked, knowing damn well her husband couldn't cook like that. He knew how to make minimal things but he wasn't no chef.

"Well Destiny made the chicken but I boiled the pasta and mixed it with the sauce. And don't be mad that she made it either."

"I'm not mad," Charm said simply.

"You say that. But then you'll be holding a grudge against me."

"Don't worry about it. I was only upset because you just seem caught up with her."

"And I am Charm. But in the way I'm supposed to be. I guess I'm just excited that this could actually work. So I've been over exerting myself to make sure Destiny won't ever feel like she doesn't want to do this for us anymore."

"You ever thought that maybe she'd get pregnant, get attached to our baby and just run off or something?"

"She can't. It's in the contract and legally even if she's carrying the baby, biologically it isn't hers so she can't claim custody over our baby. Trust me, I looked though every possibility and I want this to work for us."

"Yeah me too. I just feel like I'm young enough to keep trying on my own you know."

"Keep trying and keep failing you mean," He said. "Because you know that's what's going to happen." Charm pulled on her robe and sat at her vanity to eat her dinner.

"Fine. We do this your way. But if something goes wrong Terrell, it's all on you." He stood at the doorway and pushed his hands in his pockets.

"Maybe if you stop thinking something will go wrong, then you won't be worrying so much. But either way, it's going to happen." Charm didn't respond. He turned to leave but then he stopped and turned around.

"By the way," He stated. "Don't ever disrespect me like that in front of company again." Charm dropped her fork and blinked at her husband. He was dead serious. Because she called him out because he failed to answer any of her texts or let her know what was going on in her own home, he was pulling rank and demanding something from her. But this time she wasn't going to be the quite wife.

"Don't disrespect me in my own home in front of company Terrell, and I won't disrespect you," She countered.

"It's been a month right? You should be fully healed."

Terrell grunted lowly.

"Yeah and?" Charm asked.

"When Destiny leaves I'll show you a thing or two about respecting me." Charm leaned back and gave him a look.

"Threatening me?" She asked.

"I'm threatening your pussy Charm. Or actually it's my pussy. That's what I'm threatening. You know my favorite position. Be in it when I come back up here." He gave her a hot look before he finally left the bedroom.

CHAPTER NINE

Denzel stared at the text messages he'd sent to Gabrielle that went unanswered. He had given her time to come out of whatever funk she was in, but even after a couple days went by she still wasn't talking to him. He tried calling and she would put him straight to voicemail. Gabrielle was notorious for her tantrums but she never went more than two weeks without talking to him. So still, Denzel had time until she would finally respond. But at the same time he thought it was incredibly immature of her to be acting the way she was. Either she wanted to be with him or she didn't. All this ignoring him and blocking his calls was petty. Denzel sent one final message to Gabrielle. This one she actually answered.

I just need some time Denzel. What happened over dinner really upset me. Especially because I thought you loved me. I'll get back to you. Denzel sighed hard and replied to her quickly.

You know I care a lot about you Gabby. I haven't wanted anyone but you. That message went unanswered but Denzel figured she wasn't going to respond again. But he could take a hint. If she wanted to be left alone then he was going to leave her alone. But he just had to think about where their relationship was going to go in the future. She wanted marriage, and he simply didn't. Denzel was too restless now to go back to sleep so he called Brianna.

"What are you doing Bri?" Denzel asked when she picked up the phone.

"I'm sleeping you psycho. What's the matter?"

"Nothing, nothing. I just wanted to go paint. But I know you're not getting out of your bed right now."

"Your damn right. Now as long as it's not a pressing matter, I'm going back to sleep."

"Fine. Talk to you later." Denzel hung up the phone and shook his head. It was nearing 7 in the morning which was pretty early even for him. After a hectic few days creating more paintings at the gallery and preparing for the paint and sip, once they got home it was usually lights out for them. And he usually didn't wake up until about 9. But with Gabrielle heavy on his mind for ignoring him he couldn't brush it off at the moment. Since he knew he wasn't going back to sleep he figured he would just continue painting, but everything he was working on was at the gallery. He decided to take the chance that maybe Charm was an early bird like himself.

"Hey Denzel," She greeted in her usual bright tone. Denzel was surprised at first.

"I didn't expect you to be up honestly. Brianna was knocked out when I called her."

"My husband went to work early so I was up to make him breakfast and see him off," She chuckled. Even though he respected the hell out of Charm, he couldn't help that tingle of jealousy towards her husband. Denzel didn't even know the guy but already he hated him.

"So what's up?" Charm asked.

"I actually might not be going back to sleep any time soon so I wanted to get some of my work done. Might as well get an early start. Of course I left my work in the gallery and I don't have a key to get in. I was hoping maybe if you didn't mind you'd come down to the gallery and paint some things with me, which would also mean that I get to go inside because you have the key."

"That reminds me, I should really cut you two a key. But in this instance I don't mind the early start. I'll get dressed and meet you over there."

"Cool then. I'll see you soon."

Denzel dressed in his old jeans riddled with paint stains, with a clean t-shirt and that was it. When you were a painter there was minimal effort that went into choosing what to wear. Especially if you were going to work. That was one of the perks of his job. He didn't have to look a certain way to function well.

On his way to the gallery he stopped to get a cup of coffee for both him and Charm. He didn't know how she liked her coffee but he went to safe route and just ordered it light and sweet. Most women liked it that way. He arrived at the gallery before she did, but he only waited 15 minutes before she arrived. Denzel immediately went to her car and opened her door for her. She gave him one of those 'I can't believe you're actually doing that look', before taking his hand and letting him help her out the car.

"I figured we could use the coffee," He said. She smiled and leaned into the car to retrieve her purse and a paper bag.

"And I thought we could use the muffins," She smiled.

"I am actually a little hungry now that I can smell the banana nut one."

"Well back off. The banana nut one is mine," She laughed. He followed her to the gallery and waited while she opened it up. When she did she turned and motioned for him to go inside but he shook his head.

"Ladies first baby girl," He said. Charm rolled her eyes.

"You know, you're starting to get a little annoying. Because every time I fix my mouth to say men are dogs, your face pops up in my head and then somehow I can't say it anymore."

"But what about your husband? You wouldn't marry him if he was a dog now would you?" Charm thought about the dogging Terrell but on her a couple nights ago that she could still feel in her stomach. She shook her head to get the image out of her mind.

"In this day and age it might be our only choice to marry dogs whether we like it or not." She walked into the gallery and Denzel followed her before closing the door and turning the lock. The shades were still down so they were protected from wandering eyes. All their easels were still set up in the middle of the room so the only thing he had to retrieve from the supply closet was more paint and some brushes.

"I'm going to eat before I do any painting. I need some fuel," She said. "But if you start painting first I'll be you're admirer."

"Thanks," He said. While she sat down on a bean bag, he handed her the cup of coffee and kept one for himself. He took a few sips while looking at the painting he started the night before. All of a sudden he didn't even feel inspired by it anymore.

"What's the matter?" Charm asked.

"It just doesn't speak to me anymore. The realness I thought it would have had kind of lacks now." Charm took a good look at the man he was painting. She could see what Denzel was talking about.

"Maybe it doesn't seem real because you're trying to hide the man's real feelings."

"And what if he doesn't know how to feel?"

"Then paint that. Not knowing how to feel is just as real as knowing how to feel." Right then Denzel knew what he was doing to paint. He turned and looked at Charm before just sitting in front of her on another bean bag.

"You're incredible," He told her.

"No. I'm just a painter."

"Which makes you even more incredible. Why do you always discount yourself? You've done it when you told us about your marriage, and you do it when I try and compliment you."

"I don't know, I've never been good at taking compliments, or tooting my own horn. It's not my style."

"I think maybe you just don't get complimented enough. Which by the way, you're beautiful today." Charm frowned and looked down at her baggy boyfriend jeans and her white t-shirt.

"Seriously?" she asked.

"So very serious. You're welcome."

"Thank you," She said still giving him the eye. "I'm sorry I just don't get it. How could you compliment what I'm wearing? I mean I look like a boy."

"I didn't compliment what you were wearing Charm, I said you're beautiful today. You took that to mean I was complimenting your outfit which I wasn't. Doesn't matter what you're wearing, you're beautiful when you give me those animated looks that you always be giving me when I do something nice to you." Charm covered her mouth as she started laughing. Soon a snort left her.

"And you snort," He chuckled.

"Stop it! I try not to laugh as hard so I don't start snorting," She said. "I just know you're not talking shit about my faces, I know I can be a little animated."

"Now wait a minute," Charm said composing herself. "You talk so sweet to be a single man. Now I know there has to be a woman in your life. Except Brianna of course."

"Well it's kind of complicated," Denzel frowned.

"Ooo, tell me," Charm begged getting closer to him. He took a deep breath. Peaches. She smelled like peaches today.

"I guess I can use your advice too." He paused before he started. "Charm did your husband propose to you at a perfect time?"

"Not really. I mean, I think he proposed because he thought that I liked another man and was ready to leave him or something. So I wouldn't say it was the right time, but marriage isn't something you clock like that."

"But what if you thought he should propose and he doesn't?"

"Then maybe we're just on two different levels. You can't force that kind of thing on anyone. And if your partner doesn't want it, you either wait until they're ready or you move onto someone you know wants to be married. Is this happening to you?" Charm asked.

"My girlfriend, we've been together since high school. I practically knew her as long as I knew Brianna. Some nights ago she was hinting that I take her to this high class restaurant. I did that then she starts boasting about our anniversary and instead of the anniversary I celebrate she's here celebrating the day we met. Honestly I didn't even knew that counted as an anniversary. I gave her a promise ring in high school. She kept hinting that she wanted a new ring. And my stupid behind thought she meant she wanted another promise ring and turns out, she wanted me to propose to her."

"And you don't want to marry her?"

"There are just some things about her that aren't completely perfect."

"But not all women are perfect."

"True statement, but I don't want her to be a Stepford wife or something. I just want her to be perfect for me."

"I don't mean to pry but what's wrong with her?"

"For one she doesn't appreciate my artwork like I appreciate it. I'm not asking her to love it, I'm asking her to respect it and she can't do that." Charm knew how that felt. Terrell may not say anything about her artwork anymore but she knew he didn't respected it, and he damn sure doesn't think it produces enough income.

"So then why are you with her? If art is the number one thing in your life, and she can't respect just that, then what sense does it make?" Denzel shrugged.

"I got comfortable. And really I care a lot about her. So I just let that go. But now that she wants marriage and I don't it complicates things. Especially since the night ended with her storming off and taking a cab home. She told me she needed some time and that was it. I haven't heard from her since. I've tried calling, I've tried texting but nothing. She's done that before and come back to me in a week like nothing ever happened."

"That behavior is a little juvenile for someone who wants to be married."

"Tell me about it," Denzel scoffed.

"Well I think if you show up at her house and just get straight to the point, are we together or not, then you'll have your answer. But then again Denzel why are you even tolerating that kind of behavior? You can choose to end it too you know."

"I suppose I can," He said. "But I just know that if she calls me today I'll go running to her even if I say I don't want to be with her anymore. She has a hold on me like that."

"Did she take your virginity?" Charm asked bluntly. Denzel hated to admit it but he did.

"Yes, she did."

"No wonder you're so attached. That's your first love." There went the L word.

"I loved her then, in high school. But now it's different. I can't say that to her. I can't look her in the face and tell her I love her. I'm not sure why."

"Because you don't love her Denzel that's why. And there's nothing wrong with that. The only thing wrong is you trying to keep a relationship with a woman you know you don't want to marry and you know you don't love."

"So if tomorrow you woke up and knew that you fell out of love with your husband, would you just tell it to his face? Would you tell him right then and there and you want a divorce because you just don't love him anymore?"

"Well no. but that's because we're married. We built a life together and sometimes you can't just throw that away."

"That goes for me and Gabrielle too. We're not married but we've only been with each other."

"You took her virginity?" Denzel nodded.

"I know it might be hard to end a relationship when you've been with someone so long but sometimes it's in their best interest. Either she's going to be okay with you not wanting to marry her, or you're going to have to marry her. So I think you have a decision to make on that. I think I know what you want to do, but you just aren't ready to convince yourself you need to do it."

"Sometimes talking with women really get you in your feelings," Denzel said. Charm laughed at him. She started to get up, but he bounced up before her just to help her stand.

"Take all that feeling I just gave you and put it into your painting," She said. She tapped the wooden end of the paint brush on his chest. He took it from her and when he did their fingertips touched. The electricity in their touch was noticeable. He saw her eyes go wide and she drew away immediately but she tried to smile it off. Charm turned away from the stare of his chocolate eyes before she completely lost herself. She slapped herself on the forehead and turned to her unfinished work. She could still feel Denzel staring at her back and when she looked around he was indeed still looking at her.

"What?" She asked. Denzel had to bite back what he wanted to say to her. How could he tell a married woman he wanted to kiss her? How could he tell a married woman he wanted to know what her curves felt like underneath him? How could he even feel like that when he was obviously so stuck on Gabby? He'd just spilled his gut to her about not being able to end his relationship with Gabby and now he was thinking heavily about pulling Charm into his arms and kissing her? He had to shake those cobwebs from his head and think straight.

"Nothing," He stumbled out. "Nothing." When she looked away Denzel let out a deep breath. He seriously needed to relax.

CHAPTER TEN

Destiny pulled up to Terrell and Charm's house a week and a half after meeting them. Finally, she was moving in. With their doctor's appointments coming up soon Destiny wanted to be settled into their home. It was a beautiful Saturday morning and she was ready to get her new life started. After moving from home to home in the foster care system when she was young, Destiny always promised herself that she would never struggle the way she struggled before. But this was by far going to be her biggest payout. And she was actually going to enjoy it too. Especially being around a man like Terrell. This was going to be her most pleasurable plan.

"Hey Destiny," Terrell said coming out of the large house. He was wearing a muscle shirt and gray sweatpants. Naturally her eyes went to his lower extremities which she could guess was pretty impressive from the print it left.

"Hi Terrell. How are you?!"

"It's Saturday, that's all I can say," He smiled. "I'll help you carry your stuff in."

"Where's Charm?" Destiny asked hoping his wife wasn't home.

"I'm right here," Charm's voice called out. Destiny nearly cringed at her sweet voice. But she forced herself to smile when she looked at Charm.

"Hi Charm! Aren't you glowing this morning?!"

"Oh well thank you. I just gave myself a facial. I can give you one too." Charm left the porch and walked up to Destiny to give her a hug. Even if she was feeling a certain way about the situation she wasn't going to keep showing her displeasure. And if she kept showing she wasn't happy then only bad things were going to come out of it. So she was shooting positivity into the situation and hoping 9 months came and went quickly.

"Oh nice, I would love a facial," Destiny said. She turned from Charm and rolled her eyes after she said that. She hated acting like some nice, sweet woman. Truth be told, there was nothing but blackness inside her. After never having anyone to love her, she lost what it felt like to care for anyone or to actually love anyone. She could care less that Charm wanted a baby and she couldn't conceive. Destiny wasn't here for the feelings. She was just here for the money.

Charm grabbed one of Destiny's smaller bags while Terrell went back and forth carrying her 3 large suitcases. Charm thought it was a lot of clothes but towards the end of the pregnancy she wasn't going to be able to fit any of her regular clothes. Grabbing the other small bag, Destiny closed the trunk of her car and followed Charm inside the house.

Terrell had her suitcases in the living room so Charm put the rest of the bags there before going back to the kitchen. She'd made a big breakfast in preparation of Destiny's arrival.

"Before you get settled in your room let's sit and eat. You've been talking a lot with Terrell but you and I haven't had a good conversation."

"No we haven't," Destiny said tartly. She sat around the island and watched as Charm began to make her a plate of food. She nearly barfed just watched Charm waltz around the kitchen and be lovey dovey with Terrell while she shared out the food. This woman really thought she was all of that. Destiny was going to change that though. And she was going to love every minute of it.

"So have you ever been anyone's surrogate before?" Charm asked her, sitting across from her at the island with Terrell next to her.

"No I haven't. You two are the first couple that has picked me."

"Oh well I wouldn't say I picked you. That was all Terrell's doing."

"So are you saying you'd rather someone else?" Destiny asked. She crossed her arms ready to go tit for tat with her if that's what she wanted.

"Of course not Destiny. You seem like a very nice woman. And you'll fit in with us well. I respect my husband's choice."

"I'm glad. We want this process to be as painless as possible. Well except for the giving birth part." Charm chuckled at her words.

"So what do you do?" Destiny asked. "I saw from your clothes that you paint. Is that your job?"

"Yes it is. I have an art gallery and a company. Still building it up though. We just had a successful paint and sip session. We had 20 people come and paint with us. You should come to one of the sessions I think you'd like it."

"Oh I'm no artist. I can't even draw a stick figure. So I think

I'll pass on that one."

"Well the offer is still open anytime you want to come." Destiny nodded and sipped her orange juice.

"Well the food is delicious Charm thanks. I think I want to start unpacking my things now and get some rest. Soon we're both going to be in and out of the doctor's office getting poked and prodded. It's going to get hectic."

"Right you are," Charm said.

"Terrell can you help me carry the stuff upstairs?" Destiny asked.

"Yeah sure I can." He left from Charm's side to go help Destiny carry her things to the guest room. Luckily the bedroom was on the first floor and not upstairs near the master bedroom. While her stuff was being carried to the guest bedroom, Charm stayed behind and began cleaning up the kitchen.

With Charm staying in the kitchen it gave Destiny a little alone time with Terrell. When he brought her last suitcase into the room, Destiny unzipped one of the smaller bags and purposefully, she dropped it to the ground so the contents would spill out.

"Oh crap," Destiny gasped.

"It's alright I got it," Terrell said. He turned and bent over to help pick up the items from the bag that spilled out, but he stopped midway when he realized just what had spilled out. Destiny pretended to be embarrassed and she gathered her panties and lingerie from the floor and stuffed them back in the bag.

"You were not supposed to see that," she said.

"Don't even worry about it," He told her. "There's nothing wrong with having lingerie."

"Not even for a woman that's about to be carrying your baby?" she questioned. Terrell noticed the way she said that and it gave him pause.

"You mean carrying me and Charm's baby," He corrected her. Destiny shrugged.

"Sure," She smiled at him. She stuffed the last of her lingerie back in the bag and looked at him softly. Terrell was a bit shocked she had that kind of lingerie with her. Not that it was unusual for a woman of her age and everything to have lingerie it was just that she was going to be a surrogate. It just seemed out of the norm.

"These are just pajamas. Or well pajamas to me." Terrell raised his brows. Those were pretty sexy pajamas.

"So you wear lingerie every night to bed?" Terrell asked.

"Yes," She smiled "Doesn't Charm wear lingerie to bed?"

"No not really," Terrell admitted. "But I mean we're married we usually don't wear anything to bed."

"I guess so, but sometimes a little teasing and dressing sexily never hurt anyone."

"True I suppose." Terrell looked her up and down and wandered what she would look like in one of the lingerie outfits. His imagination took over and before he knew it, he was dazed and just lost.

"Terrell," Destiny called softly. He came to and saw her standing directly in front of him, the mounds of her breast right under his vision. He swallowed hard and forced himself to stop looking at her breasts.

"I'm sorry what were we talking about?" he asked.

"Pajamas," She smiled wickedly. "But that was what we were talking about. What were you thinking about?" Her eyes flickered down on him. Terrell didn't know what she was talking about until she pointed at his groin. He looked down and saw the hardness in his sweatpants. What in the hell was he doing?

"I'll leave you to unpacking," He rushed out. "See you later." He hurried out of the room putting a hand over his erection.

"Calm down Terrell," He breathed. "It's only lingerie! You have a fucking wife get your mind right!" He paced the hall as he gave himself a pep talk.

"Terrell are you alright?" Charm called out to him.

"Shit," He grumbled. "Yeah I'm good honey!" He called out to her. He continued pressing on his erection before Charm saw it. She was going to have a fit if she did and realized he was just coming from Destiny's room.

"Only 9 months," He said to himself. "Then you'll have your baby, and your wife. Just 9 months." He took a deep breath and left the hall and went back to the kitchen to spend some time with Charm. That's what he needed to do in the first place. Spend time with his wife, and get an erection from her. Not someone else.

"Sweetie, when was the last time we went out on a little outing?" Charm asked him when he entered the kitchen.

"Not for a while honestly. The both of us have been so busy."

"True. Which is why I'm not doing any art today whatsoever, and I think the two of us should go to the park or something and have a little picnic."

"But what about Destiny?" Terrell asked. "We're just going to leave her here alone?"

"She's not a child," Charm said confused as to why he was bringing her up.

"No but this is her first day moving in. How we just going to up and leave her like that? At least give her some time to settle in."

"So I should expect this type of answer when I suggest me and you go out? That we can't leave Destiny alone?"

"No," He said. "Don't try and pick a fight with me right now. Please." Charm just shrugged and continued cleaning up. She wiped down all the counters then washed the dishes.

"Set something up out in the backyard honey. We can have a picnic out there and spend time with each other."

"That might be my only option so sure, I'll set something up." Terrell realized even though Charm had been incredibly nicer towards the situation with them having to have a surrogate, she was easy to get snippy with him. Her attitude needed a serious readjustment.

"You're attitude has been testing me," Terrell said to her. Charm just shrugged her shoulders.

"You know the kind of woman you married Terrell. And if something deserves my attitude it will get it. Does that bother you?"

"You know it does," He stated. "So if I were you, I'd cut it out. Before you get into trouble." Charm shot him a look.

"Oh I'd love to see that happen," She scoffed. She wiped her hands on a dish cloth to dry them before turning around and looking at her husband. As she walked by him, she palmed his erection and then kept it moving. Terrell looked at her and grabbed her wrist.

"Don't play that game with me."

"Who's playing?" She asked. Knowing he'd just had an erection from another female Terrell seized his chance to use it on the woman he was supposed to be using it on. He scooped Charm into his arms and rushed up the stairs with her. Her vibrant laugh filled the house as he bounded for the bedroom.

"I should have known this is what you needed," Terrell stated as he pulled the strings of his sweatpants. "So toot that ass up baby," Charm gave him a devilish grin before taking her clothes off and fixing herself on the bed on all fours. Terrell went up behind her and pushed her shoulders down onto the bed and grabbing her hips bringing them high into the air. There was something about being with a woman like Charm. She was always willing and ready. Staring back at him was her moistened pink lips that were just begging for his attention. Terrell moved his hips forward letting the tip of his erection bump against her lips but he didn't push inside her.

"That's what you're doing?" She breathed turning to look at him.

"That's for the attitude," He said before finally pushing inside her. But he only went so deep before pulling back out of her. Charm pushed him back and slithered out from in front of him.

"I'm not playing this game with you," She snapped at him. She grabbed onto his shirt and forced him down onto the bed and onto his back.

"Think I can't take what I want?" she asked. She swung her legs over his hips, aligning herself with his erection. Terrell loved it when Charm took control just like she was doing now. She slid down onto his erection while bracing herself on his chest. Terrell had to hold back his moan as she seated herself completely. She rocked back and forth to get herself comfortable before she began to raise her hips up and down to ride him. Terrell of course couldn't help but begin to groan at her movements then. His wife was just too good, and she felt incredible.

"You don't ever get to tease me," She huffed out. "Cause you know what I'll do to you." Terrell knew what she would do to him because she was doing it now. She was gripping him tightly with her walls and all he could do was lay there gritting his teeth trying to hold himself back from popping.

"I know baby," He groaned. Charm tossed her head back as she rode herself to pleasure. Terrell's penis had always fit her perfectly and she was never left unsatisfied. Even in complete control, she was able to ride him in a way that still invoked her pleasure. His tip rubbed against her g-spot repeatedly and that's what had her eyes rolling to the back of her head. Her body began to convulse as she started to come. Terrell grabbed her supple ass and forced her to keep riding him.

"Fuck I'm coming with you," He gritted feeling her orgasm begin to trickle down onto his shaft. He let himself go, burying himself deep into her as he came hard. She called out his name in her own orgasm as her body fell limp on top of him.

"Damn," Terrell breathed. Charm chuckled and sat up slowly. She kissed him on the chin as he held her. Charm heard a squeak by their bedroom door. She turned to look quickly. The door was slightly open and that's where Destiny was standing there peeking through. She gasped when Charm looked at her and rushed away from the door. Charm hopped off Terrell quickly and grabbed something to cover herself with. What in the world was Destiny doing just watching them?

****

Destiny snuck around the house wanting to see where Charm and Terrell were without them knowing that she was looking for them. The house was so too quiet for a Saturday and she figured that maybe they had left the house or they were taking a nap. But the moment she left her bedroom, she could hear the distant gasps and rasps of sex. Destiny knew the sounds of sex anywhere. Unable to resist, she'd slowly climbed the steps towards the master bedroom. To her surprise their bedroom door was slightly open and Destiny could see clear as day what was going on inside. She crept up to the door and peeked inside. Charm was riding Terrell hard, as her breathy moans filled the room. If Charm's body wasn't swallowing up Terrell's dick then Destiny would be able to see what Terrell was working with. But she already knew it was impressive. It had to be in order for Charm to be riding it the way she was. She watched them fuck feeling herself get heated. As Charm began to orgasm, Destiny's mistake then was trying to get closer and that's when she when the door squeaked. She didn't have time to ditch before Charm spotted her.

"Shit," Destiny breathed. She rushed away and headed downstairs as quickly as possible. She tried to make herself busy in the kitchen, but Charm was right onto her. She came into the kitchen wearing a robe.

"Hey," Charm said to her. Destiny tried not to look at her but Charm came directly in her face and stopped her from wiping down the counter.

"I know you were watching," Charm said.

"Yeah? And so what?" Destiny asked. "I'm not the one who left the bedroom door open."

"But that still doesn't give you the right to just stand there watching us."

"How about apologizing to me instead of scolding me?"

Destiny crossed her arms.

"Apologize? You were spying on me and my husband and I have to apologize to you?"

"Yes. Leaving the door open like you're trying to show off or something."

"I can't-" Charm was cut off my Terrell grabbing her arm.

"We are sorry," Terrell interrupted. "I should have shut the door." Destiny nodded before looking him up and down and walking out of the kitchen. Charm looked at her husband.

"I just don't want ya'll to argue over nothing." Charm just put her hands up. She didn't even know whether to be mad, or concerned Destiny was just watching them have sex. It was downright weird.

"Whatever," Charm said.

"We were gonna do a picnic weren't we?" Terrell asked. "We should still set that up."

"Okay fine. Let me just go freshen up."

Destiny hid in her bedroom after her confrontation with Charm. That woman had some balls coming at Destiny like that. So what if she was watching them? Destiny was pretty sure she could ride Terrell better anyways. But to keep away from more confrontation she stayed in her room for more than an hour. After that, she realized she hadn't heard anything going on in the house. It was completely quiet. She left her room to investigate. Outside her bedroom it gave her more evidence that the house was seemingly empty. But in living room she peaked around the corner at the patio doors and that's when she saw both Charm and Terrell outside in their large backyard sitting down in the grass. They were caught up in their own world and for the time being Destiny was alone in the house.

She figured while they were outside preoccupied she could actually snoop around. There wasn't much going on in the main rooms, so she went straight back to the master bedroom. The moment she opened the door the first thing she saw was the large wedding photograph of Charm and Terrell hanging over their bed.

"Yuck," Destiny stuck her tongue out at the loving photo. No one was ever that happy. She carefully searched Charm's drawers and through her vanity. She took note on all of Charm's choice of perfumes and body lotions. She looked in Charm's jewelry box. The woman barely had anything in there. She didn't know why since her husband could probably afford any kind of jewelry she may have wanted. There was however a nice pair of diamond earrings and Destiny really had to contemplate on if she would be able to take it and Charm wouldn't suspect that Destiny stole it. She could earn a pretty penny from it at a pawn shop. Destiny shrugged and took the earrings. If she got caught and accused then she would have a plan for that. But if not, she was going to earn herself some bank for the pretty jewelry.

Putting everything back as it was, she snuck out of the bedroom and closed the door. Since Charm and Terrell were still outside, Destiny decided to change into some yoga shorts and a sports bra to join them outside. She wanted to be half naked around Terrell, and her plan for it was her doing yoga. Couldn't really say anything to her if she was doing something as innocent as yoga. She changed her clothes and grabbed her mat so she could join them outside.

Standing at the patio doors she watched intently as Charm and Denzel were laid out, making out and touching each other like they weren't outside and not in the privacy of their room and they had just finished fucking not too long ago. Weren't they tired of being lovey dovey? Well, Destiny was tired of it. So that's why was about to interrupt it.

"Damn ya'll," Destiny said opening the patio doors and going outside. Charm pulled away from Terrell immediately and tried to cover her breasts that were spilling from her top. She looked up and gasped when she saw Destiny wearing the tight spandex and sports bra.

"Don't let me interrupt," Destiny said. "I just thought I'd come out and do some yoga. It's nice out."

"Right but me and Terrell were hoping to just have some alone-" Terrell stopped Charm from finishing her statement.

"Just let her be," Terrell said. "She can go over there and we can be here the backyard is big enough Charm." Charm sighed and got off Terrell and just sat next to him.

"You can come out there's no problem," Terrell said.

"Thanks Rell," Destiny said. Charm looked at her then looked back at Terrell.

"Rell huh?" Charm asked. Terrell just shrugged. Charm kept looking at her husband who looked at Destiny as she walked to the other side of the yard with her yoga mat. Her ass was practically hanging out of her spandex shorts. Charm didn't mind having Destiny there with them, after all she was going to be carrying their baby, but it was like she couldn't get some alone time with her husband. And when she did, Destiny was there peeking in on them like a creep. Now she was here wearing practically nothing and her husband couldn't take his eyes off her. Charm nudged Terrell with her elbow.

"You're bold as hell," Charm stated. "Right in front of my face. Like I wasn't even riding the shit out of your dick only an hour ago." Charm stood a little fed up; and even though Terrell tried to stop her she went back into the house and slammed the patio doors shut. She wasn't going to get her husband to herself and she didn't know what frustrated her more. Destiny invading their space, or Terrell allowing her to and making it seem as if it was alright. Instead of staying in the house, she went to put on her baggy jeans and a t-shirt so she could go to the studio and paint. She didn't think it was wise that she stay. Not with the way she was feeling.

"We were supposed to be spending today together!" Terrell called out to her when he came into the house and saw her preparing to leave.

"Oh were we?" she asked.

"Why you gotta be like that?" He questioned. "All of a sudden everything I do is a problem!"

"You were just practically drooling at her ass. What in the hell you mean by why I gotta be like that?"

"Charm, I'm a man okay? I can't help it if I look. But that doesn't mean I want to touch or even do anything with her. You can't react like that for every little thing I do. Seriously. I'm your husband. Not you're little boy toy or fuck buddy. And I'm not going to take you accusing me of shit day after day. You hear me? And if we're real you're the reason she's here. Not me." There he went again, accusing her for something she couldn't help.

Charm looked him up and down. She didn't quite have the words to say to him. She just knew that this wasn't how their relationship was before. Once the babies couldn't come, Terrell was starting to be this new man. And Charm wasn't sure she liked it. She wasn't sure that she wanted to be with a man that could treat her like she was at fault for everything.

"You don't have to keep pushing that in my face," Charm

mumbled. "And just because I miscarried doesn't give you the right to gawk at another woman's ass with your wife sitting right next to you. Makes me wonder if you still hold me in the same light as you did when you said 'I do.' So you can stay here with your surrogate and I'll go do what I do best before I lose my ever loving mind by staying here." Huffing out and pushed past him. She gathered her things even faster and hurried out of the house. Right now she just needed the space and she needed to clear her mind. Only her art would do that for her right now.

CHAPTER ELEVEN

Denzel was alone in the gallery sketching on his pad. He had a blank canvas in front of him but he wasn't ready to start painting just yet. He was free sketching just to get his thoughts sorted out until he had one final idea. Most days he was in the gallery because being home alone actually depressed him without having Gabrielle to call on. Even despite her worst qualities when Denzel told her he was lonely she would be there at his side even if she never wanted to move into his loft. Just thinking about her further made him depressed. How was he going to propose to a woman who didn't want to live with him unless he had some big house? And then Brianna was giving violin lessons at the local community college so he couldn't call her and annoy her with her problems or for company.

A buzzing in his pocket caught his attention. Pulling out his phone, he had to rub his eyes to make sure he read the name of who was calling him correctly.

"Gabrielle?" He asked answering the phone.

"Yeah, it's me."

"So you finally ready to talk? This is getting out of hand you know. It's been over a week."

"It's just the way things are right now. You broke my heart Denzel. I need some time to recover from that." Denzel was flabbergasted. The last thing he ever wanted to do was break her heart.

"Broke your heart? Are you kidding me? I tell you the truth and now I broke your heart?"

"You think this is a joke or something? No I'm not kidding you," she replied hotly.

"Gabrielle you need to come to my house and let us talk. Because you can't force me to marry you and then tell me I'm breaking your heart it's not fair."

"Well I don't want to see you right now Denzel. I just can't. Not when I know you don't want to marry me."

"Wow," He gasped. "Are you seeing someone else? Because if you are we could just call it quits right here and right now. Because I'm not playing this game with you. You want me to marry you but you can't even be an adult and come and talk to me face to face." In the silence after his words he heard what sounded like a pill bottle being opened. A few of the pills shook before she gulped and took a deep breath.

"Stop trying to get a rise out of me," She said intently. Suddenly Denzel didn't even recognize the voice of the woman on the phone. She sounded completely different as if someone had taken the phone from her and was speaking in her place. The menacing voice just didn't belong to Gabrielle.

"I'll come and see you, when I'm good and ready to come and see you. And no. I'm not seeing someone else. So that means you don't get to see anyone else either. Keep that in mind Denzel." And with that, she hung up the phone. Denzel shook his head.

Something was seriously was wrong with his woman. He slammed his phone down angrily not even caring if he cracked the screen. He was a little fed up with what she was doing but at the same time he didn't see a way to rectify it. And until she wanted to talk to him there wasn't shit he could do about it.

Sitting on the ground he loosened his dreads from it's ponytail and let it fall around his face. A headache was slowly creeping into his brain and he needed as little tension on his head as he could get. It was the sound of the gallery door opening that made him look up. Charm was storming into the gallery muttering to herself. She slammed the door and locked it with the lock. She turned and stopped in her tracks when she saw Denzel sitting on the floor.

"Oh hey," She said pushing her hair out of her face. "Didn't see you there." She tried to smile and Denzel saw right through it. Obviously someone was upsetting her too.

"Hey," Denzel greeted. "Tough day huh?"

"What makes you say that?" She asked. When she went to sit down, Denzel stood and helped her to the floor. He sat back down and looked at her.

"You were throwing a mini fit just now. You expect me to believe you're fine?" She threw her hands up.

"I let this woman come live with us and I'm trying to keep the peace and I want it to work but I swear Terrell keeps doing these things that get under my skin and when I question him I look like the jealous one."

"Terrell is your husband then?" Denzel asked. Charm

nodded. She didn't even mean to blurt it out but it was on the tip of her tongue and she just couldn't help it.

"Tell me Denzel, your girlfriend you've been with her for a long time. Have you ever looked at another woman in a way you weren't supposed to? Like stare at another woman's ass or something? Is that normal for you to just 'look', and only 'touching' is problematic?" Charm asked.

"There's only one time where I've ever looked at another female and felt some sort of attraction while with Gabrielle. And even feeling that attraction made me feel guilty as hell. But I don't believe that look and not touch shit. You shouldn't be looking or touching."

"Did you tell Gabrielle you found another woman attractive?"

"No," Denzel admitted. "But I haven't done anything to get me into trouble." Even though Charm was the woman he was talking about, he didn't dare admit that.

"He did it right in front of me. And she was there wearing yoga spanks that were way too tight and way too short and he was just there staring. I of course point that out to him and you know what he says?"

"What?"

"That I shouldn't keep accusing him of shit because then he's gonna end up doing it. And that because he's my husband I should be trusting him without a doubt. But as my husband why the hell is he looking at other females?! Not only that but she was spying on us having sex and he just apologizes to her instead of telling her it wasn't right!" Charm was practically screaming at Denzel and he didn't even flinch. He just moved closer to her and handed her the unopened bottle of water he was going to drink but hadn't gotten a chance to. She took the bottle and thanked him before opening it and taking a long drink.

"Take deep breaths and relax," He said rubbing her arms. Charm nodded and took deep breaths to calm her heart down.

"I'm sorry to be yelling. I don't normally raise my voice."

"I understand," Denzel said. "And I don't mind you releasing your thoughts to me. That's what friends are for right?"

"Yeah."

"What is that about the spying?" Denzel asked.

"Me an Terrell were being intimate earlier and I hear a

sound. When I turn around she's peeking through our door looking at us. I confront her and she wants an apology. Saying that we should have closed the door."

"Well you should have," Denzel said. Charm gave him a look. "It's true. The door should have been closed but of course that doesn't give her the right to just watch." Denzel tried to avert his eyes from Charm because he was trying to mask the fact that he didn't like to hear that she was having sex with her husband. It was stupid, but he couldn't help how he felt. That was jealousy. Everything about what he thought about her was stupid because he was still fretting over Gabrielle.

"So then she's at fault for watching right? And then Terrell is at fault for sticking up for her and then staring at her ass? You know for a woman that's a real confidence breaker. Like I was just having sex with him was he not satisfied and that's why he was staring at her like that?" Denzel cleared his throat and finally looked back at her.

"I want to say something to you Charm. And I don't want it to come off as disrespectful or anything."

"Say it. I can take it," She replied.

"For one it seems like you know how to please your husband. But a man will look at another woman despite being in a relationship either because he can't help it or because that woman has something he wants. When I was attracted to that woman it was because I couldn't help it. I saw her and I felt something change inside me. Then that's when you start to think that maybe it's the universe trying to tell you something. But when a man looks at a woman because she has something he wants, it means he's unsatisfied by the woman he already has."

"Are you saying that I'm not satisfying my husband? You just said it seems like I can please him!"

"I told you I didn't want to come off as disrespectful. And it's not just sexual satisfaction I'm talking about. It's everything. Sexually you look like you can handle yourself but maybe it's something else. What if his needs have changed?" Charm crossed her arms.

"I told you I wasn't the perfect wife," She whispered. "And if something changed he didn't tell me! In fact I was giving it to him the way he likes it and he wasn't complaining." Denzel cleared his throat again. He was trying to force himself not to imagine what she looked like giving it to her husband the way he liked it.

"Either way he's still at fault for looking at another woman the way he did. But if you want to know why he's doing it and you want to stop him from doing it then you need to find out why he feels like he has to look at her." Charm nodded. She shouldn't even feel comfortable telling this man everything but strangely she was.

"Can I say something else without you possibly slapping me?" Denzel asked. Charm actually chuckled.

"I highly doubt I would ever feel the need to slap you," She smiled. "So what is it?"

"If you were my woman Charm not even Kim Kardashian's big booty could take my attention away from you. Hell, Cardi B could start stripping and threatening me with the blow job to snatch my soul to hell and still I wouldn't look at her over you. So like Jason says, your husband is kinda dumb." Charm didn't feel like slapping him at all. In fact she started laughing and snorting again. She slapped him playful and tried to control her snorting. Denzel laughed at her and caught her before she fell back. She held onto him and tried to regain control of her laughter.

"I can't even believe you," She smiled wiping the tears from her eyes. "Not even Cardi B?"

"Not even Cardi B!"

"But why though? I ain't got nothing on Cardi B!" Denzel shrugged.

"You're a gorgeous woman who paints. Why would a man like me not recognize your beauty?" He asked. "Come on, let's be real."

"Alright if that's what you think," She said.

"Come on, I think we both came here to paint, so maybe we should do that," Denzel said.

"No wait a minute. You were looking upset when I came in too. Something happened with you?"

"Oh my girlfriend finally returned my call and she said she still needs time alone because I broke her heart since I told her I didn't want to marry her. But she doesn't want to talk more about it. She simply wants to be left alone. Of course I feel like shit because I don't want to break her heart, but how could she force me to do something and when I refuse I have to feel bad that her heart is being broken?"

"That's a tough one. But if she refuses to talk what can you do? I'll tell you that you shouldn't feel bad about it. You shouldn't have to be forced to do something you don't want to. Does she think forcing marriage on you is going to make for a good marriage in the first place? You'll only begin to resent her."

"Try telling her that," Denzel huffed. "But she wants space, I'll give it to her. I'm not gonna chase after someone who doesn't want to be chased."

"Maybe that's the best thing to do," Charm said. She gathered her paints and looked at the empty canvas. Then she turned and looked at Denzel.

"Can I paint you?" She asked him suddenly. He made a face at her.

"Excuse me?" he asked.

"Can I paint you?" she repeated.

"Why would you want to do that?"

"Because I'm an artist who needs a muse. Afraid of something?" She teased.

"Don't insult me," He smiled. "Knock yourself out. Paint me." She was giddy with excitement as she turned the easel and canvas towards him so she could look at him and paint. She took his hand and dragged him back down to the beanbag and made him sit down. Denzel tried to keep his focus on something else as she leaned forward and put his hair back in a bun for him. Her perfume was sweet and intoxicating like it always was. He inhaled in deeply and it relaxed him.

"Alright, act natural," She said. Denzel nodded in understanding. He took off his sweatshirt leaving only his white t-shirt, then he grabbed his sketchpad and continued on the drawing he was working on earlier. Even if he was focused on that, every now and then he would look towards Charm. She would be staring at him intently and then look back to her canvas as she made strokes with her paintbrush. When she came out of her focus and saw him looking back at her, she would smile in a way that seemingly made him forget everything. He felt like a damn little kid that was swooning over his first crush or something. And while she was painting him, he was sketching her on his pad just the way she was in front of it.

"I can see what you're sketching," She said to him since he wasn't holding the pad up. He gave her a big smile.

"Good." She dropped her paintbrush and looked at his perfect white teeth.

"I didn't get to paint that smile," She pouted. "Why didn't you smile like that before?" He shrugged.

"Cause it takes something special for me to show my complete pearly whites. You should count yourself lucky."

"Okay see now I might actually find a reason to slap you," She said. Denzel chuckled and kept sketching.

"You sound like Brianna," He said.

"I bet if I tell her to slap you she would."

"If Jason were here he'd have my back."

"Jason wants to have more than just your back. Trust me. And you don't want to create an opening with him. Cause if he has a hold of you, he ain't letting go." Denzel let his head fall back as he started laughing.

"Stop it!" She exclaimed. "I'm painting!"

"Sorry baby girl," He chuckled. Charm rolled her eyes and continued painting. She spent an hour on it and when she was finished she entitled it 'Baby Boy'.

"Really?" Denzel asked looking at the title.

"As long as I'm baby girl you're baby boy."

"Fine. So what? Can I take this home?" he asked. Charm grabbed the painting.

"Mine," She snapped at him. She brushed him off and went to put the painting up to dry.

"Be stingy like that," He called out to her. Alone in the office to put the painting up to dry, Charm stood there gazing in the deep chocolate eyes she'd painted. Even on canvas she got that same tingly feeling inside her as when she looked into the real thing. His eyes were mesmerizing no matter how you looked at them.

"What does it mean when a woman looks at another man's eyes like it's the first time she's seeing something so captivating when she has a man of her own that should captivate her just as much?" Charm asked herself. Now suddenly she felt like a hypocrite for being angry at Terrell for looking at Destiny when she was here being drawn in my Denzel's eyes. It wasn't as promiscuous as him staring at Destiny's ass, but still it was something. Especially because she felt something inside her shift when she looked in Denzel's eyes. And then when he smiled at her; her stomach always fluttered.

"What am I doing?" She shook her head. Pulling her phone

from her pocket she looked at her messages. Terrell had sent her a text.

Please come home. Charm responded immediately saying she was coming back to him. That's where she should be at the moment. Not running away from him to be lost in another man's eyes. It was weird to her because she didn't feel attracted to him in a way that made her want to strip naked and sex him down all night. She felt that comfort Brianna told her about. But she wasn't like Brianna where she felt like Denzel was her brother. She felt his comfort and she felt his friendship that she trusted but she didn't feel like they were family. She felt like it was the start of something strong. The start of something new. Something that could lead to more than just friendship. And their friendship was so young but that didn't turn off it's intensity. That's what worried her.

She put her cell in her pocket and went back out to Denzel. He was still sitting comfortably sketching on his pad.

"Sorry to run off, but I gotta go home and talk to hubs," Charm told him.

"No problem. I think that's best for you anyway."

"Why do you say that?" She asked. Denzel didn't want to say that he was feeling too overwhelmed by her presence that he was going to forget she was even married to begin with.

"The way it was bothering you before I figure you need to talk with him about it."

"True," She said. "Don't stay here alone all night."

"Brianna's coming after her violin class. She'll keep me company for a little bit." Charm ruffled her hands through his soft dreads.

"Text me if you need anything," She said. For some reason she felt sort of bad leaving him in the gallery by himself. It was like she didn't want him to be alone.

"Where is your family?" Charm asked him randomly. He looked up at her.

"My father died from liver failure when he was only 45 because of his abuse on alcohol. But my mother lives in Florida with my aunt and I'm an only child so I don't have siblings."

"So you grew up in Florida?"

"No I grew up here. When my mother retired she wanted to live in South beach to be near the water and plus my aunt lived there too. I decided to stay here because well I'm an artist and it's L.A."

"Oh I get it."

"Why do you ask?"

"I don't know, I just don't want you to be here lonely. And I just started thinking about where your family was."

"Aw that's so sweet of you," He teased. "Don't worry about me. Brianna will be here soon. That's my family."

"Okay if you say so. Alright I'm gonna go." She backed up slowly not wanting to break contact with him but when she reached the door she finally turned around and left.

"I thought you'd be lonely," She mocked herself. Charm shook her head. What was she seriously doing?

By the time she got home again, it was almost 7 in the evening. That meant she'd talk with Terrell then start dinner. When she entered the house through the side door that would lead her straight into the kitchen she found Destiny hovering over a pot on the stove. She'd changed from her yoga spandex from earlier but now she was a t-shirt that was just long enough to cover her ass but barely. And she had nothing else on. Charm sighed hard and rubbed her eyes. Clearly there was going to be a straightening out of rules that needed to happen. But instead of saying anything, Charm just smiled and greeted her.

"Oh hey you're back! I'm making dinner again to make up from before. It was horrible with you not able to eat it. But this time I'm making fried chicken with greens and potato salad and some cornbread."

"That sounds yummy," Charm said. "Where is Terrell?"

"Maybe in the bedroom? He's been locked in there ever since you left earlier. You should take it easy on him. He adores you, you know." Charm tilted her head to the side.

"He knows why I was upset. So yeah," Charm said.

"Poor guy. He probably feels terrible." This time Charm didn't answer. She just looked at the woman then shook her head and walked off. She went upstairs and indeed she found Terrell sitting on their bed in only his underwear watching a basketball game.

"Finally you're back," He said. "I was getting worried."

"Sorry about that," Charm said. She stripped out of her clothes, keeping on her underwear she climbed onto their large bed next to him.

"I started a painting that's what had me occupied I wasn't

ignoring you."

"I'm not going to do it anymore. You know, look at her. I didn't mean it to happen before. It just did," he told her. Charm thought about what Denzel said and decided to just confront her husband on it.

"Is there something about her that makes you want to look at her?" Charm asked him.

"No," he stated immediately. "It's nothing like that. So I'm not gonna look at her at all and we'll be fine. Alright? Because I don't want to have to keep explaining myself. Got it?"

"Yeah, but I thought-"

"Alright that's the end of this conversation. You know that I'm sorry and I know that you're sorry and that's where we end it." Charm's brows furrowed.

"I know that you're sorry?" She questioned. "Is that your way of apologizing? Because if it is then I don't accept." He sucked his teeth.

"You always wanna pick some sort of fight with me. Accept the damn apology."

"And what am I saying sorry to you for? I ain't do nothing."

"Walking out every time we have a problem is doing something Charm. You run your mouth, disrespect me and then run off when I tell you the truth."

"No that's not telling me the truth Terrell. That's being a world class dick!" He snapped his head in her direction. She could tell he wanted to cuss at her but he didn't. He held it back and took several deep breaths.

"Who were you at the gallery with?" he asked her instead.

"Why does it matter right now?" Charm questioned.

"Because you smell like cologne. So unless you were at another man's house I'm going to assume you were at the gallery with someone."

"I was with Denzel. The painter I hired to help with the company." Terrell knew there wasn't a shower in the gallery only a bathroom. And since she still smelled like cologne she hadn't cleaned up. He went over to her and yanked at her panties.

"The hell are you doing?!" she exclaimed trying to stop him from getting her panties down.

"You got something to hide?" he asked her. She gasped and stopped fighting him.

"Are you serious? That's why you're acting like a crazy person right now?!"

"If you got nothing to hide then show me Charm. Show me you've been faithful." She could look in his eyes and tell that he was completely serious. He'd never done this to her before and didn't understand what would make his react this way. She didn't even realize she smelled like Denzel's cologne.

But she didn't have anything to hide. She proudly pulled down her underwear and opened her legs. His eyes went slowly from her face down to between her legs. He touched her roughly and she was dry except for her body's natural slickness. Nothing that was produced by arousal. He leaned down and pressed his nose into her. He really expected to catch her red handed. But she didn't smell like latex or sex. She smelled fresh and fruity like she always did. Now he felt stupid.

"What does it smell like huh?" She snapped at him, pushing him away from her. She yanked up her panties and began putting them on.

"I can't believe you," she shook his head. "You're staring at the surrogate like she's your next meal and now you're pushing your nose in my pussy because you think I'm the one out here being unfaithful."

"You can't fault me okay! You're the one that smells like cologne."

"Whatever Terrell. I'm over this. So like you said earlier, you won't stare at Destiny anymore and I guess I accept your nonexistent apology for staring at her. I don't even know what to say to you about what you just did though."

"You know, you're my wife. If I want to smell your pussy then I'm allowed to smell it." Charm rolled her eyes and rolled over onto her stomach ignoring whatever else he had to say.

"I'm doing to the basement to workout. Let me know when dinner is ready."

"Just tell your surrogate to let you know when she's done cooking for you. I know she's only playing nice to me because she has to." Terrell didn't reply. He simply just left the room.

Charm didn't think that her coming home would result in this. Truthfully, she thought they would have a deep conversation about how the both of them felt and then it would result in them making love all night, but clearly that wasn't the case. Not wanting to sit there alone thinking about what Terrell just did, Charm called Jason to tell him about it, but it went straight to voicemail. She didn't know what her bachelor best friend was doing. Without thinking much about it, she called Denzel. Why she was calling him, she wasn't sure. But when she saw his name in her phone she just couldn't help it.

"So if you're calling me that means you're not talking to your husband," He said once he picked up the phone.

"Actually no, we're doing nothing of the sort."

"That bad?" he asked.

"Very bad," She sighed. "I would be calling Jason but he didn't answer. And then I remembered you're waiting for Brianna so I thought you'd still be alone."

"Yeah, she hasn't arrived yet," Denzel said. "So how'd the talk go?" Charm groaned and told Denzel what Terrell said to her. On how he didn't apologize but told her to accept it, and he wouldn't stare again.

"Here's where it gets good," Charm said. "Apparently I smell like your cologne. So guess who got hit with an accusation."

"Really?" Denzel asked. "That doesn't sound like it went well."

"It didn't! Have you ever given your girlfriend the vagina test?"

"Excuse me?" Denzel was confused.

"Check her vagina when you suspect she'd been cheating. Like smell it for latex or something."

"No I've never done that. Even if I suspected her I wouldn't do that. It's a little demoralizing don't you think? I wouldn't want her to feel that way. Please tell me that's not what your husband did to you." The both of them went quiet. Denzel didn't need her confirmation to know that that's exactly what happened. He shook his head and sighed.

"You're a queen Charm," Denzel said. "Demand that either he treat you like one or he'll lose you. Husband or not, he shouldn't have disgraced you like that."

"Well, what if I was guilty?"

"But you aren't. And you know you don't sleep around with other men. So you need to demand your respect baby girl. Because you're not sniffing his goddamn balls." Charm sensed his displeasure and his anger. But she felt comforted that he cared to stick up for her.

"No I don't sniff his balls. But I did get on his case for the staring. Maybe I was acting a little bratty. Maybe he just got fed up. That's why he did what he did."

"Don't make excuses Charm." She sighed and rubbed her eyes.

"I guess you're right," She said lowly. On the other end she heard his shifting around and then the gallery door opening.

"Brianna's here," He said.

"Okay. I guess I'll let you go." She didn't want to let him go, but she didn't want to beg him to talk to her. She had her husband to worry about.

"If you still need to talk Charm I'll gladly stay on the phone with you." Oh, how she wanted to accept his offer.

"No, no. Have your time with Brianna, I'll talk to you tomorrow."

"Okay baby girl. Have a good time. My phone is always open by the way." She whispered goodbye to him before hanging up the phone. She stared at his name in her phone again until she heard Destiny was calling them to dinner. Charm put her phone away. She would never ever sleep with another man while being committed to Terrell. It just wasn't in her nature to be a cheat. But she could admit to herself that she really loved talking to Denzel. Maybe because the way she spoke to Denzel was the way that she used to be able to talk to Terrell.

Sighing, Charm got out of bed and left the room to actually have dinner. She was hungry and she wasn't going to hide in her own home even if she was having trouble with Destiny and Terrell. When she got to the kitchen she saw that Destiny still hadn't changed from her t-shirt. Which meant she was walking around with her ass basically out and not giving a damn about it.

Terrell entered the kitchen, but like he said earlier he didn't even glance towards Destiny's ass. But Charm had a feeling he was forcing himself not to. And then when she was sharing out his food and caressing his shoulder as if they were together and Charm was the guest. Still, she didn't say anything about it. She ate her food and kept her mouth shut. She wasn't interested in their conversation because it wasn't anything she could relate to and when she tried to butt in to try and understand what they were talking about Destiny just spoke over her. Right, this was going to be a long nine months.

Charm let it all go. She didn't want to fight and she was tired of arguing and being looked at like she always had a problem so she simply said nothing. That night when she went to bed with Terrell's back turned to her, she looked at her blinking phone. Denzel had send her a text. She couldn't help but smile when she read it.

Remember you're a Queen! Make sure you get treated like one and don't just lay down and roll over. Women are more powerful than that.

Reading it over and over, Charm started to feel confident. She was a queen. And this was her home. Time she started making that known. She was going to show Destiny and Terrell that she was the woman of the house. And she wasn't going to take the disrespect.

The next morning the first thing she wanted to do was take back over her kitchen. It was Monday morning so it was a fresh start to the work week and she usually woke up early with Terrell to make him breakfast anyway. That was going to be her plan, but when she awoke at 6:30 she could already smell the eggs and the bacon. Charm sat up quickly in bed. Terrell wasn't next to her. Rolling her eyes she already knew what was going to be happening when she got downstairs.

She brushed her teeth and washed her face first before putting on her robe over her naked body then she walked quietly downstairs to the kitchen. Terrell was at the island sipping coffee while Destiny was cleaning up the plates from their breakfast. Again, she was wearing short satin shorts which when she bent over Charm could see she was wearing no underwear and a tank top with no bra.

"Good morning," Terrell greeted her. They hadn't talked about what happened the night before but he did kiss her good night and now he was greeting her this morning. Charm didn't want to start the day off wrong so she just swallowed her pride. Approaching him, she kissed him lightly on the lips. He seemed shocked at her affection but he didn't pull back. He kissed her back, pecking her on the lips lightly before kissing her on her neck. That was her sweet spot and he knew it. Charm pulled away from him then and smiled.

"Want some food?" he asked her.

"No actually that's not what I want right now," She said looking at him deeply. Terrell raised a brow while he stood from the stool he was sitting on.

"Well what do you want?" Terrell asked her. When Destiny looked over at them, Charm had untied her robe a little showing that she was naked underneath. Destiny gasped but didn't say anything.

"Well it's still early." She said seductively putting her leg up around his waist. He grabbed her ass and held her close to him.

"And I think we should both be apologizing to each other. And we love to apologize this way don't we?" she asked.

"You know if we start that, it's gonna be hard for us to stop right?" Terrell asked her.

"So I guess we shouldn't waste any time. Cause I'm not stopping until you're completely satisfied." This was the wife he missed. Now it wasn't about only having sex when she was ovulating, but they were actually going to enjoy unplanned love making like a couple should.

"Oh yeah, let's go," He said ready to carry her.

"Wait," She laughed. "You go to the room I'll meet you there. Let me get a quick bite of food so I can keep my energy." Terrell slapped her on the ass and hurried towards their room.

Charm closed her robe and crossed her arms looking at Destiny. She had a sour look on her face.

"Well good morning," Destiny said.

"It's about to be a very good morning," Charm said teasingly. She stepped towards Destiny.

"Listen, I appreciate you being our surrogate a lot. It means the world to me and Terrell. But that doesn't excuse you from certain behavior."

"I don't know what you're talking about," She said.

"Okay well first thing, you need to start wearing a little bit more clothes. I don't wanna tell you exactly what to wear but if you can bend over and I can see your whole vagina then that's a problem for me. Second thing, I'm the woman of the house, and I don't really appreciate you basically trying to beat me to my own kitchen. Again, I won't restrict you to cooking, but naturally I cook most nights and every morning before Terrell goes to work. So I feel like you're trying to compete with me or something."

"No that is not what I am trying to do. I didn't know that's the impression you got," Destiny said. "I'm just here trying to give Terrell the baby you can't give him." Destiny knew how she said that and it was on purpose. Charm was standing there talking about she's the woman of her house and she couldn't even have a damn baby. Destiny was going to remain as kind as possible but she wasn't afraid to take shots either since Charm was trying to compete with her.

"Baby or not Destiny, I'm the one wearing the ring." Charm flashed the ring in her face. "Know your place and this will be the easiest 9 months. Otherwise, me and you are going to have a unique relationship. You think about that. In the meanwhile, my husband is waiting for me upstairs. Oh and this time I'll make sure I close the door." Charm winked and turned to leave.

Destiny slammed her hand on the island. She paced back and forth for a few minutes before she left the kitchen and headed to their bedroom. Did Charm really have the nerve to be shoving sex in Destiny's face? Destiny couldn't take that so she went right to their bedroom and carefully put her ear to the door knowing it might not be a good idea. And it wasn't. Her mouth fell open when she heard Charm moaning loudly. Terrell was grunting and calling her his baby over and over again. Destiny shook her head and backed away from the door. Charm may have won this round, but for what Destiny had planned, this was the only time Charm was going to come out on top. So she could have fun with her husband now, because soon that was going to be all over.

CHAPTER TWELVE

After Charm had laid out some rules, Destiny actually backed off a little. She wasn't racing Charm to the kitchen to cook first and she wore more clothes around the house. She kept to herself and when she wasn't watching TV in the living room she was in her room locked away. Even if Charm kind of wanted to be closer to the woman who was going to carry her baby she wasn't going to force a relationship.

But the process to have the baby finally started and Charm had to admit she was kind of excited. Both she and Destiny went to get a medical exam to make sure the both of them were healthy. Destiny was in good shape to carry a baby, and Charm's eggs were healthy enough to be fertilized. Even Terrell had gotten a checkup as well and his sperm was healthy. It was more proof to Charm that it was her body that was rejecting childbirth since Terrell had healthy sperm. But now that didn't matter. They were making moves to actually go through with surrogacy and it was no use in dwelling on anything else but this. After their checkups and results the next step was synching her menstrual cycle with Destiny so Destiny's body would be able to support Charm's eggs. So now they were both on medication to synchronize their cycles and once they were in synch Charm would start taking her medication to stimulate her egg production. Then afterwards she'd be ready for her eggs to be taken out of her body and fertilized before being put into Destiny's uterus. Just knowing they were one step closer to having their baby created put a calm on the situation with Charm and Destiny.

While Charm was doing laundry on a late Friday night at the end of the week Destiny was in the living room with her legs crossed on the couch eating out of a carton of ice cream. Terrell was sitting in his favorite armchair watching TV. But he had a bunch of papers on his lap continuing his work from earlier in that day. She had some of Destiny's clothes in the laundry basket folded so she went to Destiny's room to leave them there. She never went into the room after Destiny moved in because she wanted to give the woman privacy. At least she kept the room clean. Charm dropped the folded clothes on Destiny's bed when something caught Charm's eyes. She looked at the night table stand and found her diamond earrings sparking back at her. Charm gasped and quickly grabbed the earrings before storming out of the room. She went back to the living room to confront Destiny.

"Can you explain why you have these?" Charm asked showing her the earrings. Destiny looked at her.

"You were snooping around in my room?" Destiny asked standing up. "What the heck? Can't I have privacy?"

"Don't turn this on me," Charm stated. "Tell me how you got my earrings that were in my bedroom in my jewelry box?"

"Um they weren't in your damn jewelry box. I found them outside on the patio and you weren't home so I put them down in my room because I didn't want to go into your bedroom. I even forgot I had them in the first place!"

"You expect me to believe that?" Charm asked. "Do you think I'm stupid or something?"

"Oh trust me, you might not be it now but you're gonna look stupid soon enough."

"What in the hell is that supposed to mean?" Charm gritted. Destiny didn't mean to make that slip from her mouth but it drove her crazy to have to act like the goody two shoe when she knew she could take on Charm.

"Terrell, it's not fair that she was snooping in my room," Destiny said.

"What you calling on him for?" Charm asked. "This is between me and you. And I wasn't snooping. I was dropping off you laundry that I just washed for you in case you didn't notice I was doing chores all damn day."

"Oh well my bad. Because last time I tried to help you told me you were the woman of the house and the wife. So you put your own foot in your mouth and you're going to have to deal with it. Terrell, tell her she can't go through my room anymore."

"Your room is part of my house," Charm stated. Terrell stood up.

"Look you two should-"

"Stay out of this," Charm cut Terrell off. "Tell me the real reason you have my jewelry," Charm stated. "Right now."

"You know what," Destiny said. "I actually don't have to put up with this shit. And I'm not going to sacrifice my body and carry around a baby for an ungrateful woman who's accusing me of thievery!"

"Whoa hold up wait!" Terrell shot out of his chair. He yanked on Charm's arm pulling her out of Destiny's face.

"Let's not do anything crazy right now," He said. "Destiny I'm sorry okay? I'll apologize for Charm just don't walk out on us now. We're almost close to getting this done. Please."

"She needs to apologize," Destiny said. Charm rolled her eyes.

"Charm," Terrell gritted. "She's doing us a big favor by carrying our baby. She said she found it outside and was holding onto it to give it back to you. Apologize to her."

"I can't even believe you right now Terrell. And she's not doing us a damn favor. We're paying her to carrying this baby. Which means she's doing a job."

"Jobs can be quit Charm. So unless you want me to walk right now, you'd better apologize," Destiny said. Charm couldn't even believe this woman was giving her this ultimatum.

"You've-" Terrell grabbed her up and glared at her.

"I'm telling you to apologize Charm right now. I'm not going to lose the chance at having my baby because of your ego. Do it." Charm ripped herself out of his grip.

"I'm sorry Destiny," Charm said sarcastically. "And thank you so much for finding my earrings for me."

"Now that's more like it," Destiny said. Charm looked at her husband.

"If anyone didn't know us it would seem like you gave her your vows and not me," Charm spat out. Here she went again with the bullshit. Terrell just couldn't catch a break from her. And he had enough of her trying to ruin their chance at finally having a baby.

"Yeah well if that's the way it has to look then that's just the way it has to look Charm," He snapped.

"And I don't care how angry you get at me for saying this, but we need her. Whether you want to face that fact or not. Because for the past four times you've miscarried all of my babies!" He shouted at her pointing a finger in her face. Charm tried to back away but he only followed her with his harsh words

"How do you expect me to feel knowing that I have to turn to another woman instead of who I married to give me a baby? But since that's the case I'm not going to let you ruin our chance, hell *my* chance at finally having a healthy baby. And if you can't carry our child then you need to back off and let someone who can, do it." Terrell's chest was rising and falling harshly as his words spewed from his mouth. When he finally had a chance to stop and think he realized his mistake. He thought Charm would be furious at him for saying what he did. And he could handle Charm being furious. But it was quite the opposite. She held her head down and tears rolled down her face. That he didn't know if he could handle. But what he said wasn't lies.

"I didn't choose to miscarry," She said lowly.

"I'm just saying-" Charm shook her head. She took several deep breaths and wiped her eyes. When she looked at Destiny, the woman was smiling smugly as if she was enjoying seeing Charm break down. Just looking at the woman provoked anger out of Charm. She lost herself for a moment and the first things she could think of doing was lunging at Destiny.

"Do you think this is funny?!" Charm screamed. She tried to get her paws on Destiny but Terrell held her around the stomach keeping her away from Destiny.

"You don't know what any of this feels like!" Charm could feel the tears leaking freely down her face. She elbowed Terrell in the side of the head until he finally let her go. She shoved him hard before slapping him.

After glaring at him, she hurried to their bedroom to change into a pair of joggers and a clean t-shirt.

"Charm don't leave," Terrell tried to coax her. She shot him an angry look with bloodshot eyes and a tear painted face. That was all the answer he needed. She wasn't going to stay. Not after what he just said, or what Destiny did to her.

"She was being rude to me," Destiny said to Terrell when he threw himself back onto the armchair.

"Yeah but you weren't being nice either. Calling her stupid, what are you thinking Destiny?"

"I'm thinking that I need to defend myself when I'm being called a thief. All those thing you said to her was right Terrell. She has to put all her problems to the side and realize the bigger picture. Which is the baby the both of you want." Terrell just shook his head. He shouldn't have said that to his wife. Even if he was thinking it. He knew she wouldn't be able to handle it. What in the hell was wrong with him?

"Why does she always run off when shit gets tough?"

Destiny asked. "It's gonna come back and bite her in the ass."

"Destiny please," Terrell waved her off. Destiny walked over to him. She stood behind him and began massaging his shoulders.

"I didn't mean to upset you," She said. "I would never want to cause problems between us."

"No, this was all my fault," Terrell said. "I was the one who said those awful things to her."

"Not like they aren't true. She's a tough woman, she'll get over it and come back and forgive you. Don't worry about it." Terrell just shook his head and sighed.

****

The gallery was empty when Charm arrived. She was thankful for that because she didn't want Brianna or Denzel seeing her in the state she was in. The tears had stopped pouring from her eyes, leaving them bright red and puffy. She retreated to the back of the gallery and into the office where she set up a blank canvas to do another painting. Truly painting was her way to sort her mind out and relax. The words that Terrell said were playing over and over in her head and she just found herself getting more and more hurt. How does the man you love say those kind of things to you? Especially about something not in your control? She found that she had to ask herself that too many times. Charm couldn't help it that she miscarried. She took vitamins, she took medication, she read books to make sure she was doing things right but time and time again she just kept losing her baby. What was she supposed to do about it? Feeling her tears well again she took a deep breath and started painting. She looked in the corner of the office where her painting of that pregnant woman was hung up that they'd used for a paint and sip. She chuckled to herself and shook her head.

"You'll never be big and round with a baby." She said to herself. "You'll never know what it's like to feel a baby kick or what it's like to use the bathroom ten times at night because the baby sits on your bladder. You'll just never be woman enough." Without her even realizing it, her hand was moving and she was stroking across the blank canvas creating another painting. Only this time, it wasn't as happy and glowing as the miracle of birth. It was just the opposite.

The only thing she would ever feel when it came to having a baby is blood between her legs, cramps from the pain of her body rejecting her baby, and the crushing of her heart when she realized just what was happening. The memory of what her baby looked like when it was pulled out of her body in bits and pieces at the hospital came flush to her mind. And so she painted it. She painted the sorrow of a woman sitting down with blood soaking her thighs and a dead baby in pieces between her legs.

"Charm are you here?" the sound of a man's voice ripped her out of her own thoughts. She quickly wiped her face and looked at the time. She'd been at the gallery lost her in thoughts and drowning in her sorrow for over an hour. Her painting wasn't finished completely but the idea was there.

"Charm?"

"I'm in here!" she responded. Her voice sounded foreign to her. She cleared her throat and wiped her nose and face. Denzel came to the office door smiling, but that faded away the moment he saw her.

"Why are you crying?" he asked immediately entering the office.

"It's nothing really. I'm a woman we cry for nothing."

"No don't give me that Charm. Tell me what's the matter." He went up to her behind the canvas and that's when he looked at the painting.

"Dear lord," He said looking at it. His heart felt like it would actually break just looking at the sadness of it, and then thinking about it being Charm he felt even worse.

"I just got so inspired I actually started crying," She said. Denzel knew she was lying. She was awful at it.

"Come here," He said. He sat her down in the office chair and got on his haunches in front of her so they were eye to eye.

"Why would you paint something like that?" he asked.

"I don't know I just thought it would be a good idea," She shrugged. His eyes turned cold. The chocolate depths of them frozen.

"Charm I'm never really a stern kind of man but when people lie to me, especially people I care about it pisses me off. I'd rather you tell me to mind my business than to sit and look me in the eyes and lie to me. I'm not going to force you to tell me something you don't want to but I'm not going to be lied to either."

"I don't want to talk about why I drew it," Charm said lowly.

"Okay that's fine. So then why are you crying?"

"Because…someone said something hurtful to me and I

couldn't handle it so I started crying and I haven't been able to stop."

"Who said it? Male or female? If it's a woman I can get Brianna to take care of it. And if it's a man I'll handle it for you. Who are they and what they said to you?"

"No Denzel you can't handle it," She sighed. "And it was Terrell. We were having a little argument and well he took it too far." Denzel tightened his fist.

"Husband or not baby girl I can still rock his jaw for hurting you. Did it have something to do with that?" he asked pointing to the painting. Charm blinked, not used to this kind of attitude from Denzel. The last thing she'd ever say about him was that he could ever hurt anyone. He was just that carefree and full of spirit.

"Yeah it did," She admitted. Denzel could put two and two together and realized she drew that painting because she'd experienced it before.

"I know you're not stupid and you can figure out what happened."

"You lost a baby," He said. Charm nodded and wiped another stray tear.

"I dealt with it you know. And I'm doing what I have to do to move on. It's not easy."

"Of course it's not," Denzel said rubbing her arms.

"But for Terrell to throw it back in my face that it was somehow my fault brought back all those emotions and I lost it again. So I came here and just started painting."

"Do you know that it's not your fault?" Denzel asked.

"Yes."

"So then don't put yourself down baby girl."

"It's just the fact that he said it. That he would say something that hurtful to me. I'm not superwoman you know. I can be hurt. He just thought I'd be angry at him or something. How he couldn't see that this would hurt me, I don't know."

"I'm so sorry he said that to you Charm. And you shouldn't sit here crying over something you're trying to deal with because he decided to throw it back in your face." Charm blinked back more tears. Denzel wanted to hug her but he was afraid to be that close to her. The fact that she was with a man who kept making her feel like shit over and over again, Denzel was really starting to get pissed by it. Charm didn't deserve that type of treatment.

"Are you interested in going home anytime soon?"

"Oh no, definitely not," Charm answered quickly.

"Good. I think I have something that'll take your mind off all of this. Brianna was supposed to meet me here she should arrive soon. Call Jason up and tell him to come too."

"Denzel then they would all want to know why I was crying and I don't want to go over it again."

"Baby girl I got your back okay? Don't worry about it. Just go wash your face with some warm water and your eyes won't be so red anymore if you put a warm rag on it. And although your painting is beautiful it's downright heartbreaking so I'm going to put that in the basement and cover it up."

"Okay," She said nodding. He leaned forward and kissed her forehead before standing up to get her painting.

"Denzel," She called out to him.

"Yeah?" he asked.

"Thanks," She said. "You're always here to make me feel better."

"A queen needs her royal court sometimes," He commented. "Now go on wash that face. Oh and no more crying. Got it?"

"Yes my liege," She mocked him. Denzel rolled his eyes.

"Go your little ass in the bathroom." Her laughter filled the room.

"Last time I checked I had a good sized peach," She said going into the bathroom.

"You ain't lying about that," She heard him mumble.

"What was that?" She asked poking her head out of the bathroom. He looked at her sharply.

"Nothing," He rushed out. "Go on." He lifted the painting and hurried out of the office to escape her piercing stare.

While she washed her face with warm water to try to ease the redness of her eyes, Denzel waited out in the gallery for Brianna to arrive. When she did Denzel filled her in on what happened.

"Charm didn't have such a good day today," He told her. "Let me show the painting she was working on when I got here." Denzel quickly led Brianna down to the basement and uncovered the painting. Even's Brianna's eyes watered when she looked at the painting.

"Please tell me she didn't go through something like this," Brianna said. Denzel just shook his head.

"I don't know when it happened but she said she's still

dealing with it and after arguing with her husband tonight he pushed it back in her face as if he was blaming her for what happened."

"That son of a bitch," Brianna shook her head. "So we're going over there so you can rock his jaw right?" She asked. Denzel chuckled and shook his head.

"No, she doesn't want me to. But I'll leave it at that. But she's still a little upset and Jason is gonna come here too I thought we'd take her out to a lounge and just show her a good time. Take her mind of things."

"I'm down for that. You didn't even have to ask."

"Okay good." Denzel covered back the painting and led Brianna back upstairs.

"Denzel?" Charm was calling out to him.

"I'm right here baby girl, I didn't go anywhere," He said to her. She turned seeing him come from the basement.

"Brianna," Charm smiled. Even though she was smiling Brianna just saw the sadness on her face. Poor woman. Brianna walked to her and hugged her tightly. Charm did the same wrapping her arms around Brianna needing the comfort.

"What's all this lovey dovey mess going on without me?!" Jason called out entering the gallery. Charm let go of Brianna and ran to her best friend and hugged him tightly.

"What the hell happened?" He asked looking at her face.

"Just Terrell. He was taking Destiny's side again. And he was treating my miscarriage like it was my fault. I don't know I just couldn't handle it. I came here to try and calm down but then Denzel came and saw the state I was in."

"Terrell need to act like he got some sense," Jason snapped. "I swear I'm going to slap the hell out of him." Charm gave Jason a look.

"Jase, not that I don't appreciate the notion but you know Terrell would probably kick your ass." Jason thought about it for a moment.

"Alright then fine, I swear I'm gonna get Denzel to slap the hell out of him," He corrected. Charm smiled and looked over at Denzel who was nodding confirming what Jason was saying.

"Enough talk about what happened," Denzel said. "Charm, we're going to take you out. Show you a good time."

"But I'm not dressed to got out," she said looking down at the joggers she was wearing.

"You look beautiful Charm. You don't have to change anything," Denzel assured her. It was a stark difference from Terrell. Because Terrell would have forced her to change into something else.

"Oh well I don't want to take you guys away from whatever original plans you had to begin with," Charm said.

"We never have plans," Brianna said. "And besides, this is what friends are for. So come on we're going out and none of us are taking no for an answer."

"I hate to get on your bad side Brianna so fine let's go."

"I'll drive," Denzel said. Everyone followed him out then piled into his dark gray SUV. He opened the passenger door up front and motioned for Charm to get in. She thought Brianna would sit up front but Brianna only winked at her before getting in the back. Shrugging, Charm got in the passenger seat.

She didn't know where they were going, but they drove for about 15 minutes before they turned into the parking lot of a lounge that looked to be real popular.

Denzel told her to wait in the car while he went around to the passenger side and opened the door for her again. He took her hand and helped her out of the SUV, before opening the back doors and helping Brianna out of the SUV too.

Charm was a little nervous about going in this place wearing joggers and a t-shirt, but while the place had bright lights, inside it was a chill spot where everyone inside was relaxing and enjoying the good music and drinks. Denzel got them a large booth were they all climbed in and ordered drinks from the waitress. Even though she felt like she wanted to drink she knew it wasn't going to solve any of her problems, so just ordered a virgin daiquiri while Denzel ordered a soda. Brianna and Jason of course ordered their drinks not worrying about the fact that Denzel and Charm wanted to be the sober ones. After ordering drinks they ordered a large platter of wings to share between all of them. When the food arrived Charm sat back and just watched as the three of them began eating and talking freely.

Charm's phone buzzed in her pocket and of course when she looked it was Terrell texting her. Sighing she decided to open the text and read it.

I want you to come home Charm. Every time we have an argument you run off on me. That's not going to solve anything. Shaking her head Charm replied.

I'm with Jason, Brianna and Denzel. I told you not to wait up for me. Damnit Charm, you're my wife and I'm telling you to come your ass home! And then you wonder why I have to vagina test you when you get home.

Charm sucked her teeth loud enough to catch the attention of the others. Denzel took her phone away from her and turned it off before putting it in the middle of the table. He didn't have to say anything for Charm to understand he didn't want her to be bothered by Terrell. She left the phone in the middle of the table.

"Eat," Denzel said to her softly.

"I don't have an appetite right now," She sighed. "Sorry." Denzel gave her a stern look ready to get on her case when Jason called out her name.

"Charm listen to what they're playing!" he shouted to her. Charm paid attention to the music in the lounge when she heard the Mary J Blige song.

"It's her favorite song," Jason informed them. Denzel looked at her.

"This is your favorite song for real?" he asked her. Charm smiled weakly at him and nodded.

"Yeah it is. I love 'Real love'."

"Let's go dance then." Denzel began scooting out of the booth. Charm looked at the people on the dancefloor.

"No, no," She shook her head.

"Why not?" Denzel asked.

"I just-" Rolling his eyes, he grabbed her arm and dragged her out of the booth with him. He brought her out to the middle of the floor. Charm hugged herself and just stood there looking at everyone else dancing. When she finally looked at Denzel he gave her a goofy smile before he started dancing. Charm couldn't help but smile at the way he started dancing smoothly even though he was the only man on the dance floor. This song was a woman's anthem, but that didn't stop him from dancing to it. Some of the women on the dancefloor noticed him and began sashaying their way over to him to dance with him. Next thing Charm knew there were three women circling him and dancing. Her mouth opened at how quickly he attracted women to him. More than the woman surrounding him, she was surprised at the feeling that came over her. She was sure she didn't want to dance when he brought her out on the dancefloor but seeing him with the other women she wanted to be selfish and have him all to herself.

"Excuse me," Charm said cutting in between them. She began swinging her hips to clear the space so she could get close to Denzel. When they were close, he grabbed her hand and twirled her around. She laughed at the movement and continued to dance with him. She honestly loved the fact that they weren't slow dancing and staring into each other's eyes like Omar Epps and Sanaa Lathan did in love and basketball. Because dancing like they were made her forget her worries. And to her it sounded completely insane but she wasn't falling for Denzel in a romantic way. Not yet. She was falling for his friendship. And she should be worried about this. Very worried.

"I want in on some of this action," Brianna said joining them on the dancefloor with Jason at her side. The four of them continued dancing even when Mary J. Blige stopped playing. Skin hot and sweaty, they finally retreated to their booth where Charm actually had her appetite back and she began eating the wings. She saw when Denzel nodded in approval and relaxed in the booth bobbing his head to the music.

They spent a couple hours at the lounge before Denzel drove them back to the gallery so everyone could retrieve their cars and go home.

"Thanks a lot for this guys," Charm told them before she got in her car. She didn't know what she would do without them taking her out for the night.

"We're tired of telling you we got your back," Brianna said. "If you'd ever let me I'd smack fire out of Terrell. All you gotta do is tell me." Charm laughed.

"Trust me I will. Goodnight ya'll. Night Denzel," She said softly. Denzel smiled at her as she got in her car and then drove off.

"Alright now I'm leaving," Jason said. "I've got a date with my nail salon that I cannot miss!"

"Are you okay to drive?" Denzel asked.

"Eh it was only one drink!" Jason kissed Brianna on the cheek and tried to do the same with Denzel but the man backed up.

"You ain't gonna give it up easy are you?" Jason asked. Denzel waved him off.

"I swear you get on my nerves." Jason laughed as he walked down the street to where he parked his car.

"Imma get you one day!" He called out. Denzel shook his head and looked at Brianna.

"I don't care that he's gay but if he tries to kiss or hug me again he's the one that's gonna get his jaw rocked."

"Oh calm down. He's just messing with you." Brianna crossed her arms holding herself against the slight chill of the night.

"Come on, it's chilly." Denzel put his arm around her and walked her to where she parked her car. Brianna leaned against her car and looked up at her best friend. He had a look in his eyes that gave Brianna pause.

"What are you thinking?" She asked.

"Just about Charm going home and if she's gonna be alright."

"She'll be fine Denz."

"I don't know. Just the way I found her today and then that painting she drew. Sometimes I wonder if she's really fine." Brianna shook her head.

"Denzel I warned you," She scolded him. "She's a married woman! And you're crazy if you think that a woman like her would dare cheat on her husband so you can have her."

"I know what the situation is," Denzel said. "You don't have to spell that out to me."

"So what are you going to do?" Brianna asked. "You know I love you Denzel but I don't wanna see you push Charm into confusion about what's right and what's wrong."

"You know I won't do that. And besides I'm not trying to get involved with her. I'm just trying to be her friend. Same like I did with you."

"Yeah but I was a skinny girl that wore glasses. Charm's smoking hot with the perfect tit to ass ratio."

"I-I hadn't noticed that bit," Denzel said.

"We all know you're lying when you start to stutter," Brianna teased.

"Just get in your car Brianna. I'm ending this conversation," He stated. She snickered at him knowing he would have ended the conversation quickly.

"Goodnight Denz," She smiled. "And honestly it was real good what you did for Charm tonight. I'm proud to call you my bestie."

"Thanks Brie." He hugged her then opened her car door for

her and helped her get in before closing her in. She drove off waving leaving Denzel in the street alone. Even though everyone else had went home, Denzel didn't feel like going home. So he went back to the gallery and used his key to unlock it and go inside. He found his sketchbook of that drawing he did of Charm. Something sparked in him and without much consideration, he got out a clean canvas from the supply room with some paint and began to paint a new portrait of Charm. He didn't know if he was overstepping by what he was going to paint but he hoped that if he did decide to show Charm she would appreciate it. Instead of that horrible scene she'd painted that was covered up downstairs, he drew a woman still saddened by the loss of her baby, but at peace with the fact that her baby was an angel now. Denzel depicted that very image onto the canvas. It took him hours to get through the entire painting and he was going to show it to Charm when the time was right. Hopefully she would receive it in the right way. Because Denzel never wanted to do anything to upset Charm. Unlike her husband apparently.

CHAPTER THIRTEEN

After the argument Destiny had with Charm she was kind of pissed that Charm had found the earrings in the first place. That meant that Destiny couldn't pawn them for some cash. That was a whole week ago and on the other hand, Destiny was gleeful when she got Terrell to side with her and force Charm to apologize. It fed that darkness inside her that needed it's dose of chaos. But the tit for tat was over with. Destiny had a plan she need to fulfill. But that argument she had with Charm was the game changer. Charm barely spoke to her, looked at her or even really desired to spend any time with Destiny, and for Destiny that was perfectly fine. She wasn't really talking to Terrell either and that too worked for Destiny. Because she could slip in and take Charm's spot easier.

"Charm I'm home!" Terrell called the moment he entered the house. Ever since the argument he'd been sucking up to her to get their relationship back to how it was, but Destiny didn't see that happening. She sat around the island in the kitchen eating a sandwich when Terrell came in. It took her five minutes, but Charm entered the kitchen. He tried to kiss her but she turned her face so his kiss landed on her cheek. On the inside, Terrell was rolling his eyes but on the outside he was expressionless. He didn't know what else to do to get Charm to come around. He'd apologized already.

"Listen ladies, I booked the appointment for the lab so we can get your eggs Charm. And after they're fertilized with my sperm then they'll be ready to be put inside you Destiny."

"When is the appointment?" Charm asked.

"In two weeks. Have you been on your medication to synch your cycles?" Terrell asked.

"I have," Charm said. "I got my period soon after I started taking the medication." Terrell looked at Destiny.

"Same,' Destiny lied. "Have you been taking the medicine to stimulate your egg production?" Charm turned and looked at Destiny.

"I have. My period should be done by the time the appointment comes around."

"Good. There's two different appointments. One to retrieve your eggs Charm and then one to put them inside Destiny. Once the eggs are fertilized Destiny will go in." Destiny didn't know how fast everything was going to begin to move now. She realized her time was limited and she had to make fast use of it.

"Alright," Charm shrugged. She was ready to leave the kitchen.

"Wait Charm where you going?" Terrell called after her.

"I'm tired Terrell," She sighed.

"If you weren't at the gallery all night for the past couple nights then maybe you wouldn't be," He said. Even though she always came home late smelling like that damn cologne, Terrell never gave her a check again. He just realized Charm wouldn't step out on him. But the fact that a man was part of her company again was a little irritating.

"I don't complain when you stay at your office late Terrell. So don't throw those stones at me."

"What do you want from me Charm?" He sighed. "I'm trying to make things right and you just won't let me." Charm had to admit she wasn't her normal self with Terrell. In the end she wanted to forgive him and just move on from his horrible words but then sometimes she just remembered what he said to her and she just couldn't help but retreat into herself. Call her weak, but that's how she felt.

"Do nothing Terrell," She shrugged. "You've done enough." With that she turned and walked away. In the bedroom her phone was buzzing with messages from the group chat she was in with Brianna, Denzel, and Jason. When she looked the three of them were arguing over Cardi B versus Nikki Minaj and who was the better rapper. It actually made Charm laugh at the back and forth banter. She added her two cents.

This whole conversation is dumb. We all know Remy Ma is the best. Of course she got complete backlash but that's what she wanted. She didn't know who was the better than who. In her opinion all three women had something about them that made them worth talking about. Sometimes it was always about competition instead of just being about talent. But Charm loved that she had people to have pointless conversations with instead of drowning in her sorrow about Terrell.

"She's gonna forgive you," Destiny said to Terrell once she saw the look on his face after Charm walked off.

"She's really starting to frustrate me." Destiny shrugged.

"That's your wife," She said.

"Yeah, tell me about it." He flopped down on a stool around the island.

"I know she's probably going to be mad I'm offering, but you want something to eat? I can warm up some left overs."

"Thanks I appreciate it," He said. Destiny smiled at him and got up to warm up the food Charm cooked the day before. As she walked by him, she closed her silk robe.

"What's that you're wearing?" he asked her. Destiny looked down.

"A robe," She replied.

"Not your clothes," He smiled. "I meant your perfume. It smells nice." Destiny giggled inside her head. She knew he would like it because it was the same perfume his wife wore. Destiny had went out and bought the same lotions, perfumes, and body mists that Charm wore.

"Oh thanks," She commented. "It's what I wear to bed."

"I thought you wear lingerie to bed?" he teased.

"Very funny," She scoffed. "Lingerie could do your marriage some good right now."

"I doubt that's going to help. But now that she told me she was on her period it makes sense why she doesn't even let me touch her." Destiny should have her period too but that was if she was on the medication like she was supposed to be on. She was on a different kind of medication however, but that was just part of the plan.

"That's why they say marriage is hard work and less sex," Destiny said to him. Terrell gave her a look.

"Less sex?" he laughed.

"I'm just saying, not like I was listening out or anything but when I moved in I thought I was going to hear you guys doing it every damn night. So far I can see that it doesn't happen every night." Terrell had to think about that one. Since Destiny moved in they only had sex a couple times and it's been a couple of weeks. Maybe that's why he was a little uptight. Maybe that's why he was easily frustrated when she began acting out.

"Well maybe we just don't do it because you're here. Sometimes Charm is very shy."

"Yeah right." Destiny scoffed thinking about the time the

woman purposefully had sex with her man because she was threatened by Destiny.

"Watch your mouth that's still my wife," Terrell smiled.

"I'm just saying." Destiny placed the warm plate of food in front of him, leaning over him a little so her breasts touch his shoulder. He didn't jerk away from her or tell her to back up so Destiny didn't back up. She stayed there for a couple moments and watch him begin to eat his dinner before she backed up.

"How come I don't see you really talk on the phone or go out with friends?"

"Because I don't have any," Destiny said. "I've always really be a loner."

"Why did you decide to go into surrogacy?"

"Well there's obviously a money factor but then there's the fact that since I've been alone I like to help people and their families. I was in the hospital getting a routine checkup when I saw the brochure about surrogacy and I don't know it caught my attention and let's just say the rest is history."

"I hope you'll still feel this good about surrogacy once the pain of childbirth hits you."

"Don't remind me," she laughed. "But I'm up to it. I'm actually excited even if Charm isn't really excited about it." Terrell realized that it did seem like Destiny was more excited and it wasn't even her baby. But then again Charm was always upset at something so that was probably preventing her from being excited about anything.

"Well I'm excited," Terrell said.

"If you weren't then I would be seriously worried. But as long as I've got your support then I think I can make it." She sat back in her seat and watched him eat. He gave her a look and smirked while he kept eating.

"So what do you say we watch a movie and have some popcorn after you finish with dinner? I'm not tired and I'm kind of lonely. Especially with the no friend's things."

"Actually that sounds pretty good. I'm just gonna take a shower and all then come back and we can watch something. If you ever get bored here by yourself just tell me. I'll try to keep you as much company as I can," He said.

"I appreciate it," She smiled. She sat there and kept smiling at him as he finished his dinner just thinking about her plan finally coming to fruition. She just couldn't wait.

****

Terrell and Destiny spent the rest of the night watching TV before she fell asleep. He didn't want to leave her on the couch so he picked her up in his arms and carried her to her room. In his arms, her fragrant smell wafted to his nose. The subtle fragrance was familiar to him and he could only think about the fact that he liked it. She was easy to carry and fit in his arms perfectly it seemed. In her bedroom, he set her down softly on the bed. She curled up and Terrell put the covers over her. He brushed her hair out of her pretty face. Sighing he shook his head. He was overstepping and he knew it. So he immediately backed out of the room and left. Charm was fast asleep. He still got in next to her and pulled her close into his body. She snuggled into his chest. This was where he should be. And if Charm didn't continue to push him away then they would have no problems at all.

He didn't know how much time to give her in order for her to get over what he said, and he didn't want to get into another argument with her and cause more damage but it was getting tiring to have to deal with her emotions. She was acting like a child instead of a grown woman and he was beginning to get more than just frustrated. In the morning, she woke up at the same time that he did. She gave him a simple kiss on the mouth.

"I'm going to make you some coffee," She said softly.

"Wait," He said pulling her back into bed. She looked at him.

"Are you excited about having this baby?" he asked her. She rubbed her eyes.

"Truthfully, I am excited but not as excited as I would be if I was carrying the baby myself. But I'm not going to ignore the fact that we have the chance at finally having a baby."

"You have to just accept the fact that we're not going to have a baby the normal way. If things were different with your body then fine. But it's not. It doesn't mean you have to be less excited." Charm backed up.

"There you go again blaming me for this." Terrell shook his head.

"I don't know what you want me to say Charm. We've done the tests, I have healthy sperm and yet for some reason the baby just never happens."

"Wow, so it's all my fault then?"

"Just accept the fact that it has to be this way," Terrell said. "You can't be upset with me, you can't be mad at me. I want all of that to end."

"Terrell you can't just say shit like that to me and expect me not to have a response to it. It's not easy you know. But whatever, I should just learn to accept I can't be woman enough for you." Charm slid out of bed. "I'll go make your coffee. Get ready for work you don't want to be late do you?" She didn't wait for response. After brushing her teeth, she left the room still wearing her short nighty to make him coffee. But of course again, Destiny was in the kitchen already brewing the coffee. Charm crossed her arms.

"Good morning," Destiny greeted.

"Morning," Charm said. Destiny got out the bottle of pills and handed it to Charm.

"Don't forget to take the medication."

"Yes I know. I don't need you to remind me. But thanks." Charm took the bottle and took her medication. Destiny slid her a cup of coffee. Even if Charm didn't look to be in the mood, Destiny played nice because she had her plans in mind and she didn't want anyone to ruin her moment for her.

"Working today?" Destiny asked.

"I work every day," Charm said.

"Right." Destiny sat down and the two woman just looked at each other. It was awkward but Destiny didn't care. 20 minutes passed when Terrell came into the kitchen. Before Charm could move to get him his coffee, Destiny jumped up and beat her to it. Charm just threw her hands up and sat back down. What was the point in even trying? And plus, she didn't feel like arguing either. So she just left it alone.

"I have a big client today and if I make this sale it'll be the biggest I've ever made," Terrell said.

"Which one?" Destiny and Charm asked at the same time. Terrell looked between the both of them praying they didn't start fighting but the both of them just stayed quiet.

"It's a mini mansion they just built up. A lot of us have been trying to make the sale but so far all the families back out because of the price. I'm hoping my shot at it will be successful."

"I'm sure you'll do well," Destiny said.

"Just remember your wife's name," Charm spoke up. "You have plenty of it and will do great." Terrell smiled at her.

"I think I can find my charm." Even if she was upset at him, she had to give him good vibes so he would go into work and give it his best shot. She knew he loved being in real estate and she supported him completely. Terrell grabbed a muffin and ate it while sipping his coffee. When he was ready to leave Charm actually hugged him tightly. It was actually a real hug. It surprised him but he held her tightly then leaned his head down to kiss her. She tried to move her head again but Terrell wasn't going to allow it this time.

"Kiss me Charm. Stop denying me that simple pleasure." She gazed up at him and this time she didn't move when he leaned down to kiss her.

Destiny rolled her eyes and watched as Charm and Terrell tongued it down right in the middle of the kitchen. He reached down and grabbed her ass, squeezing it in the little nighty that she was wearing.

"I'm still here," Destiny cleared her throat. Charm pulled away from him and backed up and smiled with embarrassment.

"I'll probably be a little late tonight but I'll keep you updated." He gave her a quick peck before he left the house.

"Well, I'm going to go to the gallery soon so yeah," Charm said leaving the kitchen. Destiny shrugged and sat back down. She stayed there until Charm came back downstairs dressed and ready to leave. She was talking on the phone and not even paying attention to Destiny.

"I'm on my way Denzel stop being so dramatic." She laughed at something he said and walked out of the house. Denzel huh? Destiny smiled to herself and finally left the kitchen.

In her bedroom she dug into her drawers for her tests. After reading the instructions, she tested herself and waited for the results. Staring down at the result of the smiley face she smiled to herself. It was time. No matter what happened, her plan had to take effect tonight.

Since she was alone in the house for what was going to be most of the day, Destiny went to work. She went into the master bedroom and raided through Charm's clothing. She found nighty's and robes that she took to use for later. She had some money in her account already which was an advance for taking the job for Denzel and Charm, so she went back to her room and quickly got dressed. She drove to the nearest hair store and bought the perfect short haired wig that looked exactly like Charm's hair. She didn't even know why the woman didn't get extensions or something. Her hair was cute and all, but long hair was everything nowadays.

With the wig, and with clothing that belonged to Charm, Destiny was ready. Now all she had to do was wait for the right moment.

CHAPTER FOURTEEN

Terrell slammed his fist down on his desk in anger as he read the email he just received. He had succeed in every single house and apartment he'd shown that day. Everyone had agreed to sign off on the purchase. But here he was waiting for the last confirmation of purchase. And it didn't happen. The biggest client he'd ever had didn't opt for the house that Terrell had showed him. Instead, he opted for a house across town that was in a much better neighborhood and was going to be worth more in time. Terrell didn't know how he completely forgot to scout out other houses being sold for less the price but had the same amenities as the house he was trying to sell. And to make it worse, the client had purchased the home from a completely different real estate agency.

"Tough loss," Terrell's boss said coming into his office. "I thought for sure we'd have the buyer and a new promotion to give to you."

"Right so if you know we have none of those why are you in here right now?" Terrell asked, his anger teetering over the edge.

"Mind your tone," He ordered. "You may be the best agent we have but that doesn't make you untouchable."

"Then go head and fire me. Think I can't start my own company? Think I can't do better on my own?"

"Is that the route you want to take? Don't you have a family you're trying to start that's going to need some support?" Terrell began packing his things up. He had to get out of there before he actually said something that would in fact cost him his job.

"You know what, it's late, I been here all day I think I need to go home."

"I think so too." Terrell grabbed his things and stood to leave. Before he walked through the door he turned to look at his boss.

"I'm trying to close up my office," he said.

"Oh yeah I forgot. You lock your doors like you're some big executive."

"You would too if you were making as much money for this company as I was," Terrell said. Terrell may not be the boss right now, but he knew if he kept the numbers he had going he was liable to take the boss's spot. And that's why the boss was in his face now gloating about Terrell losing that sale.

"We'll see about that," He said walking out of the office. Rolling his eyes, Terrell locked up and left immediately. It was 8pm which was late to be in the office anyway. But his excitement to be home was dashed when he pulled up and Charm's car wasn't in the driveway. He didn't even have to call or text her to find out where she was. He knew she was painting and perhaps he was just going to have to wait up for her so he could tell her about this bullshit of a day he had.

"There's the infamous real estate agent," Destiny greeted him. "I know you made well on that sale." It was nice to have her around so at least he didn't come home to nothingness when Charm was still in the gallery.

"Actually, I didn't get the sale," Terrell admitted. "Which means I didn't get the promotion to head of the company and I'm just back at square one."

"Square one? Wouldn't square one be fresh out of college trying to pursue your license in real estate?" Terrell chuckled.

"You're right actually. It just feels like square one."

"I know what you need," Destiny said. She took his hand and led him to the living room and pushed him down on the large leather couch. She knelt in front of him and took off his shoes, then stood to take off his blazer.

"Don't worry, I'm not trying to undress you completely naked," She smiled at him as he unbuttoned the top buttons of his shirt.

"I just want you to relax."

"No worries I get it," He said.

"Good. Now just stay here I'll be right back." Destiny hurried back to the kitchen. She retrieved two glasses, put ice cubes in them and then retrieved the bottle of whiskey from the liquor cabinet. She was ready to go back to the living room when she saw his phone on the counter. Putting the items down, she grabbed up his phone and opened a text message to send to Charm.
Honey, when are you coming home?
I should be finished by 11 tonight. Jason got us a job doing a pop up art class at the community center. We're just trying to finish planning what we're going to do for the job. How did the sale go? Did you do well?

I did great! I remembered what you told me this morning and it worked out fine. Take your time honey I'll be here when you get in.

Destiny smiled at her deviancy. This was her moment. She had more than enough time before Charm came home. That's all the time she needed.

"This is what the doctor ordered," Destiny sang bringing the glasses and bottle of liquor into the living room.

"On a weekday?" Terrell questioned.

"Come on, you already had a really intense day. No reason why you just can't have a little drink, loosen up a little. Plus, you'll sleep like a baby and wake up tomorrow refreshed."

"I think you and I have two different meanings to a hangover," He said.

"We're drinking to feel good, not to get drunk."

"Is this even good for you?"

"Don't worry. I'm not pregnant. Yet. And I don't wanna hear anymore. You're going to have this drink with me. I won't take no for answer."

"Seen as I have no choice, go head. Pour." Destiny smiled and poured them each a glass of the liquor. She watched as he took a sip then groaned in delight and tilted his head back in full relaxation mode. Destiny bit her bottom lip as she just stared at his handsome features. Suddenly he turned and looked at her.

"What?" he smiled.

"Nothing," She laughed. "Actually there is something I just don't want it to come off in the wrong way."

"Just say it."

"I'm a female who likes men," Destiny said. "So it's only quite natural that I sort of think you're attractive. And I just like looking at you." Terrell sat up slowly.

"I appreciate it," He said. "But you know that in no way shape or form I'd want to cheat on my wife right? I mean, we're trying to start a family. That's why you're here."

"No I get it completely. I wouldn't dare impose anything on you." He nodded and sunk back down into his relaxed position. So much for that. He'd completely shut her down. Simple. Plan B.

"Finish that up," Destiny said finishing off her drink. "Don't tell me you're a lightweight." Terrell scoffed and tipped back his drink finishing it in one gulp.

"I'll be right back let me get you some more ice." Destiny

got off the couch and took his glass with her. Since he was resting back with his eyes closed, she tip toed to her bedroom to get something before she tip toed back to the kitchen. She added more ice to his drink and returned to his side on the couch. She didn't take her eyes off him as she poured his drink and dropped the drug she'd been holding onto for the right time into his drink. It fizzled a little but settled into the glass.

"Here," She said giving it to him. He sat up and took the glass. Destiny watched intently as he sipped it.

"I wonder how long it's going to take for Charm to come home. I needed her comfort."

"Relax, don't worry about Charm you have me."

"Yeah but," Terrell blinked and cleared his throat. Destiny helped him sit back as the date rape drug started to take effect on him.

"She's my wife. She should be here," He mumbled. He took another sip and Destiny held the end of the glass keeping it tilted so he could finish the whole thing.

"Yeah, sure," Destiny said. "Come on, we should go to the bedroom."

"For what?" He drawled out.

"You'll see," Destiny smiled. She stood and took his arm yanking until he started to get up. She'd given him enough of the drug to make him out of it but not that much where he couldn't move on his own. But she knew his vision was blurred. She draped his arm over her shoulder and walked with him upstairs to the master bedroom. Once inside she pushed him to lay down on the bed. He just flopped down onto his back and didn't try to move.

"Wait for me here," She ordered. She ran back downstairs to her own bedroom where she rubbed her skin down with Charm's lotion and sprayed herself with the perfume that Charm wore. Then she changed into the short haired wig and put on a small nighty she stole from Charm's closet.

"Perfect," She said looking at herself in the mirror. "Oh Terrell," She called leaving her bedroom and walking up to the master bedroom. She entered and watched him struggle to lift his head.

"Charm, honey," He drawled out. "You're home."

"Yes baby. I came home for you." She crawled onto the bed climbing on top of him. "Baby make love to me."

"Oh Charm." Terrell started fumbling with his belt to try and unbutton his pants. "I need you right now." He began babbling about his day at work but Destiny just ignored him. She helped in unbutton his pants and gasped when his arousal spilled out.

"Damn Terrell. I should have known a man like you was blessed," She breathed. She yanked off his pants completely them tugged at his shirt. Even though this was just part of a plan she found herself eager and getting aroused at the anticipation of having him inside her. She leaned over and kissed him on the mouth. His kisses were sloppy because of the damn drug but she didn't care. She liked kissing his pouty lips. Leaning up she took off her nightgown where she was completely naked underneath. To push him further along, Destiny shimmied down his body and licked the tip of his engorged erection. He jumped in response but didn't stop her from taking him into her mouth completely. Damn he tasted good. And feeling him in her mouth further raked up her own arousal in a way she didn't anticipate. She was gushing between her lady lips something that never happened to her before. She'd never met a man that actually made her lose herself like this. And she wanted more. She pulled his penis from her mouth and crawled back up his body. Straddling his hips, she balanced herself on her feet in a squat position and seated herself on his erection. She couldn't help the real moan that actually left her mouth when he filled her up. Oh it felt so damn good. So good to have her muscles clenching and fitting around something so big. Terrell's hands went lax around her hips as the drug continued to course through his system. But Destiny didn't need his help. She laid her hands flat on his chest and began riding him slowly at first. The tendrils of pleasure sprouted out from her tailbone and through to her core as his large head rocked against her g-spot.

"Wow Terrell. You've got an amazing dick," She breathed as she bounced on him harder. He didn't respond to her. His eyes were halfway closing.

"No, don't fall asleep," She slapped him across the face. "Feel me!" She gritted clenching her walls around his dick. She grinded on him as she leaned over to kiss him sloppily.

"Wake up," She snapped. "Please. You have to come inside me. I'm not going to stop until you come inside me!" He began moaning even though his body remained lax.

"Yes," She moaned. Her eyes began to flutter shut as she hit her g-spot with his dick one too many times. Her orgasm erupted over her taking her by surprise.

"Don't come Destiny," She scolded herself. But it was too late. Her legs began to lock up as her stomach quaked. Terrell let out a loud grunt as her muscles continued to clench him in her release. The orgasm was so powerful and such a new feeling to Destiny that she saw stars when she closed her eyes.

"Oh my god," she breathed. She fell on top of him breathing heavily. That was the best sex she'd ever had, even if he hadn't stroked her himself. His size was good enough for any position. She was in a fog of her own pleasure before she realized she actually had a plan to be thinking about. She hopped off his amazing dick quickly. She could see the remnants of sperm dripping from his tip. She looked between her legs and smiled realizing he'd come inside her completely.

"Good job Terrell," She smiled patting his stomach. She looked at his softening penis and licked her lips. She wanted another round just for the hell of it, but when she looked up at him he was knocked out cold.

"Don't worry. You'll get to have me again. And besides-" Destiny stood and looked at her naked figure in the mirror and imagined herself with a round belly. If the medication she was taking did what it was supposed to do then her belly would start to swell.

"I'm going to be having your baby."

CHAPTER FIFTEEN

"I think we're all good," Brianna said flopping down on a beanbag. "We're ready for this job at the community center."

"I don't know what I would have done if it was just me," Charm said. "No way would I have been able to pull anything off. But thanks Jason for getting us this job. You're the best."

"That's what I've been trying to tell everyone," He said fanning himself. Charm looked over at Denzel who was unusually quiet. He kept looking at his phone and then looking off into space. Last week when he took her to that lounge she began to see him in a new light. Because she realized how dangerous her feelings towards him were becoming. She didn't dare touch him because she knew that was cheating. And she even felt like a cheater because of her thoughts too. And now just staring at him across the room, she felt herself getting lost again.

He was wearing a pair of joggers that hugged his legs and his butt in the right damn way. The lump that was his groin was thick. Charm had to bite her lip when she gazed at it. If he was thick and he was soft imagine when he was geared up and ready to go? His locks were always pulled from his face and today he had it up in a sloppy bun showing off his straight and clean shapeup. His biceps were tight in the black T-shirt he was wearing that said 'Thing 1'. Charm looked at the shirt Brianna was saying that said 'Thing 2.' She laughed at it and suddenly she had a crave for that kind of corniness. She wanted to do something like that with Terrell even if it was corny but her husband wasn't that type of man. Denzel though he was that type of man. Charm shook her head and took a deep breath. Just be his friend Charm. Not lust after him.

"Earth to Denzel," Charm called out to him. He turned and looked at her.

"What's up?"

"You okay? You seem very distracted. You're never distracted."

"I am a little, sorry."

"Is it Gabrielle again?" Brianna asked. "You keep unclenching and clenching your fist and I don't wanna be around if the incredible hulk is coming out." Charm was confused.

"Incredible hulk?" Charm asked.

"Calm and subtle over here has an alter ego. Major anger issues when he's provoked." Charm would have never guessed that Denzel even had anger issues. He'd never displayed any sort of animosity in her presence. And he seemed embarrassed that Charm now knew about it.

"Brie shut up," He snapped at her. He didn't want Charm to know about his problems. Not in that way.

"Shutting up," Brianna said. "So what's the deal with Gabby?"

"She just randomly texted me and said she's at my place waiting for me," Denzel replied.

"Oh, now she wants to talk," Brianna scoffed. "Baby bye. She can kick rocks with that."

"Brie," Denzel sighed. "Just chill out."

"So what you gonna do? Go running to her like you always do?"

"Case you forgot that's my girlfriend. Of course I'm gonna go to her. I've been waiting to talk to her even if she is being immature."

"That's bullshit. She hasn't been your girlfriend for what? Like three weeks now because she's been off doing god knows what? You didn't even know if the two of you were still dating or not. Now she snaps her fingers and you go running like a little dog?"

"It's always the single ones that got so much shit to say about someone else's relationship." Brianna gasped.

"Seriously? I'm just looking out for you Denzel. You know that. You don't even want to be with her! Why do you act like you love her?"

"I don't act like I love her Brianna. I've never told her I love her, but she knows I care. That's worth something ain't it?"

"I'm not buying it Denzel. Because I know who you're really in love with. And it ain't your so called girlfriend." Denzel's brows went up and he immediately stalked over to her.

"Don't you dare say anything else," he gritted. "I do not love her. I'm with Gabrielle."

"You think it matters that you're with another woman? The heart wants what it wants and it aint Gabby." Charm felt incredible awkward watching them argue. It was like a friend who went over to another friend's house and they started arguing with their parents.

"Wait just a minute," Denzel said. "Weren't you the exact same one telling me that I had no chance with this woman? That I need to quit feeling anything for her?" Denzel didn't want to argue about this now because if Charm figured out they were talking about her being the one he loved there would be a huge problem.

"That still doesn't mean you don't love her."

"Stop saying that. I don't love her. I haven't known her long enough to even think like that. I don't know why you're always trying to stir the pot."

"Whatever. Go back to your girlfriend. And when she dips off on you again, don't come running back to me complaining about her not talking to you again."

"Okay hold on," Charm finally spoke up. It was too awkward to stand there and watch best friends fight. She had to say something. She stepped in between them and pushed them away from each other.

"Denzel, Brianna has a point. At some point in time Gabrielle can't just run off on you and then come back and expect everything to just be all and well. You have to set that straight. And Brianna, you can't tell him not to want to be with Gabrielle. He has deep feelings for her. It doesn't make him an animal because he goes back to her."

"Well then it makes him stupid," Brianna snapped. Brianna backed up some more and grabbed her purse.

"I'm out of here."

"Brie don't-" Denzel grabbed her arm but she snatched it away. "Leave me to my lonely single life."

"I didn't mean-" She turned and walked out of the gallery slamming the door as she left.

"Now look what I done," He said.

"You're best friends Denzel. She won't stay mad forever. Remember that. And remember what we talked about considering Gabrielle. She wants marriage and you don't. Think about that." Denzel nodded. But he didn't look convinced about anything. When Charm looked at Jason, he was motioning for Charm to continue talking to him.

"Wanna go for a walk?" She asked Denzel softly. "To clear your head?"

"With you?" Denzel asked.

"Yeah with me, unless you don't want to," She replied.

"No, no that's fine. We can go." They paced up their things and left Jason at the gallery. Denzel lead the way, choosing a direction for them to go in. Denzel switched sides with her standing closer to the street. Charm smiled and shook her head. He was truly one of a kind. For a while they just walked next to each other quietly.

"So you're in love with someone else?" Charm asked him finally.

"No," He sighed. "Or well, I don't know. Love is kind of crazy word to be honest. I care a lot about the person but that doesn't mean I love her."

"Maybe it does and you're just not allowing yourself to believe it." Denzel exhaled loudly. He got quiet as they continued to walk to vacant dark street. Even if they weren't speaking, her warmness and sweet smell was very comforting. When a bicyclist came whizzing by them on the sidewalk, Denzel grabbed hold of her hand and pulled her towards him to get her out of the way. She bumped into his chest. They were frozen at the contact, just gazing in each other's eyes. The electric pull that was coursing through them was unlike anything they'd ever felt. He never held Gabby and felt his heart beat irregular. He never got lost in her eyes. And as if under a spell he began leaning down towards her. Her soft lips like an aphrodisiac calling him towards them.

"Denzel please don't," Charm begged. "I can't become one of those unfaithful women. I'm just-I'm just trying to be as good of a friend as you've been to me." Denzel let her go immediately. He remembered that Brianna had warned him not to put Charm in a position like this. It wasn't fair of him.

"I didn't mean to do that," He said backing away from her. "Forget about it okay? I would never want you to do something that you'll regret because you became a woman you're not. And I promise you Charm it won't ever happen again."

"Who-who's that woman you think you're in love with?" She asked him softly. He shook his head.

"I think you know," He replied lowly. "I think I should go home and talk with my girlfriend," He said.

"Oh-al-alright," She stammered. He felt so stupid about what he'd just done that he wanted to just run to his car and drive off, but they were two blocks away from the gallery and he wasn't going to leave her alone to walk back by herself. So he pulled up his big boy underwear and just walked with her. They were quiet and said nothing to each other but unlike before the energy was different. He couldn't get too near her. Not after what he'd just done. When they finally got back to the gallery, Denzel couldn't leave any faster.

"Talk to you later Charm," He said hurrying to his car.

"Denny," She called out. Denzel stopped at the nickname she'd given him. He turned and looked at her. She was just standing there on the sidewalk, wearing leggings and a big t-shirt but looking like an angel that fell from the sky in his eyes.

"Yes Charm?" He asked.

"I'm not mad," She said. "I won't hold anything against you and I don't want our friendship ruined."

"Me either Charm," He smiled. "Me either." They gazed at each other for a moment longer before Denzel finally got in his car and drove away.

Jason watched as Charm entered the gallery, walking as if she was in a trance. He looked at her questioningly but she just began packing up her things to go.

"Where's Denzel? And what happened?" Jason asked.

"He tried to kiss me," Charm whispered. It was more to herself because she still couldn't believe that he wanted to kiss her. The emotions running through her were all over the place. She was angry at herself for breaking a vow to her husband by even being close to another man that he would attempt to kiss her. Then she felt weirdly intrigued that he even thought of her in that light and he wanted to kiss her. But it was wrong on so many levels. Charm felt like a horrible wife. And she wanted to get home to her husband. That's where she needed to be.

"Oh my god, you didn't let him kiss you?" Jason gasped.

"Of course not Jase! You know I couldn't do that to Terrell!"

"After the way he's been treating you he deserves it," Jason scoffed. Charm fanned him off.

"I should probably get home. Terrell had a big client he won over today so I wanna go celebrate a little with him. That's where I should be."

"Alright fine. Suit yourself," Jason said. Even if she was headed home, Charm couldn't help but think about how that conversation was going to go with Denzel and his woman.

Denzel sat parked in front of his home for ten minutes trying to get himself together. He'd just tried to kiss another woman when he knew his girlfriend was waiting for him. He felt ashamed. And he felt like a cheat. But nevertheless he had to confront Gabby.

The loft space he lived in was large enough for him to hang all his paintings and even do some work from home and that's why he loved it. Plus he had the perfect view. Gabrielle however didn't see anything cute in the one bedroom loft.

"Good to finally see you," Denzel said when he entered and found her in the kitchen eating a salad.

"Well good you're finally here. I've been waiting for hours."

"Yeah well I was working." She continued eating as if what he was saying wasn't of interest to her.

"So you came here not to bother to talk to me?" he asked.

"No. I came here because I want something from you." She took one last bite then stood from around the table. She removed the trench coat she was wearing and that's when Denzel saw she was only wearing her panties underneath.

"Ohh," He said understanding flowing through him. He leaned against the door frame.

"You want to have sex with me," He said.

"Clearly."

"I thought you would have wanted to talk."

"Sex now. Talk later," She demanded. And if you don't come on I'm going to start getting impatient. And I don't think you want to see me get impatient."

"Right," Denzel nodded. "Go to the bedroom," he ordered her. She walked away seductively. He knew he should be talking to her and not about to sex her down after weeks of not seeing or speaking to her, but right at that moment his second head was overpowering his first. Not only was he sexually frustrated and a little angry after what just happened with arguing with Brianna, he needed to do something to take his mind off what he'd just tried to do with Brianna. What better way to let some steam off that just hard sex? He damn sure wasn't about to go to a gym so sex was the only option. And it would perhaps get Charm out of his damn head for once.

As he walked to the bathroom he stripped off his dirty paint filled clothes. He was already rock hard just thinking about having Gabrielle after so long. Even though she'd been ignoring him, he could always count on an amazing sexual experience with her. He showered quickly and didn't even bother covering himself up as he went to the bedroom. Gabrielle was naked on the bed waiting for him.

"I'm getting impatient," She said tapping her fingers on the bed and opening her legs.

"Have you been with anyone else while you've been gone?" he asked her. He didn't know if he trusted her to be faithful since she was gone for so long. She shrugged and smirked.

"I don't know, maybe." Denzel rolled his eyes at her. He didn't want to play her stupid little game. Since she didn't want to answer his question he retrieved a condom from his drawer and opened it with his teeth before sliding it down onto this erection.

"Face down, ass up," He ordered her.

"No foreplay?" she asked.

"You said you were getting impatient right? So face down, ass up and let me give you your nut."

"Seems like I'm not the only one who needs a nut, grumpy," She mumbled. She assumed the position, spreading her cheeks wide in front of him. Denzel dragged her down to the edge of the bed so he could remain standing. He tested her wetness and finding that she was wet enough for his entry, he pushed into her slowly.

"Yes," she hissed. "Don't be easy. Just put it in and fuck me." With her walls stretching around him, Denzel entered her swiftly. He pushed her head down into the bed to further arch her back as he began to do exactly what she wanted him to do. He held her at the waist and drilled into her body repeatedly giving her the strokes he knew she liked and knew would make her come with the quickness. And for him, giving her those powerful strokes was relieving the tension he had in his own body. Her moans, and screams of passion fueled his movements inside her. When he closed his eyes, a flash of Charm's face came to his mind. He faltered a little and immediately opened his eyes.

"No don't stop," Gabrielle begged. Denzel blinked and continued what he was doing. How another woman was in his mind when he was already inside his woman was baffling to him. And when he did close his eyes again, it wasn't just Charm's face he saw. It was Charm bent over in front of him, drawing on his penis with her clenching walls, and calling his name as she came hard. He opened his eyes again and there was Gabrielle instead of Charm. His pleasure was mounting when he had his eyes closed, and now that they were open his pleasure was receding. He wanted to orgasm badly but it was like he physically couldn't. He knew Gabrielle would start to complain since when she had her orgasm she got lazy, but Denzel couldn't come. Or well maybe he could, but it was just wrong to be there stroking another woman's insides and be thinking about Charm. Cursing loudly, he closed his eyes. In order to keep himself from shouting Charm's name, he bit his fist and continued pumping. In his mind he was inside Charm, being one with her. He could feel her heartbeat through her insides as it helped her give him pleasure. He squeezed her ass and his orgasm finally rolled over him, breaking through whatever strain he was just experiencing. And it was complete bliss. Oh he felt magnificent. Until he opened his eyes and Charm wasn't beneath him, Gabrielle was. He couldn't believe that just happened to him.

Gabrielle crawled to the top of the bed and flopped down. She was pissed at Denzel for not trying to marry her, but at the same time no other man was good enough in bed to her. Denzel was the whole package. So if she had to stick around and force him into marriage then she was going to do that. One way or another Denzel was going to be her husband.

"What's the matter?" she asked him seeing he hadn't even moved from where he was standing at the end of the bed.

"Nothing," He cleared his throat.

"You know, you're lucky I don't get offended by you wearing a condom. We've been dating way too long for that."

"Yet for a couple of weeks you weren't around so I need to protect myself since instead of just answering my question before you were trying to be cute."

"Whatever," She sighed. "Well I think I should get my things and go now. This was just what I needed."

"I thought we were going to talk," Denzel said. "And you could just spend the night you know."

"You know how I feel about this place," She said. "And there's nothing really much to talk about. You know why I was upset and had to take a break. But now I'm back and our relationship can go back to the way it was."

"See that's the thing Gabby," Denzel. "You want marriage and I'm not ready for it. So it's like we're going down two different paths. You think it's fair that we stay together and drive each other crazy?"

"Don't worry. I do want marriage but I'll be alright. Maybe soon you'll want marriage too and we'll go from there. If not, then we'll do the right thing. Are you ready to give up on us?"

"No, but-"

"I don't want to hear buts. It's alright. I'll call you in the morning." Denzel just shrugged. No use in trying to continue a conversation where she was going to continue remaining nonchalant. He could get what she was saying but there was just something inside him that said something wasn't right. He just didn't know what. But for now he just wasn't going to think about it.

"You can come home, but later," Denzel said.

"Excuse me?" she asked. Denzel went for another condom as he felt himself getting erect again.

"You've been gone for three fucking weeks Gabrielle. You ain't leaving until I physically can't nut anymore." Denzel was determined to fuck his girlfriend until he stopped thinking about Charm. He reapplied the new rubber and got in bed. When he laid on his back, Gabby took her cue to hop on top of him to ride him. She rode him slowly and tentatively. It wasn't doing the trick. He was still thinking about Charm. Sitting up, he grabbed Gabby under the chin and pressed her cheeks together puckering her lips.

"You better ride me like you fucking mean it," He gritted to her. With his urging she got on her feet, squatting on his erection.

"That's it," He grunted as she began riding him hard. Denzel kept his eyes open and forced himself to find pleasure in his girlfriend rather than closing his eyes and finding pleasure in Charm's image in his head.

CHAPTER SIXTEEN

Charm rushed home. She put what happened with Denzel to the back of her mind because she wanted to focus on Terrell. She wanted to show her support from him getting that client. She knew it meant a lot to him and bringing home her thoughts of what another man tried to do wasn't going to be a good idea.

Even though she couldn't quite get over what he said to her she wanted to be there for him for something that was important to him. She hoped that he was still awake waiting for her and he didn't think she was neglecting him. Getting this client meant big things for him. It meant that he could potentially get the promotion he badly wanted. He was a hard working employee for that company and if he started running things the company would only get better. She started to think about the bottle of champagne in the fridge that she could pop for him before he got to bed.

Entering the house, she found the kitchen light was off but Destiny was in the living room watching TV. She was snuggled in a pink fluffy robe with a smile on her face that seemed to have nothing to do with the movie she was watching. It was almost creepy.

"Hey Destiny," Charm greeted.

"Hey," She said looking at Charm. "I've been waiting for you to get home."

"What's up?"

"Um, it's Terrell." Turning off the TV Destiny stood. "He didn't make that big sale today so he was a little upset. I didn't know what to really do about it and I thought if he had a drink he'd just go to bed and start fresh in the morning. Only, he didn't stop drinking. I told him I'd call you but he shouted at me and said not to and just carried on. He passed out not too long ago upstairs. Thought you should know."

"He didn't get the sale?" Charm was confused. "Why would he text me that he did?"

"I think he did have it at first. And then he got a message and I don't know that's when he got upset and started drinking more."

"Shit," Charm shook her head. She felt terrible that she hadn't been around for him.

"I wish he or you would have called me so I would have

known." Charm continued shaking her head and hurried off to get to the bedroom. Just like what Destiny said, Terrell was knocked in the middle of their bed. He was wearing boxers but that was it.

"Oh Terrell," She sighed. She got in bed next to him and caressed his face. "I'm so sorry I wasn't here for you." She laid down next to him and just held him even though he was probably too deep in sleep to feel her. But still, she just laid there and hold him.

****

Terrell blinked his eyes open. The sun was shining through their windows and even if he would have liked it on another morning, this morning he hated it. His head was pounded so bad his actual skull hurt. But among the pain he smelled Charm's sweet perfume and he realized she was next to him.

"Good morning baby," She greeted leaning over and looking at him.

"Charm," He muttered. "Jesus I have a migraine."

"Well that's the hangover talking," She said. "But don't worry, I have a light breakfast for you and some Gatorade." Terrell sat up slowly grabbing his head. He had no idea what the hell happened last night. The last thing he remembered was having his first drink of whiskey but that was all. Everything else was a big blur. Terrell looked at Charm.

"Did we have sex last night?" he asked a vague memory of his dick being rode coming to him.

"No," She laughed. "You were passed out when I got home."

"Oh." Maybe it was just that he had a wet dream. "Guess I took too many drinks," He said realizing he'd probably drank himself silly.

"I'm sorry about the sale," Charm said running her finger over his cheek. "You're going to be the boss of that office soon anyway. It's not like they have anything you have." Terrell smiled.

"Thanks baby." He sat up some more. Even if she never outright said she forgave him for what he said, he appreciated her being at his side like this.

"You know, I missed this," He said. "Us." Charm looked down while smiling. She touched his arm and slowly caressed it.

"Me too. There's been too much bad blood between us." Charm smiled. "Do you think you're able to even go to work? If you go with a hangover it's not going to look good for you," She said.

"You're right," He admitted. "And I feel nauseous as hell."

He grimaced and got out of bed. He stumbled over to the bathroom before emptying his guts out in the toilet.

"I think you need to stay home," Charm said coming in the bathroom behind him.

"I know, I will." He stood straight, flushed the toilet then brushed his teeth. He couldn't even imagine what would have gotten into him to get that drunk. Especially on a weekday when he had work the next morning. It wasn't like him.

When he went to use the bathroom, he pulled his penis from his underwear and noticed it was sticky. It was only ever like that when he had sex and didn't take a shower afterwards.

"Are you sure we didn't have sex?" he asked her.

"Terrell, I'd know if you were poking at my uterus. Trust me." He laughed and the notion further shook his skull.

"Lord," He said holding his head.

"I'll get you some medicine. Shower and come lay back down." She left the bathroom then so he could take his shower.

Standing under the hot spray Terrell struggled to figure out what the hell happened to him. The more the thought about it, the more the vision of Charm on top of him, riding him plagued him. Was it really just a dream? Because Charm wouldn't lie to his face saying they didn't have sex if they did. There would be no reason for her to do that. And in fact, she had her period. And she would never agree to have sex with him while on her period. Never. Terrell just shook his head. He already had a headache and trying to figure this out when it might not even be real in the first place was making his head hurt further. If no harm was done then it didn't make sense to dwell on it.

"I forgot how a hangover feels," Terrell said leaving the bathroom. Charm was in bed sketching while she waited for him to come out of the shower.

"I bet you did," She smiled at him. "Come sit down." He flopped down onto the bed. She turned and gave him some painkillers and the Gatorade. He didn't have an appetite yet so he held out of the food for a moment.

"I called the company and told them you were sick already for you," She told him. "I'll stay here with you all day too."

"Oh no don't do that," He sighed. "Just let me get over it a little then you can go and get work done at the gallery. I'm sure when I wake up again I'll feel much better." Charm leaned over and kissed him on the forehead. With Charm next to him he was out in no time.

****

Charm got to the gallery by 5pm that afternoon and she planned to head home no later than 10. Four solid hours she could get some good work in. Denzel and Brianna were in the gallery working on their paintings. When she entered Denzel looked up at her and smiled but that was it. She smiled back at him and she was grateful that at least nothing was weird between them. But she realized she should have been worried about Brianna and Denzel's relationship.

Unlike how they painted before, now the gallery was completely quiet. There was no music and they weren't even dancing like they usually did. Jason was at a company party for the marketing company he worked for so Charm was literally on her own in trying to get Brianna and Denzel back on the same page. She hated to see them angry at each other.

"Didn't think you were going to come," Brianna spoke first. "You never come this late."

"Yeah, Terrell wasn't feeling well today so I was taking care of him. He's better now so I decided I could still come and finish my painting for the community center job. You guys okay?"

"I'm perfectly fine. It's Casanova over there who isn't."

"Brianna," Denzel snapped looking at her. Brianna rolled her eyes. She liked to give Denzel shit even when she'd forgiven him for something. Last night when she left the gallery she'd already forgave him when she got home. But then he'd sent her a long text that morning apologizing and she forgave him even more. She could never stay mad at Denzel because he would never say anything that would hurt her that bad. And even if he did she knew his temper was wild.

"You two need to cut it out," Charm said to them. "I thought you would have forgiven him already."

"I didn't say I didn't. He just hadn't talked to me," Brianna said.

"I sent you a long ass text that you haven't even answered and you expected me to think you forgave me?" Denzel questioned.

"But you know I don't stay mad at you Denzel. You know that." Denzel looked at her with his mouth open.

"That don't mean nothing!"

"Don't even get into it," Charm ordered. "Hug. Right now."

"I'm not gonna-" Brianna started.

"Go. Hug. Him," Charm gritted. Brianna gave her a look before going over to Denzel.

"He has to hug me back!" She protested.

"You'd better hug her back," Charm turned her glare to him. "Don't play with me." Denzel gave Charm a long look and saw she was completely serious. But she was right. Besides he had a lot he wanted to tell Brianna. So he opened his arms and Brianna launched into them hugging him tightly. They stood there hugging for well over a minute before pulling apart.

"Spill tell me what happened with Gabrielle last night," Brianna rushed out.

"She was there basically waiting for me to come home so we could have sex. She didn't want to talk and insisted the sex happened."

"And you gave in didn't you?" Brianna asked.

"What else was I supposed to do?" he asked. "I was sexually frustrated and I'm a man, I'm not going to turn it down. What you think I'm made out of, steel?"

"You really had sex with her?" Charm gasped her interest peaking. She got close to them so she could hear.

"I thought you were going to talk to her about the marriage and all that stuff?" Charm asked.

"I wanted to. Then my bigger head took over and I didn't see the harm in it," Denzel answered.

"It's not that big," Brianna mumbled. Denzel snapped in head in her direction.

"Why you gotta do that every time my dick is mentioned?"

"Wait? You've seen it?" Charm chuckled.

"I walked in on him naked and he didn't go to cover up. I mean, it's a good size but I've seen bigger."

"Don't play with me," Denzel said. Brianna held her hands up and snickered. "Back to what I was saying," He said. "I couldn't help myself so I went with the sex first. Only when I tried to talk to her afterwards she was just brushing it off."

"Brushing off? She disappeared and claimed you broke you heart and now she's just brushing it off?" Charm asked. "That doesn't seem right."

"She claims that if nothing changes down the line then we'll deal with it but for now she just wants to be normal." Charm didn't like the sound of that.

"I'm not buying it," Brianna said taking the words right out of Charm's mouth.

"What about what you want?" Charm asked him. "Your mind is already made up. Why continue on when you know you're never going to want what she does?"

"Because I figure something might change," Denzel said. Even he didn't believe those words.

"What's that you said about lying?" Charm questioned. "You don't like being lied to and well neither do I. So don't lie to my face."

"Yeah and don't lie to yourself either," Brianna added.

"You know it's already a struggle having one female friend. I don't know why I decided to go out and get another one." Both Charm and Brianna laughed at the face he made. The both of the held onto each other and walked away laughing.

"So you really saw his junk?" Charm whispered to Brianna.

"Yes! And he didn't even bother to cover up he just stood there in all his glory!"

"I can still hear you!" Denzel called behind them. The both of them began laughing harder and turned to look at him.

"So?!" Brianna laughed. He shook his head and looked at Charm. She was smiling and looking down but as if feeling his stare, she looked right up at him. She pushed hair behind her ear and blushed a little. Denzel was assaulted by the memory of what happened to him the night before. He realized he missed a vital piece of information he didn't tell Brianna.

"Bri," He called to her. "Come here real quick." She left Charm across the room and came to him. Charm sensed they wanted to talk about something in private.

Once Charm had turned her back and began getting her things ready to continue painting, Brianna turned to him.

"What?" She asked. He leaned over to whisper to her.

"You were right about the L word with me and that other woman." Brianna gasped. "I don't know about the L word but something happened."

"What?" He pulled her further away so Charm wouldn't be able to hear.

"I tried to kiss Charm last night." Brianna covered her mouth as her eyes went wide.

"You did what?!" She exclaimed. "How in the hell did that even come close to happening?!"

"I don't know! I pulled her close to me and then next thing I know we're staring each other down and then I'm leaning down towards her to kiss her." Denzel tried to keep his voice in a whisper.

"But she stopped me. And it was right of her to do that. I didn't want to become the unfaithful wife. Just in that moment I couldn't help myself.

"That's freaking insane," Brianna shook her head.

"Oh there's more," Denzel said.

"More?"

"It was me and Gabrielle last night. And at first it was good. I was hitting it from the back and it felt amazing. But the minute I close my eyes guess who popped up in my head. Guess who I imagined I was hitting from the back and making them scream like no tomorrow? And guess who couldn't have an orgasm when I stopped thinking about that person?"

"Are you kidding me?" Brianna shrieked.

"Shush!" He snapped.

"Are you saying you only got off because you were imagining you were sexing Charm?" she whispered.

"Yes." He admitted.

"Denzel," She sighed. "You got it bad. I didn't know it was this bad, but damn! What the hell you gonna do?

"I don't know Briana. I don't know." He sighed. He looked towards Charm who was again wearing baggy jeans and a t-shirt and he couldn't find her anymore gorgeous. And she was still off fucking limits.

CHAPTER SEVENTEEN

Charm was nervous as she sat in the laboratory waiting for the doctor to come in and take her eggs out of her body. At first she wasn't thinking too much about it but then the closer it got the more her nerves began to creep into her body. Now that it was finally here she didn't know if she was excited or just plain old nervous. Her relationship with Terrell after he lost that sale was actually better than it was in the last couple weeks and she really wanted to keep it that way. He hadn't said any more hurtful words to her so that actually helped.

"So the procedure should go nice and easy. We'll put you under then go in and get your eggs. Dad here will give us a sperm sample so we can fertilize your eggs." Charm took a deep breath and nodded.

"Okay, I'm ready." She held onto Terrell's hand as she was given the anesthetic and it was lights out for her.

"You sure it'll be fine?" Terrell asked the doctor as Charm went out.

"Yes it will be. Here's your cup for the sample." Terrell took the cup. "You can use the room at the end of the hall." Terrell nodded and left the room. Destiny was sitting in the waiting area and stood when Terrell came out of the room.

"Sample time," He smiled at her. He waved the cup at her then walked down to the room at the end of the hall. Destiny watched him go. She stayed where she was twiddling her thumbs. Ever since their sex session Destiny was smitten. She wasn't going to lie. Feelings like jealousy and arousal kept plaguing her and it was something she had ever dealt with before. When he kissed Charm, Destiny always had to leave the room because she swore she wanted to smack Charm over the head with a heavy object or something. And then when she saw Terrell, her stomach would flutter and when he smiled at her she would swear she was going to faint. She wanted him for much more than what her original plan was. Now things were completely different.

Looking around the hall, no one was paying attention to her so she slowly began to inch her way down to the room Terrell had just went into. She stood outside of the door just waiting until she finally had the courage to go in. When she did, she closed the door quickly behind her. Terrell jumped and tried to hide his exposed penis from her.

"Jesus Destiny, what are you doing?" he asked. Destiny looked at his penis and smiled. The memory of it inside of her took over her conscience. She couldn't think about anything else. Instead of answering him, she just kept getting closer to him. And when she was close enough she reached out and took his hand from his penis and placed her hand on him. He took a sharp intake of breath.

"Destiny," He warned. "This isn't right. And you know it." She began stroking him while looking him in the eye.

"Just let it happen Terrell," She shrugged.

"I-I can't," He gritted. "I'm married."

"And this is for your wife isn't it? This sperm that is going to come shooting out of you is too important for you to waste. So don't let it go to waste. And if you didn't want it to happen Terrell you wouldn't have even let me touch you." Terrell didn't know what was wrong with him but he didn't stop her. Or well it felt like he couldn't stop her. He gazed into her eyes and he just let her continue to stroke him. What surprised him was the pleasure of it. She began stroking him faster and faster. She pushed down the top of her dress so he could get an eyeful of her breasts. With her free hand she popped her breast out of her bra.

"Taste it," She whispered.

"No," He rasped. Holding the back of his head, she forced his head down until he was suffocating on her boobs. Finally, he slurped her free breast into his mouth. Destiny moaned and continued stroking him. He suckled on her breast like a new born baby. When he got through with one he popped the other one out from her bra and began suckling on it. It was like his appetite was insatiable.

"Do you remember any of it?" She moaned.

"Any of what?" he gritted looking up from her breasts. Destiny didn't answer him. She leaned into him and took his bottom lip into her mouth. She bit it before sucking onto it then kissing him. He couldn't push her off because he was succumbed by the release that jetted out of him. Destiny grabbed the sample cup and made sure to catch each drop that came from him. He grunted as his penis throbbed in her hand. His breathing was ragged as he emptied himself. And when it was over he brought angry eyes to her.

"Why would you do that to me?" he asked. Destiny didn't answer. She lunged and him and kissed him deeply again. He fought her for a minute before he just gave up. He gave into the kiss. Her lips were sweeter than he thought they would be. And though they weren't pouty like Charm's they still fit his lips fine. She put his hand on her ass and he grabbed it. Her supple peach had his erection beginning to rise again. When Destiny felt his erection she pulled away from him.

"That's why I did that to you," She said pointing down at his erection. "Charm doesn't have to know. We can have each other." Terrell angrily stuffed himself back in his jeans. He couldn't believe he did that.

"If you utter a word of this to Charm I swear Destiny-"

"Keep your threats Terrell. I know." Terrell grunted in anger and grabbed the specimen cup from her before barging out of the room. How did that just happen?! Even if Destiny tasted good and he loved the feel of her supple ass she wasn't there for him to have sex with. She was only there for him to have his baby and that was it. And now he had to deal with the fact that he knew he wanted to sleep with his surrogate even if he wanted to be faithful to his wife.

For the rest of the time at the lab he just paced back and forth not really sure what the hell to do. When Charm came to and the procedure was over all they had to do now was wait until the eggs were fertilized and at a certain stage before they were planted in Destiny. Charm was completely excited about this finally being done, but Terrell was only blinded by what had happened with Destiny. And his nerves were all over the place. He didn't know what had gotten into him. And if Charm sensed any of his infidelity then their relationship was going to crumble.

"Is everything alright?" Charm asked him as he helped her into his car once they were leaving the labs.

"I'm fine, why do you ask?"

"You look like you're thinking hard about something."

"No, I'm good baby." He cleared his throat and looked at Destiny who was getting in the back of the car. She smiled and winked at him as she got in the car. Terrell only shook his head and hurried to the drivers side to get in. He just knew that Destiny was going to hold this over his head.

When they got back home he helped Charm to their bedroom because he didn't want to be around Destiny. He couldn't handle what he'd just done. However the time he wanted to spend with his wife was cut short. Charm was still sleepy from the procedure so once he had her in bed she was sleeping in no time.

"Terrell," Destiny sang from outside of the bedroom door.

"Go away!" Terrell snapped at her. Charm groaned and turned over at his shout but she didn't wake up.

"Don't ignore me now," She teased. Terrell got up from the bed quickly and went to the door. He flung it open and pushed Destiny back before leaving the room and closing the door.

"What if Charm was awake?" Terrell asked. "What are you trying to do?"

"Nothing," She leaned against him and touched his chest. "Your dick felt so good in my hands," She whispered. "I wonder how it would feel inside me." Terrell shook his head. He wondered what the inside of her would feel like too. For years he'd just had Charm. What if he got to sample something new for a change.

"No, stop it," Terrell gritted. "It's not going to happen Destiny. Get that through your thick skull. Stop trying to seduce me because it won't work."

"But it already has," She smiled eerily at him. Terrell just looked her up and down before opening his bedroom door and retreating back inside the bedroom.

"No it hasn't!" He gritted. With that he slammed the door in her face. But he knew that wasn't going to be the end of it. And her words haunted him.

Over the next few days he hated to be alone with her. Because he was afraid of being alone with her. And not afraid because he thought she was going to pounce on him or something. He was afraid because like at the lab his control might not be there and he would let her do whatever she wanted to him. And his eyes would stray. When she was wearing her night gowns or just wearing regular jeans he would look at her ass and he couldn't stop himself from remembering how they felt under his palms. She still smelled so sweet and something about her was just distracting. At this point Terrell was starting to fear that it would only get worse when her stomach would begin to swell with Charm and his's baby. Because maybe he wouldn't be able to differentiate that she was just the surrogate. He hated the fact that this was happening to him when he was finally about to get his baby with his wife. Why was he so weak at controlling his libido?

Things were a little shaky because a couple days after the procedure, Charm was back to her normal self. Which meant that she was going to the gallery daily to continue her own work. And whenever Terrell came home from work and her car wasn't in the driveway, he had to sit in his own car to prepare himself to be alone with Destiny. He'd avoided Destiny as best as he could up until that moment.

"Good night Terrell," She greeted. She was wearing a short nightgown even though it was only a little after 6pm. The silkiness of it hugged her curves. Terrell stopped in his tracks to admire the way it fit her body.

"You've been running from me," Destiny said. "But now it's just us." Terrell shook his head, snapping from his drooling fantasy. He needed to get away from her.

"Right," Terrell said. "I'm going to bed," He stated.

"It's still early," She called out. "You know, you've been avoiding me as if I'm not about to be carrying your baby," She said.

"What you did at the lab Destiny-"

"You're the one that got the hard on. So you wanted it like I wanted it."

"No, that's not true."

"Terrell I've been thinking," She said walking up to him. She circled him while looking him up and down.

"Do you want to have sex with me?" She asked seductively. Terrell swallowed hard. "Don't you want to feel something different for a change? Charm may be good but don't you think about the other kind of women out there? The kind of woman at your disposal? Right here in front of you?"

"No Destiny. Why are you doing this?"

"Look, you give me a vibe and now you want to act like you don't feel it but I'm not gonna play that game with you. So I'm going to tell you, if you want me. All you have to do is take me."

"What I want you to do is carry my child. That's all."

"I will," She winked. She turned and walked away from him swaying her hips in a way that Terrell couldn't stop staring at. How was he going to survive 9 months of this?

CHAPTER EIGHTEEN

Denzel couldn't take his eyes off Charm as she was painting on a small canvas. Ever since he told Brianna what happened with the whole sex thing and the kiss, he hadn't really been able to forget it. He tried his best not to make her feel uncomfortable by his staring but he couldn't help staring. But since that happened weeks ago, she didn't let their relationship change. And she hadn't been complaining about any issues with her husband so Denzel had to assume everything was perfect in her life. Which meant that he would never have a chance to be with her. And he needed to just give it up. Maybe being with Gabrielle was what he needed to focus on.

"I haven't seen you eat," Charm said looking back at him. He blinked.

"Oh yeah, I didn't have an appetite."

"Well I'm ordering pizza so don't let me eat a pie by myself."

"Okay sure I'll eat with you." Denzel told her. She put her paintbrush down then came to sit next to him while she ordered the food on her phone.

"How come lately Brianna and Jason haven't been staying here too long leaving only the both of us here alone?" She asked.

"Good question," Denzel said. But he kind of knew the answer. Which he didn't get because Brianna was completely against him and his feelings he was developing for Charm. And well Jason, Jason was just following along because he wanted to stir the pot too.

"Do you ever wish you weren't married?" Denzel asked her. Charm looked at him sharply surprised by the question.

"Sometimes I do yeah when things get hard, but I don't regret being married. I love Terrell."

"Do you think you can love more than one man at a time romantically?"

"No I don't think that. Love is a powerful thing. Something like that can't be shared between multiple men. What's with these questions huh Is it about the fact that we nearly kissed?" Charm was a little nervous. What if he'd realized she had thoughts about him? Did he know that sometimes she got lost in his eyes?

"No, not just that," he sighed. Denzel looked at her and he

just couldn't hide it anymore.

"Charm, I'm attracted to you," He admitted. "I love your friendship and that's the only reason why I would even put myself through being close to you knowing well it'll start getting hard for me to pretend that I don't want you." Charm cleared her throat. She didn't know what to say. In fact she was afraid to say anything. He wanted her. Oh my god, he wanted her. And Charm began to blush feeling like a school girl who found out that the boy she was crushing on was crushing on her too.

"I'm not here to take you from your husband or corrupt your marriage. When I tried to kiss you I don't know what came over me. But I'm simply attracted to you and that's just the way it is. But I value our friendship more than anything and I won't jeopardize it." Charm tried to control her breathing as he admitted what he admitted to her.

"What about your girlfriend?" Charm asked.

"Nothing," Denzel shrugged. "I still very much care about her. This is the first time something like this has ever happened."

"Wow. So I was the woman you were talking about before huh?" Denzel nodded.

"I know it must be hard to admit but I won't make things weird between us. As long as you promise not to make it weird either," She smiled at him.

"When have I ever made anything weird?" he teased. She laughed and hugged him. There was a slight tingle inside her from his confession. She couldn't help but to blush and gush like a school girl.

"I can confess something," She said to him. "If I was single and you asked me on a date, I'd say yes." Denzel smiled at her.

"Good to know," He said. "Even if I want to be selfish I don't want to wish bad on your marriage. And I hope you two will be married for a lifetime."

"That's actually really sweet of you. I'm surprised you wouldn't be wishing something bad on us."

"Why would I do that? I don't want to see you hurt. I told you, I value our friendship more than anything. If I can't be your lover Charm, then I'll be your friend." This time she did more than blush. When they embraced again, she felt the petals of her arousal beginning to open. It wasn't just her cheeks that were blushing. Her lady parts were too.

"Can I confess something else too?" she asked. Denzel nodded at her. "When I'm in your presence you make me feel different. Like different than my own husband makes me feel. When I rush off on you it's because I can't handle the fact that what I'm feeling is wrong and that I'm cheating on Terrell. I don't want to be that woman, but you just make me feel, I don't know you just make me feel wanted. And sometimes it's not sexual, but then sometimes it is. I get aroused. And it's wrong of me I know that." Denzel was stuck. How was he going to respond to that?

"Um, I don't know what to say," He finally spoke.

"There isn't much else to say Denzel. We just feel a whole bunch of shit but at the end of the day we're committed to other people. I wouldn't hurt Terrell by acting on how I feel towards you. Because if he ever cheated on me I'd be devastated."

"I know Charm. And like I said, I'm not asking anything of you. I just felt you should know how I feel and well now I know how you feel. And I'll try to be as normal as possible around you."

"Thanks Denzel," She smiled. Even though it should have been weird, it wasn't. They actually sat there and talked until the pizza was delivered. Being the man he was, Denzel paid for the food when it arrived. They had one slice each when someone began banging on the gallery door. Charm and Denzel looked at each other.

"Who would that be?" Charm asked.

"I'll open it. Stay right here." Charm nodded and watched as he went to open the door.

"What are you doing here?" Denzel asked when he opened the door and found Gabrielle standing there. She pushed her way through entering without an invitation.

"I've been texting you all-" she stopped when she spotted Charm on the ground. Charm stood quickly.

"And who is this?" Gabrielle asked Denzel.

"Gabby this is Charm the woman me and Brianna works with. And Charm this is Gabrielle."

"Just Gabrielle?" she asked. Denzel gave her a look. "I'm his girlfriend."

"I know," Charm said. "Denzel told me a lot about you."

"Humph," She pouted. "Denzel let's go."

"I'm working," He said.

"No you're having pizza and relaxing. So let's go. I want to be with you tonight. So if you don't want me to get impatient, then come on."

"Just like you don't want me to see you impatient, you don't want to see me get angry Gabrielle. I said I was working."

"And you've been neglecting me all day. So what now huh?"

"Go to my house and wait for me to get home."

"It's not a damn house. It's a one bedroom loft." She looked Charm up and down. "Enjoy your date."

"Gabby don't do-" she turned sharply and walked out of the gallery. Denzel felt so embarrassed at Gabby's behavior.

"Well she's pleasant," Charm said.

"She loves control and when she doesn't have it, she acts like that." Denzel shook his head and locked the door behind her.

"And that's who she wants me to marry," Denzel shook his head.

"Don't feel bad about it," Charm said seeing the way he couldn't look her in the eye.

"It's just so embarrassing," He said. "And here I am telling you how much I'm attracted to you when I have a goddamn girlfriend."

"Sometimes you can't help what you feel Denzel. And you're not the only one who confessed something like that. It's worse for me because I have a husband. But not all relationships are perfect."

"And yours isn't? I know that sometimes you and him argue but you wouldn't still be with him, and love him if your relationship wasn't perfect." Denzel saw a faraway look in Charm's eyes. She changed the way she was sitting, pulling her knees up to her chest. She looked away from him as her thoughts consumed her.

"Charm?" Denzel questioned. He went over to her and sat in front of her so he could read her expression. It's funny how he got good at that. After a moment she turned her head and looked at him. She rest her chin on her knee caps.

"He doesn't treat me like the queen said I am anymore. I come into the gallery and the first thing you tell me Denzel is that I look beautiful. I wake up in bed next to my husband, kiss him and then we proceed on like we always do. I don't remember the last time he told me I looked beautiful. All I remember is him telling me that I need to dress a certain way around company or when I'm with him. I ignored it until you started doing it. Ever since my miscarriage it's like I've become less of a wife in his eyes. I know that he loves me. He just doesn't show it like he used to. And I'm struggling to understand why it's changed between us." Denzel reached out to brush her bangs from her eyes.

"Gabby doesn't want to move in with me. She doesn't like the fact that I live in a loft because it only had one bedroom and apparently her closet is bigger than my bedroom. She wants to leave her place and my place behind and live in a luxurious ass house where then she'll decide if she wants to mother my children. Plus, she doesn't think my art is real work to her. So making a thousand dollars at the end of the week from a paint session, or working for the community center, and that wedding gig we got isn't enough for her. I feel like an idiot because I'm attached to her and I know that our relationship isn't the same anymore. Sometimes it's not as easy as we think to recognize what's wrong with our relationships or even end them." At the same time the both of them inhaled and exhaled. Nothing else had to be said. They understood what they were dealing with and it was another level of connection for them.

CHAPTER NINETEEN

After having that talk with Denzel, Charm really couldn't take her mind off him. She already thought about him heavily, but now as their connection just became deeper she was further enthralled by him. Oh there was so much more to learn about him, so much more they could experience together and the craving that Charm had to experience those things with him was scary. And she hated the fact that he was in an unhappy relationship. So much so that she wanted to be the one to fix everything for him. But how could she do that if she was in a confused state herself. Charm never had to question her marriage because she never found herself battling attraction to another man. And now as she was trying to start a family with Terrell through Destiny, she had to completely forget about what she felt for Denzel. Because starting a family and being a wife to her husband and a future mother was more important than giving into temptation. She just had to focus on the bigger picture.

"You're not at the gallery today?" Destiny asked, coming from her bedroom. Charm was sitting on the couch lost in her thoughts. They'd been working late and frequent at the gallery and Charm just needed a little bit of a break. Especially after her deep conversation with Denzel.

"No," Charm replied not even giving her an explanation.

"Damn, I thought I would get Terrell to myself today." Charm side eyed Destiny but the woman only smirked and plopped down in Terrell's favorite chair.

"Have you and Terrell....you know?" Charm asked her. She didn't know what happened between her surrogate and her husband when she wasn't home. And after what Destiny just said, Charm was a little suspicious.

"Of course not!" Destiny exclaimed. But the sarcasm under those words again made Charm get defensive. If she could resist temptation for the sake of her family, Terrell ought to be able too.

"Charm!" Terrell shouted from their bedroom. His heavy footsteps came down the stairs. His eyes were wide with excitement.

"We have embryos!" He screamed. "The lab just called me!" Charm stood and covered her mouth.

"Really?" She asked.

"It's ready for implantation! I set an appointment for tomorrow so the embryos can be put inside Destiny. We're finally going to have our baby!" the excitement in his voice pierced through Charm. Her thoughts of Denzel slipped away, and she shared a moment of happiness with her husband. Because their child was what was important. Before Charm could advance to hug Terrell, Destiny popped up from the chair.

"I'm so happy for you guys!" She squealed jumping onto Terrell and hugging him tightly. He kept his arms to the side as she hung from his neck. But then when she pulled away the two of them shared a gaze that made the alarm in Charm's head go off.

"Are you sure the two of you aren't fucking behind my back?" Charm asked. Terrell shoved Destiny away from him.

"What?!" He exclaimed. "What would make you ask something like that?" Charm shrugged.

"I think that's obvious," She replied.

"No it's not fucking obvious Charm! I can never win with your ass. We finally got embryos to have our fucking baby and you wanna stand there accusing me of cheating? Yet still you can be at the gallery all night with that fucking painter?"

"Wow," Charm shook her head. "What you so defensive for?"

"I'm defensive because my wife won't stop accusing me of shit. Accuse me one more time Charm. I dare you." He pointed a finger in her face.

"Or else what?" Charm asked crossing her arms.

"Or else I'm gonna give you a reason to accuse me Charm. If you want me to fuck her so bad, I'll fuck her all night long and give you something to be mad about." Charm looked her husband up and down. So much for him not saying anymore hurtful things to her.

"Whether you like it or not Charm, she's woman enough for me in this moment. And you're not. So we're gonna have this baby and I don't wanna hear no more cheating accusations. I'm through with it. We're going to the appointment tomorrow and we're finishing this procedure."

"Too bad I'm not woman enough for you when all I wanna do is be the best wife I can be. I always come back to you no matter the horrible shit you say to me. But think. If I'm not woman enough for you, why are you trying to start a family with me? Who's to say I'd be woman enough to be the mother of your child?"

"Because you're wearing that," He pointed to the ring on her finger. "And I've already invested my time in dating you, and loving you Charm. I don't want to start over with no one else. You're the woman every other man would want."

"So is this some competition to you?" She asked. "All I want you to do is love me Terrell."

"And we wouldn't be here if I didn't." He closed the distance between them so he could lean down and kiss her on the cheek. Charm just stood there, tears forming in her eyes. She didn't know if she was crying because he said she wasn't woman enough for him, or because he could be that horrible to her and still say he loved her. After he placed a kiss on her cheek she backed away from him. Without saying anything she brushed by both Terrell and Destiny and walked back up to their bedroom. She sent a text to the group chat saying she felt sick and she wasn't going to be at the gallery today. Even if she wasn't physically sick, her heart was hurting.

"See, she's onto us," Destiny said once Charm was gone. She rubbed Terrell's chest. "And I don't think she's going to be accusing you anymore after that threat."

""I'm not fucking you," He said taking her hand from his chest. "Even if I wanted to Destiny, I'm not losing my wife to you. Carry our baby and that's it." He pushed her away from him and headed towards the basement so he could workout. What he thought was supposed to be good news turned sour all because Charm had to ruin it.

****

By the next morning, Charm barely spoke with him, but she woke early prepared to go to the lab. As she sat at the edge of their bed he saw when she looked at her phone. A warm smile came to her face. Terrell hadn't seen her smile all morning so he was immediately suspicious.

"You okay baby?" he asked.

"I'm fine," She replied without looking at him. Terrell stalked over to her and snatched her phone out of her hand. She didn't make any move to try and grab it back from him. She only stared up at him.

"Who are you talking to?" he asked. He looked down at her phone to see that she was in a group chat. It was of all the people she worked with now asking if she felt better and wanting to know if she wanted them to come to the house to spend the day. Charm replied that she was fine and she would be with Terrell for the day and they continued talking about other things. Again, Terrell felt stupid for grabbing her phone up like that. But the way she smiled made him think she was having another kind of conversation. But when he searched she had other conversation threads but they were all innocent. Clicking on the Denzel conversation thread, all they talked about was paint supplies, what they were going to eat, and jobs they were planning on doing.

"Finished?" Charm asked quietly reaching her hand out. Terrell placed the phone in her hand.

"I know you probably deleted some messages off your phone," He said.

"You can go online and check Terrell. I got nothing to hide. What you saw is what it looks like when someone actually cares about another person. Maybe that's why you're looking so confused."

"Care? You don't think I care about you Charm?" He asked. "Do you know how much money this process is costing us? If I didn't care I wouldn't be footing this kind of bill. If I didn't care I wouldn't be doing this just so we could have a family. And if I didn't care I wouldn't be working my ass off day in and day out just so you can spend your time splashing around in paint like some teenager. So think about that." Charm wasn't surprised.

"Right," She said nodding. She stood from the bed. "We're going to be late for our appointment." She didn't have the strength to argue. Not again.

"Charm, baby," Terrell sighed. He knew he'd said the wrong thing again. But that's what he got for speaking too much truth. He stood in front of her and cupped her face in his hands. She looked up at him, her eyes already misty.

"I hate when we're like this," He said. "I don't wanna fight, I don't want to argue I don't want none of this. We're starting a family! It's finally happening! I was us to be happy." He brushed the tear that left her eye with his thumb.

"I say all those things baby but you know I love you," He whispered. Charm didn't understand why, but it was as if she needed to hear him say he loved her. Once it trickled out of his mouth she was weak with emotion. He brought her close and held her tight. All Charm wanted was for him to show he loved her. And to know that he wasn't falling out of love with her because she wasn't giving him a baby.

"Feeling better?" He asked her, rubbing her back. She nodded into his broad chest. "Okay let's go." He kissed her forehead and led her out of the room.

"Wait here let me get Destiny," He said leaving Charm in the living room.

"Hey Destiny are you ready?" Terrell called from outside of her door.

Destiny stayed where she was sitting on her bed. She pretended to be excited the day before but she already knew she wasn't going to accompany them to the lab. She knew she couldn't get an embryo put inside her because hopefully she had one growing inside her already. It was too soon to tell if she'd gotten pregnant yet so she had to hold off on going to the lab. And she was going to do everything in order not to get trapped into going to the lab.

"Hey Destiny?" Terrell knocked on her door. Destiny quickly laid down and got under the covers. She groaned as if she was sick. Terrell gave up on knocking and went inside.

"Oh my god are you okay?" Terrell asked.

"I don't know. I just feel a little ill. Maybe it was something I ate," she groaned.

"Charm!" Terrell called. Charm entered the room after a few minutes. She eyes the scene in front of her and knew immediately that something was wrong. Terrell was on his knees next to the bed stroking Destiny's hair.

"She's sick," Terrell said. "We can't take her for the implantation if she's sick it won't be good for the baby."

"But how long are they going to hold the embryos? You so valiantly pointed out how you're spending a lot of money on this," Charm said.

"Don't be inconsiderate," He said. "They can keep them frozen until she's ready.'

"Okay fine. We'll wait."

"I'll get you some medicine Dest," Terrell said stroking her hair again. Charm hummed and just left the room. She was bummed that this was holding them up. At this point she just wanted her baby. And once she had her baby Destiny would be gone and everything could return to normal with her and Terrell.

"I'm sorry," Destiny said lowly after Charm left the room.

"Oh quit it. Don't apologize. You can't help if you're sick."

"I just know you want the baby bad and I don't want to hold you up from it." Terrell sat next to her on the bed and brushed her hair from her face.

"I want you to be safe too," Terrell said. "So worry about getting better and we'll think about the baby." She smiled tenderly at him and for a moment Terrell couldn't get up to leave. He swore up and down he wasn't going to cheat on Charm but he really didn't believe it anymore. His only question now was how was it going to take before he finally gave in. Unable to just sit there and look at her without touching her, Terrell forced himself to stand and leave the room. Charm was pacing the living room.

"You okay honey?" He asked her.

"Yeah. I just-all this waiting. I'm just ready to get this done."

"Don't blame her about this."

"I'm not!" Charm exclaimed. "Why are you so defensive of her that quickly?" Terrell sighed. He was pretty defensive for absolutely no reason. He felt like he needed to protect her.

"I'm sorry," He said.

"Yeah, I bet you are," She snapped at him. She rolled her eyes and walked off. He stayed where he was but he heard the bedroom door slam.

"Great job Terrell," He scolded himself.

CHAPTER TWENTY

Destiny could only play sick for a couple of days. After that the jig was up but she still needed time. But she had to do something to keep Charm and Terrell off her back about going to the lab. The embryos were there waiting for her. Every morning Charm was questioning if she was feeling better and the third day of her lie she knew Charm was going to be onto her if she didn't think of something new.

"I'm going to the lab today," She announced walking into the kitchen. Charm was giving Terrell slices of bacon while he sipped on orange juice.

"What?" Terrell asked. "You made an appointment?"

"I woke up this morning feeling loads better. Which by the way thanks Terrell for taking care of me. I figured then I'd just go to the lab and get things on a roll."

"But why didn't you tell us you were planning on going?" Charm asked. "We both want to be there."

"Charm's right, Destiny. I have clients today so I can't cancel my house showings but you should have let us know ahead of time."

"I already thought about that," Destiny replied. She came over to the island and hopped up on a stool.

"I'd take some orange juice Charm," She said. Charm cocked her brow at Destiny's tone. Oh so she wanted to be cute? Charm went to the fridge and pulled out the carton of orange juice. She slammed the carton in front of Destiny and gave her a smile. Destiny rolled her eyes. She looked at Terrell and continued what she was saying.

"I figured I could go without you for the first procedure because I have to have two procedures done. The first procedure is just the implantation but the second procedure is for confirming the pregnancy and seeing how far along I am. That's probably when the two of you could be present. What you think Terrell?"

"Well I think," Charm spoke, seeing that Destiny was trying to cut her out of the conversation. "I think you should have told us you were doing this before making those plans. It's not up to you to decide what appointment we want to go to. Maybe Terrell and I wanted to see the first procedure too."

"I knew Terrell was going to be busy. You can blame me for trying to get this done without anymore complication!"

"Don't even start up," Terrell warned both the women. "Charm is right, but Destiny I appreciate the sentiment. Either way, there's nothing we can do. You're going to the appointment and we'll be at the next one. Simple. That one does seem like the mist important."

"Which is what I thought," Destiny said shaking her head at Charm. "Not many things pleases you huh?" She asked Charm. "Guess sacrificing my body isn't enough for you." Destiny gave Terrell a look before hopping down from the stool and sauntering out of the kitchen. She heard Charm and Terrell talking after she left but she paid no mind. Soon after that, Terrell had to get going. And an hour after he left Charm was gone. Destiny sat back and kicked her feet up. She didn't make no damn appointment. She'd only said she did on a day she knew Charm and Terrell couldn't come with her. So if they weren't coming with her then she didn't actually have to go. So she sat there all day watching TV and feeling giddy that yet another plan worked. And just because she was confident about where this was all headed, Destiny took a sexy selfie of herself, making sure her boobs were popping out of her top and she sent that picture directly to Terrell. He never answered but she knew he was either staring at it, or thinking about it. And that was good enough for Destiny.

****

Gabrielle rolled off of Denzel's body. The both of them shuddered as their releases raced over their bodies. Denzel pulled the condom off his softening penis. He got up to dispose of it but when he returned to the bedroom Gabrielle was tossing a pill in her mouth. She quickly put the pill bottle away when Denzel came into the room.

"What is that?" He asked her.

"Just vitamins," she replied not even looking at him. But Denzel didn't take his eyes off her. She made a pained face and held the bottom of her stomach.

"Did I hurt you?" Denzel asked worriedly going over to the bed and sitting down next to her. He rubbed her tummy to try and comfort her.

"No, just been having random phantom pain I guess," She mumbled. "The sex was fine trust me." Denzel didn't believe her. He gave her a look and continued rubbing her stomach.

"You're not pregnant are you?" He asked her. She scoffed.

"You know I'm not," She said. "I'd never let myself get pregnant and you haven't proposed to me."

"Wow," Denzel exclaimed. He moved his hand from her stomach then moved away from her completely. He remained quiet as she started getting dressed to leave.

"Stay the night with me Gabby," He said to her.

"You know I don't want to stay here," She said.

"You can come here to fuck me though but you can't spend the night with me?" She threw her arms up.

"Fine! I'll stay!" she grunted. She flung her clothes to the side as if she was a child having a tantrum.

"You know what," Denzel said. "Don't stay. I won't force you. I don't have time to deal with you immature ass attitude."

"I wasn't immature just now when I was riding your shit now was it?"

"You know, that's all we do right? Fuck each other then proceed to argue right after. I'm getting tired of this endless loop."

"So what? You trying to break up with me because of this? Or is it because of that bitch you paint with?"

"Bitch? That's a strong ass word Gabrielle. You don't even know her." Gabrielle decided she wasn't going to stay to please him. She couldn't stay. Because if she did, she was going to have an episode and he was going to see why she had to pop those pills.

"After ten damn years this is what the fuck I get," She muttered. "Count yourself lucky Denzel! Not too many women would be dealing with your shit." She dressed quickly and got her bags ready to go.

"If I've spent ten years already with you Denzel, then guess what?" She spat.

"What?" he asked.

"You're fucking stuck with me whether you like it or not. I'm not going to give you ten years of my life and end up with nothing. So we're gonna be together forever. And you know you'll never want to be without me." Denzel just say in bed with his arms crossed. He couldn't believe she was saying this. Some of it had truth. He knew being with someone for ten years was a big deal. And sure, he should have been asking her to marry him. But was it his fault that he simply felt that Gabrielle wasn't going to be a good wife to him? She was barely a good girlfriend. Even if it would be hard to end their relationship, Denzel knew that eventually he would have to. No matter how she thought they were stuck with each other, Denzel knew they weren't. He just wasn't going to propose to her. He knew that for certain. And he should have suckered up the courage to tell her right then and there their relationship was through but he said nothing. He just watched as she gathered her things and angrily stormed out of his place. The front door slammed with the might of her anger. When had things gotten this bad between them? Denzel couldn't pin a point down but that wasn't going to change the ultimate outcome he knew was going to happen.

CHAPTER TWENTY-ONE

"How's the thing going with Destiny?" Jason asked Charm. All four of them were in the gallery preparing for another art class later in the week but Charm seemed removed from everything. It was just her either. Denzel was spaced out. Because the two of them were hardly talking, it meant that Brianna nor Jason spoke either. And that just meant the whole gallery was silent. Jason figured whatever was on her mind it had to deal with the surrogate. Truth be told, Jason and Brianna knew Denzel and Charm was attracted to each other and they wanted to prompt that relationship. But with Charm being hitched the way she was, she would never cheat on Terrell. No matter how he treated her.

"It's going," She replied lowly. "She went to get my eggs inside her. Now we have to wait a week or so before we go back and see if it was successful."

"So are you happy?" Jason asked her. Charm didn't answer that question. But her silence was all the answer Jason needed. He knew she wanted a baby, but there was something in her that was taking away her happiness from the moment. He just didn't know what.

"Denzel seems pretty upset too," Jason told her. Charm immediately looked over to Denzel. He was painting the image of a dark and rainy day. Funny thing was that's how she felt on the inside. Without further prompt from Jason, Charm stood and went over to him. He touched his shoulder. He jumped at her touch and turned to look at her.

"You alright?" she asked lowly.

"Relationship problems," he replied.

"Tell me about it," Charm sighed. "Me and Terrell, we're um. We're starting a family again. Or at least trying to." Denzel raised his brows when he looked at her again. She saw the genuine happiness in his eyes for her news, but she didn't miss the fleeting sense of sadness that came in his expression. It did something to Charm knowing that even if he was disappointed he wasn't going to let it overshadow his happiness for her as a friend.

"That's great Charm. I'm real happy for you. So are you pregnant right now?"

"Oh no!" She exclaimed. "Not pregnant. But perhaps in the future a baby will be here." Denzel stood and opened his arms.

"If you're not afraid to hug me," he teased. She laughed and fell into his arms, hugging him tightly. She didn't know why she told him about the baby but she figured she might as well have. And then when she had a newborn at her side but she hadn't had a belly, then she'd reveal that she had to use a surrogate.

"I only told you my news so you'd hug me," Charm teased him. He laughed and pulled away from her.

"You do not have to reveal something like that to me just to get a hug. You know I'd hug you regardless."

"And it seemed like you needed a hug too," She smiled. "Have you decided anything about Gabrielle?"

"It's probably not going to work out," He said. "I don't think I'll ever want to marry her."

"Because you don't want to be married or because it's her?"

"Because it's her," He sighed. "Because like Terrell, if I was dating you Charm I would put a ring on it quick. Then I'll keep filling your belly with my babies." Charm couldn't help but put her head down and laugh into her hands.

"You're crazy," She smiled. "But I appreciate that compliment." Taking his compliment was way better that Terrell's underhanded way or telling her he loved her.

"Thanks for coming over here to talk to me," He said. "That just brightened my day." She'd come over here and told him she was going to have baby by her husband and that still didn't depress him further. Charm was impressed by it and she felt that his feelings for her were not only out of pure attraction. He just simply cared about her. And that was something Charm truly appreciate. It took her mind off of anything undesirable when it came to her marriage and Destiny.

****

Once Charm and Denzel broke that ice and they came out of their slumps, the day in the gallery returned to normal. It was lively, fun and it brought it all back to the fact why the three of them loved to paint. She let all her worries drip away from her and once she did, nothing bothered her. As long as she went to the gallery and saw Denzel's warm smiling directed at her, she was fine. While waiting on Destiny to have her 2nd appointment to confirm the pregnancy, Charm didn't bother the woman or even pay attention to anything she was doing.

One morning a week after Destiny had the first procedure done, Charm woke up to Terrell tapping her on the shoulder. She rubbed her eyes and turned over to look at him.

"I'm leaving now," He whispered to her. Charm rubbed her eyes and looked at the time. It was indeed time for him to go to work but she didn't smell food or coffee.

"Wait, did you eat something?" she asked trying to get up.

"No," he said. Charm hadn't been waking up early anymore because when she did Destiny was already there making her husband breakfast.

"Destiny didn't rush to make you anything to eat?" Charm asked.

"No, she's still asleep too."

"Well why didn't you wake me up Terrell? I would have made your coffee and something for you to eat."

"I figured you needed some sleep. Don't worry honey I'll pick up some Starbucks." He leaned over and kissed her on the forehead. "I just wanted to tell you I was going before I left. Go back to sleep." He rubbed her shoulder and stood from the edge of the stood. She watched as he buttoned his blazer and left the room. Sighing, Charm turned over and went back to sleep.

This time when she awoke again, it was after 10 in the morning. With late nights in the gallery she knew that Brianna, Jason, and Denzel weren't early birds so none of them were going to be awake and working unless planned. Charm took her time, stretching and getting herself prepared for her day. She combed her short hair noting that it was growing out past her shoulders again and it was time for her trim. She never liked her hair to get too long because her father told her it made her look like her mother, and Charm did not want to look like that woman.

After her shower and greeting dressed she realized that she hadn't heard Destiny moving around downstairs. Wondering what happened to the woman that wanted one up Charm at every moment. But down in the kitchen it was vacant. Nothing seemed touched or that Destiny had awoken before Charm did. Even if she didn't like the woman Charm had a heart so she wanted to make sure Destiny was alright. Charm left the kitchen and headed towards Destiny's room.

"Destiny," She called. She knocked on the door softly. When

she didn't hear anything she pressed her ear up against the door. It was the sound of retching that made Charm open the door without getting permission. Destiny was sitting on the edge of the bed vomiting into a plastic bag.

"Oh crap," Charm rushed into the room. She pulled Destiny's hair from her face and held it as she continued to vomit. When she finally emptied her stomach of it contents she just breathed heavily for a few minutes before picking her head up. Charm helped her up and walked with her to the bathroom. Once there she tied the vomit bag in another bag while Destiny washed her face and brushed her teeth.

"I will never miss throwing up," Destiny said once she was done.

"I don't think no one will," Charm commented.

"Thanks for helping out," Destiny said.

"I thought you were over your stomach bug?" Charm asked.

"I am over my stomach bug," Destiny replied. "I haven't been sick all week until now."

"Well then," Charm started. "Guess the implantation worked. Think you're pregnant?" Destiny paused for a moment before finally speaking.

"I guess it is working," She said. "But we'll know for sure once we get back to the lab in a couple days."

"You gonna be good?" Charm asked her. She seemed dazed out so Charm just stood there waiting until she answered.

"Yeah, yeah, I'll be good," She rushed out. "Gonna go back to bed and just rest. I'll be fine trust me."

"Alrighty." Charm backed out of the bathroom and left Destiny to her own devices. She was going to head to the gallery soon anyway.

Destiny stood alone in the bathroom looking at herself in the mirror. She hadn't thought about the reason she was throwing up until Charm mentioned it. Once Charm was clear out of the bedroom and on her merry way, Destiny rushed back into her bedroom and dug through her top drawer. She emptied everything out until she reached the box of pregnancy tests at the bottom. She stared at the box, a smile coming to her face. She couldn't believe this was real. She hoped that it was real.

Back in the bathroom her hands trembled as she tore up the box. She'd never peed so quickly as she did in that moment. She followed the instructions after she peed on the stick and was crossing her fingers as she leaned over the bathroom counter waiting for the results of the test. Hearing the beep she looked down at the test.

"Yes!" She squealed. She looked down at her flat stomach. "Oh my god it worked," She gasped. With the fertility medication she was taking instead of synching her cycles with Charm, she'd managed to get her own egg fertilized with Terrell's sperm. Now she was going to be connected to Terrell and his money for a long time. That was her original plan but now it was much more than that. She didn't want just Terrell's baby. She wanted Terrell. And now with his baby in her tummy Destiny knew she could get him.

Charm wasn't home when Terrell arrived, and Destiny had to resist the urge to shout in his face that she was finally pregnant. But she didn't. She sat in the living room wearing her favorite lingerie.

"When are you coming home Charm?" She heard Terrell on the phone. "I'm your husband if I want you home then I don't need to have a reason. Damn." She heard him suck his teeth and then he was coming in the living room. Just like she expected he stopped in his tracks and dropped his briefcase. Destiny sipped her apple cider and winked at him.

"What are you doing?" He stuttered. She shrugged.

"Drinking apple cider." Terrell was nearly drooling at the pink teddy Destiny had on. Her breasts were falling out of the top practically and the garter belt she had on was making Terrell's hand itch. The image of sliding the panties off and fucking her from behind with the garter belt on raced through his mind.

"Destiny why the hell do you do this?" He questioned.

"Does it bother you?" She asked.

"You know that it does," He gritted.

"Why?" she asked getting up. She walked over to him and walked circles around him. He stared at her every move. She stood in front of him and took his free hand. He let her place his large hand on her ass.

"Want some of this?" She asked.

"Destiny just-"

"Terrell I'm back!" Charm called out. The entrance to the house in the kitchen opened and closed. The fright on Terrell's face made him unrecognizable for a second. He tore his hand away from her ass and pushed her back.

"Go the fuck in your room before she she's you!" Terrell

gritted. Destiny didn't want to run but she knew she couldn't get caught yet. But before running off she palmed his growing erection. She heard Charm's steps coming closer and that's when she dashed off to her room. She hurried and locked herself in with a big smile on her face. Charm could have her husband now, but Destiny was close to taking him away from her.

CHAPTER TWENTY-TWO

Charm was smiling from ear to ear at the end of their art class. It was filled to the max with adults who were actually serious about art. Without Brianna and Denzel, Charm would have been missing these chances to make this kind of money in her art because she couldn't handle a big class by herself. Not when it was so hands on. And she wanted every participant to feel as if they were getting attention. As Denzel was packing his stuff away Charm was peeking over at the way his biceps curled when he lift things up. But apparently she was staring too hard because after a minute he picked his head up and looked at her. Charm dropped paintbrushes in her effort to hurry and look away from him, but that didn't matter. He'd already caught her. She cleared her throat and just smiled at him.

"Damn Charm, should me and Jason leave so you and Denzel can hump like rabbits for the rest of the night?" Brianna teased. Cham threw a paintbrush at her.

"Shut up!" She blushed.

"You the one staring a hole into him. What, your horny or something?" She asked. Charm thought for a moment. She was in fact a little sex deprived. She hadn't made love to Terrell in over a month because of their constant disagreements. So yes, she had to admit that her hormones were a little heavy.

"Maybe I am," She responded truthfully. Denzel gasped and stared at her. His eyes raking her up and down.

"Don't even think about it Denzel," Brianna warned him. "Miss hot draws is still hitched and you in the same boat." Denzel only shook his head at that. If he was given a chance to be with Charm he wasn't so sure that he wouldn't break up with Gabrielle even sooner. But that was impossible. Charm was starting a family with her husband and Denzel had no chance at the woman who made him feel different.

"I hope you don't have a wood over there thinking about something," Brianna said to him. He shot her a look. Brianna backed up immediately laughing.

"You know what," Charm said. "I think I'm just going to go home. Guess I need to cool my hot draws and actually show my husband some love."

"You don't have to," Jason said. "I'm sure Denzel would love to cool your hot draws for you."

"Oh come on guys," Denzel finally spoke. "Leave her alone. Let her go." He flashed a smile at her and she nearly lost her composure. Oh hell no, she really needed to leave.

"I'll see you guys tomorrow." She hurriedly gathered her things. Denzel went to the door and held it open for her as she walked by. His cologne drowned her and made her want to turn back and bury herself in his chest. But instead of being that extreme Charm just looked at him.

"Gabrielle is a lucky girl," She said.

"And you aren't?" he asked. Charm shrugged her shoulders. Sometimes she was, and sometimes she wasn't. But that didn't matter now because she was putting that aside to finally give her husband much needed attention.

"Well he's a lucky man," Denzel told her. Charm smiled and nodded at him before walking away quickly before she did something she would regret. She just needed to get home.

****

Terrell was trying to eat his dinner peacefully that Charm had cooked the night before but Destiny was sitting across the island from him, staring. He bit into the ribs slowly and licked the sauce off his lips. Destiny sat forward as if she was a hungry dog that wanted his ribs. But Terrell knew it wasn't that. After what she pulled a couple days ago, and Charm came home and nearly caught them, he'd been avoiding her. He couldn't risk letting Charm catch them. That just couldn't happen. He tried to act as normal around her.

"Do you want some?" He asked her motioning to the ribs. He pushed the plate towards her. She picked up one of the ribs and ate it teasingly slow. She licked her fingers, sucking them in a way that made Terrell's arousal jump.

"What you looking at like that woman?" he asked. He couldn't stand her stare anymore.

"Just a sexy ass man," She responded.

"Please don't start that," He said. "Don't try that. Not after what happened the last time."

She pushed the plate of ribs back towards him and walked off while licking her fingers. But Terrell didn't think she would give in so easily. She was up to something.

Destiny went to her bedroom. She was through with the

games and the waiting. She was going to have him tonight. After finding out she was carrying his baby those few days ago she was keeping herself in check. But now she was sick of keeping in check. She wanted to make love to the father of her baby. She knew he loved lingerie and his favorite color was red. So inside the room she changed into a red teddy but left the underwear part off so she was naked underneath and he would be able to tell she was. She stayed in her room and called out to him.

"Terrell come here and help me with something!!"

"What's up?" He called back.

"Just come here!"

"Destiny don't try and play that game with me! I know you're up to something!"

"Don't be a little bitch. Come here!" After a few moments she finally heard his footsteps approaching the bedroom. When he came inside he halted and looked her up and down.

"I knew it," he said swallowing hard.

"Is this cute? I'm trying to decide which one to wear. That's what I wanted you to help me with." Terrell shook his head trying to clear the cobwebs and see reason but he couldn't. All he saw was the sexy woman in front of him wearing the lingerie that his wife didn't wear for him anymore.

"It's-It's cute," He sputtered.

"Are you sure?" she asked.

"Red, that's my color." He whispered. Destiny strutted up to him. As she did, he began backing up. He could back up all he wanted, he wasn't going to get away from her this time.

"Where ya going?" she asked teasingly following him. He began shaking his head again but continued backing up. He went from her room, through the hall and back towards the living room. He maneuvered the house looking over his shoulder even moment or so and then looking back at her to make sure she hadn't gotten any closer. But each time, she was closer.

"Destiny please don't do this," He begged. But she didn't listen. She pulled her teddy up showing more of her naked bottom half. His breath caught as he looked down to her womanly core staring prettily back at him. He backed up until he hit the back of the couch. She continued walking towards him and because he was stuck against the back of the couch she pressed her body against him. She went on her tip toes and began unbuttoning his shirt and kissing on his neck.

"You want this Terrell, you know you do. Just give it to me."

"I can't Destiny, I can't."

"Charm won't be home any time soon. Just take a small feel of me please and then I won't ever ask again." Her hands went to his pants that she unbuttoned. His erection was quick to come bouncing out. And when she wrapped her hand around it he trembled.

"Just one time," Destiny begged kissing him. She made him grab her ass. He clenched the softness and moaned. She let his hand marinate there before she started to lower herself in front of him. She got on her haunches to lick his dripping tip. His pre cum coated her tongue in that magnificent taste she loved. She wrapped her lips around his tip sucking softly and teasing him.

"One time Terrell. Please. I'm so fucking horny. I want you so bad." Terrell looked down at her teasing his tip and his control just snapped.

"Fuck," He groaned. He lifted her roughly in his arms and carried her back to her bedroom. But they didn't even make it to the bed. The first wall he could get her up against was the first wall he used. He pressed her face first into the wall. She threw her ass back, arching for him as he tugged down his pants harshly. With force he thrusted up inside her. The difference between his wife and Destiny was immediately noticeable as he fit himself deep inside her. But pussy was pussy wasn't it?

He gritted his teeth as his hips worked with a mind of their own. He couldn't stop thrusting. Terrell knew this wasn't right. He knew he was messing up big time. But with that all in his head he still couldn't stop himself from thrusting into her. He held her hips and with his eyes closed he pounded into her. He could feel her walls quivering around him and that enticed him to keep going. He couldn't stop until he felt he come all over him. Their raspy breaths filled the air around them to the point where they heard nothing else. Not even the front door opening and closing.

"Fuck Terrell fuck!" Destiny cried out. "It feels so good!" Charm froze mid-step. The mail she was holding in her hand fluttered to the ground Her head immediately turned towards Destiny's bedroom. There was no thought in Charm's brain. But she felt her feet moving directly towards Destiny's room. Her footsteps were quiet as she went down the hall. But there was no door the burst down for Charm to find out of her husband was really doing what it sounded like they were doing. Charm stared directly into Destiny's bedroom. Her heart was racing so fast she felt like she was about to faint. Tears clouded her eyes as she watched her husband screw their surrogate against the bedroom wall. Destiny's eyes were closed in ecstasy with her mouth wide open. Charm refused to stand there and be played like this. No matter how bad things have gotten cheating was just crossing the line. And if Destiny was going to be shouting for pleasure because of her husband, then she could have him.

"I'm coming!" Destiny shouted scratching up the wall. This was completely different than their first time. Terrell was actually in control and thrusting inside her so hard Destiny felt like she was going to pass out from the orgasm that was barreling through her. Not only that, but she could feel Terrell swelling with his own release. She just wanted him to finish inside her, filling her with his essence. The same essence that gave her the baby that was in her stomach.

"Come for me," She groaned tossing her ass back at him. He slapped her ass and watched her cheek jiggle. Curse words left his mouth as his own balls began to choke. He was two seconds from spilling his release when he felt something hard hit him in his back. His hips halted when he heard a small squeal. Dread filled his body. Looking up he saw Charm standing in the doorway of the room tears falling from her eyes. The look she gave him as she shook her head and covered her mouth ripped his heart to shreds. No. This couldn't be happening. He pulled out of Destiny's body quickly.

"Charm it's not what-" Before he could finish his statement she was picking up a glass picture frame. She threw it at him before she ran from the room crying her eyes out.

"Oh my god," Terrell gasped. "No, no." He punched the wall he was just fucking Destiny against.

"SHIT! Charm wait!" He tripped over his pants as he tried to pull them up. Righting himself he tucked his wood in his pants and ran after her. She was in their bedroom hastily packing a bag. She was literally shaking with her tears.

"Baby please listen to me," He begged.

"Don't baby me!" She screamed. She climbed onto the bed so she could knock their wedding photo off the wall.

"I'll never hurt you! You remember when you said that to me?" She cried. "You fucking liar! In our own home?! How could you do that to me?"

"Baby I don't know it just-it just happened! It meant nothing I swear! I love you so much."

"No. This isn't love. You're a cheat." She continued packing up her stuff. Terrell felt so helpless watching her grab her things and packing them away. The way she cried tore his heart into pieces.

"Please don't leave," was all Terrell could say. Destiny ran into the bedroom. Terrell wanted to lock her out because he knew she would only make it worse, but Destiny wasn't going to be locked out. She forced herself into the room.

"Charm!" She called out. Charm looked at the woman. She was pissed and wanted nothing more than to charge at Destiny and just fight her uncontrollably but it wasn't just her fault. Terrell was just as guilty and he could have just not had sex with her. He made that choice.

"The both of you can go to hell," Charm spat.

"Don't give up on us Charm! We've been together all this time and-"

"Now how long we been together matters?!" she shrieked. "I just caught you balls deep in another woman. Did you even think about hurting me? About our marriage?"

"It meant nothing," he said. "It was just a fuck."

"Just a fuck?!" Destiny shouted. "How can you say that Terrell? You've wanted me since the moment I stepped foot in this house!"

"You know I love my wife Destiny! You forced me to do this and you know it!"

"That's bullshit!" Destiny said.

"I'm not going to leave my wife for you Destiny. Charm please believe that."

"I don't want you Terrell," Charm cried.

"But what about us and the baby?" Terrell asked. "She already went and got it implanted in her we can't just throw that away. We-we have plans for our future. She's more than likely pregnant already!"

"We have plans for the future?" Charm gasped. "So while I'm up at three in the morning feeding the baby, you're in Destiny's room fucking her to hell and back?! I don't fucking think so!" She looked at Destiny and shook her head.

"You carrying our baby Destiny doesn't change what you

two have done. And you're still a cheat Terrell and I can't-"

"Wait," Destiny snapped. Charm hushed up finally. "You were right. I am pregnant. But I'm not pregnant with your baby Charm. I'm pregnant with Terrell's baby." Charm looked at Terrell who was viciously shaking his head.

"She's lying," Terrell exclaimed. How would that even be possible?! This is the first time I've ever had sex with her and I didn't even finish! And you went to get the embryo implanted in you, you told us you did! So if you're pregnant it's with Charm's eggs and that's it!"

"I am lying but not about the baby. I didn't get the implantation. Only told you I did because I wasn't ready to get them and the two of you wouldn't hop off my back about it. So I lied."

"So then how are you saying you're pregnant with my kid Destiny? This is the first time I've ever put my dick inside you!" Charm looked back and forth between them. She was still packing up her shit.

"No Terrell don't you remember. We had sex a month ago. When you lost that sale to the big client." Charm realized something then.

"Excuse me?" Terrell gasped. "No, we didn't have sex. I would remember that," He exclaimed.

"No but the next morning you kept asking if I we had sex and I kept telling you no," Charm said. "Apparently you couldn't remember who you were fucking."   Terrell put his hands on top of his head. What in the hell type of twilight zone was he in right now.

"Wait. Wait. Wait," He finally spoke. "So you're saying you're pregnant? As in your egg? That the baby is ours?"

"Yeah that's what I'm saying. We're gonna have a baby." Terrell took a breath and looked at her stomach. This was not the way he was supposed to get his family. But now that there was a baby involved he wasn't going to deny it. Especially when all his babies never survived.

"I'm not getting rid of it Terrell so don't even think of asking that," Destiny rushed out.

"No! I'd never ask you to do that. If that's my baby I want it." Charm looked between them. She realized then she was the odd man out. Terrell was finally having a baby. And it was with the woman he was having an affair with. She could hardly catch her breath. And once again, not being able to control it, she burst out into tears. She grabbed the suitcase she was packing and pushed past the both of them to get out.

"I want a divorce!" She cried out as she hurried away. "I'm done with you!" All she could imagine was Terrell holding a newborn baby by a woman who could actually carry and birth his child. And she could do none of those.

"Charm please don't!" Terrell called out after her following her. "Baby please don't leave me!" He grabbed her arm for a chaste second, feeling her soft skin before she slipped out of his reach. She ran out of the house and dumped her suitcase into her car. Terrell could only watch as she backed out of the driveway fast.

The road was blurry because of her tears but she knew where she was going because she'd driven the same route almost every day.

Terrell watched her car motor down the street. Destiny came to his side coaxing him to come back inside. That's when it started to sink in that he just lost his wife.

CHAPTER TWENTY-THREE

Denzel sat alone in the gallery on a beanbag with his sketch book in hand. He wasn't really drawing anything. He was just daydreaming. Brianna and Jason had left a little bit after Charm did, but Denzel didn't want to leave. He didn't feel like being burdened by his girlfriend at the moment. All he could think about was Charm however. Even though he said he wasn't going to do anything to disrupt her marriage Denzel couldn't help but to feel jealous. Just now the way she wanted to go home to Terrell made Denzel wish he had that kind of excitement inside him to go home to Gabrielle. But he just didn't. And it rightfully depressed him.

He realized he was avoiding her because he didn't want to eventually say the things he needed to say to her. Denzel rested back in the beanbag when he heard someone at the door. He paused for a minute and listened. There was no one he expected to come there but then he rolled his eyes when he thought that it must have been Gabrielle again. If she showed up ready to fight with him again, he didn't know how he was going to act. He got up from the beanbag and went to the door.

But it wasn't Gabrielle at the door. Charm was on the other side of the door desperately trying to open it. She was twisting the knob so angrily that she couldn't get the door open. Then again she wasn't just angry. She was crying uncontrollably. Denzel quickly opened the door for her.

"Charm-" She pushed passed him dragging her suitcase, but tipped over her own feet and ended up on the ground. Denzel closed the front door and ran to her. He knelt down next to her so he could pick her up. But she wasn't giving and effort to come off the floor. He'd never seen her like this before. It was worse than the time he caught her upset and drawing her painting about the miscarriage. It made Denzel fear the same thing had happened again.

"Baby girl what's the matter?" He asked picking her up and holding her.

"Terrell, he-he-" she couldn't even get the words out.

"I'm here Charm. Sshhh." He held her tightly pressing her head against his chest and just allowed her to cry on him.

He didn't know how long they stayed in that position, but he didn't even want to move. He just wanted to comfort her. And she too needed it because she didn't move to let him go. After some time, her cries turning into sniffles, and then her sniffles turned into hiccups.

"Charm?" When he looked down at her he saw her eyes were closed. He caressed the side of her face. This poor woman. How could Terrell ever hurt her this much? Denzel gathered her in his arms and carried her further into the gallery. He sat back down and leaned against the wall and put her head to rest on his thighs.

"Hey Jase, something happened with Charm. Can you come to the gallery?"

"What? What happened?" He shrieked into the phone.

"I don't know, she didn't tell me. But just come please."

"I'll be there in ten minutes." Denzel sat there and massaged Charm's hair until Jason was unlocking the gallery door and rushing in.

"Is this her suitcase?" He questioned.

"Yeah. She burst in here crying uncontrollably and all I could do was hold her. And she just cried herself to sleep. She said Terrell did something but she didn't say what." Jason turned and gave Denzel his back as he pulled his phone out.

"What did you do to her?" Jason gritted. "You son of a bitch! Just save it! She's never coming back to you I swear!" Jason hung up the phone.

"He doesn't want to admit what he did!" Jason paced back and forth. He threw his hands up.

"Look, Charm will tell us what Terrell-"

"Terrell?!" Charm jumped from her sleep in fright looking all around her.

"No baby girl it's just me and Jase." Her eyes were damn near swollen shut from her crying. Denzel didn't like this. Not one bit.

"Lay back down sweetie. It's okay." She nodded and rested her head back onto his lap falling back to sleep quickly.

"We have to get her somewhere so she can sleep for the night."

"Of course I can take her to my apartment. But I don't want to wake her and I live on the 5th floor. I can't carry her."

"No worries, I'll come with you." Denzel gathered her in his arms again and headed towards the door to walk out with her while

Jason rolled her suitcase out behind them.

He put Charm in his car and followed Jason to his apartment. On the way there he texted Brianna so she knew what was going on. Every few minutes he looked over at Charm who was stull sleeping, but her face was drawn into a frown as if she was dreaming about the very thing that got her so upset in the first place. Denzel didn't want her frowning. Not even in sleep.

Jason's apartment had two bedrooms so he carried Charm to the guest room where he tried to rest her down in the bed. But she woke up and grabbed hold of him.

"Where am I? Is Terrell here? I don't want to be here with him! Please take me somewhere else!"

"No, no Charm. There's no Terrell. You're at Jason's apartment." He hushed her by caressing her face.

"No one here is going to hurt you."

"Please don't leave me," She whimpered. "Please stay with me Denzel." How could he say no to that? He looked at Jason.

"It's fine with me. You can stay here. I have extra toothbrushes and all of that. She needs you." Denzel only nodded.

"Text Brianna and tell her I'm staying the night here. She can come over in the morning." Denzel looked back at Charm's pleading eyes.

"I'll be here for you," He said to her. She breathed a sigh of relief that helped her let him go and actually lay down on the bed. Denzel got in with her and put her against his chest. She was asleep again soon after but this time her frown was gone.

"Are you falling in love with her? Like Brianna told me?" Jason whispered to him. Denzel looked up at the man.

"Look at me. Tell me what you think," Denzel answered.

"I think that now Charm's heart is broken. And if you really are falling for her then you'll help her heart heal. But don't force her into anything. She's going to be so confused about her feelings and I think that she just needs you to continue being her friend. Then it'll come together for the both of you."

"I still don't understand how I can fall for someone that I've known only for months," Denzel said looking down at her sweet face. He didn't know how he fell for her but he knew the moment he laid eyes on her that there was just something different about this woman.

"Love doesn't wear a watch," Jason said. He began backing

out of the room. "See you in the morning don't be afraid to ask me for anything you need."

"Thanks Jase. For helping me to help her."

"That's what bestie's are for. And yes I'm talking about you too." He smiled and left the room, closing the door on the way out. Denzel waited until he felt Charm was deep into sleep before he inched away from her. He got out of the bed and stood to take his jeans and his t-shirt off. He leaned over her and unsnapped her jeans and pulled them off too, and then pulled off her T-shirt. In her condition he couldn't even look at her in a sexual way. It just wasn't right. But he wanted her to be comfortable and if he wasn't comfortable wearing jeans to bed then she wasn't going to be comfortable either. Once she was down to her underwear he pulled the covers over her then got back in bed next to her and continued holding her soft body against his.

CHAPTER TWENTY-FOUR

Charm's eyes slowly blinked open. The sun was wafting through the window in the room. She could smell Denzel's cologne but the bed was empty next to her.

"Den-" she cleared her throat. She'd cried so much her voice was hoarse. Before she tried to call out to him again Denzel came into the bedroom with a tray of food.

"You're awake," He smiled. "I was going to wake you up if you weren't." Charm only nodded since she didn't think she could talk yet.

"Jason left those over there for you so you could freshen up," Denzel said pointing to the lounge chair under the window. Jason had taken her night shorts and tank top from her suitcase and folded it up on the chair. Charm got out of bed slowly and went to the bathroom so she could take a shower. Her mind was still fuzzy about everything that happened the night before. But if there was one thing she remembered was the image of Terrell thrusting into Destiny and the pleasure on her face. Hot tears began falling from her eyes again. She never imagined something like this could hurt so bad. And to make it even worse, he was having a baby with her.

Wiping her eyes, Charm finished showering and wrapped the towel around her body before going back to the bedroom. Denzel smiled at her when she entered. She gave him a weak smile in returned. Seeing that she wanted to get dressed, Denzel excused himself to give her some privacy. While he waited outside, Jason and Brianna came to the room. Jason was carrying a large cup of hot chocolate.

"She loves hot chocolate," He said.

"She's changing in there, let's give her a few minutes." After she was finished dressing, she opened the door and walked back to the bed and got in.

"Here you go boo," Jason said handing her the cup of hot chocolate.

"Thank you," She replied hoarsely. Denzel got in bed next to her while Jason and Brianna sat at the end of the bed. For a moment everyone just watched her sip her hot chocolate and then start to eat the food Denzel had brought up for her. Charm knew they were all waiting for her to come clean about what happened. And she knew that talking about it might help her overcome the situation. She set her mug down and pushed her food away.

"I caught Terrell cheating on me," She said finally. As she figured there was a collective gasp. "I got home and I heard sounds and I went to investigate. And right there against the wall, he was fucking the woman who was a guest in our house." Denzel shook his head. He rubbed Charm's back to comfort her.

"You've got to be fucking kidding me," Brianna breathed angrily shaking her head.

"I should have known this would happen. I was so stupid to think it would work out in the first place," Charm shook her head.

"Charm you don't need Terrell or Destiny. Fuck them!" Jason spat.

"Well they're the ones that don't need me," Charm said. "She's pregnant with his baby."

"His?" Jason asked, hinting about the surrogacy.

"Yes. Just his."

"I can't believe this," Jason said. "Charm I'm so damn sorry." Charm wiped the tear that came from her eyes then laid down, resting her head in Denzel's lap. He immediately began running his hand through her hair. The motion felt good and it allowed her to stay calm.

"I suppose it is what it is," She said dully.

"So what now?" Brianna asked.

"I guess we'll get a divorce and that will be that."

"You'd better take him for all he got," Brianna snapped. "He shouldn't be able to just do that to you and get away with shit to easy!"

"I don't care about that. He could keep his money and everything. I want nothing to do with him.

"But you have to do something."

"I don't know. He's going to have a baby. It seems petty that I try and take money from him."

"I can't believe you," Brianna gasped.

"What?"

"The man just cheated on you, broke your damn heart and you're thinking about not being petty? About taking his feelings into accommodation? Nah, fuck all that. And fuck him. If you ain't gonna do something Charm. Then I will. I can make his life a living hell!"

"I don't want you to get into any trouble either," Charm said. "It doesn't matter what he did to me. I don't want you to come out of yourself in the name of revenge." Brianna crossed her arms.

"I can't guarantee I won't do something if I ever see him. I'll tell you that right now." Charm was quiet.

"Does anyone have art supplies?" she asked quietly.

"I have a canvas and some paint in my car," Denzel said. "Do you want to paint?" he asked. Charm nodded.

"I'll go get it form the car," Brianna said.

They waited while Brianna got the canvas from Denzel's car. When she returned with the items, Charm sat up and took them from her. The whole room was quiet as she set up her pallet and started a painting on the small canvas.

"Look, I've got to get to another violin class," Brianna said. "But I'll be back here later to make sure you're alright. Or I can still go to your house as teach Terrell a thing or two." Charm just shook her head.

"No it's fine Brianna I promise. I'll see you later."

"Alright then if you insist," She breathed. "See you guys later." She went around the room hugging and giving everyone a kiss before she left. Jason had to get to work soon but he was wondering if he should call out to stay with Charm.

"You're not working today Jason?" She asked him.

"I'm supposed to but if you want me to stay here with you then I will."

"No, don't miss your money for me."

"I'll stay with her Jason. Not like I have to report to anyone to work. And I can take the day away from my paintings," Denzel offered.

"You sure?" Jason asked.

"I'd like that," Charm whispered looking at Denzel.

"Okay fine, I'll head to work. I showed you around already Denzel so make yourself comfortable." Jason came over to the bed and hugged Charm.

"Keep your head up beautiful," He told her. He flicked her nose before leaving the bedroom. Charm sighed and continued painting. Denzel rested back and looked over her shoulder at what she was doing. After a half hour he gasped at the image that was coming to life.

"Come on Charm why would you be painting that?" He asked, looking at the image of two people having sex against the wall.

"I can't get it out of my head. He had her face first against the wall and he was thrusting into her as if his life depended on it or something. Like he'd never had sex with a woman before when he had a whole fucking wife that laid next to him in bed every fucking night!" Charm was gripping the paintbrush so tight she almost broke it.

"Let it go," Denzel said trying to take the brush from her. She glared at him for a moment before she finally let it go. He took the painting from her and placed it on the floor next to the bed.

"I don't like you drawing that kind of shit," Denzel said. "This and the miscarriage one isn't the type of painter you are."

"It's not about the type of painter I am. It's about the fact that I am able to express myself no matter the circumstance." Charm gave him a look.

"Well I don't like you expressing yourself that way. You're hurting yourself even more."

"How would you feel if you walked in on Gabrielle having sex with another man?" Denzel's brow went up.

"I'd be pissed the hell off," He said.

"What would you do to get over it? To move on? Because I feel so stuck. I don't know what to do but to keep thinking about it over and over again."

"You're trying too hard," Denzel answered. "You're not going to move on today. Or Tomorrow. But eventually you will. What you have to remember is that you're a woman of worth. One man's garbage is another man's treasure. Through all that pain you just have to find the silver lining." Charm looked at him. Her eyes landed on his lips and not really sure what came over her, she leaned forward to kiss him. Denzel saw her sweet lips coming at him and he wanted so bad to grab her up and kiss her plump lips but he didn't. He grabbed her by the chin to stop her from leaning forward. She opened her eyes a little and looked at him.

"What's the matter?" She asked huskily. "I thought-I thought you said you were attracted to me?" Denzel sat up fully and made her sit up too. He faced her so he could look her in the eye.

"Charm trust and believe I am attracted to you. I wasn't lying about that. But for one thing technically Gabrielle and I are dating. I can't kiss you." Charm suddenly felt stupid. She held her head down but Denzel made her look at him again.

"I forget. You're not like my husband."

"And then that's the second thing Charm. I need for you to come to me and want me for the sake of wanting me. Not because you feel like you need to do something to make you forget about what your husband did, or to get back at him. I know you're hurting Charm, but this isn't the answer. If you're not going to want me because you have feelings for me then what's the point?"

"But-but I do have feelings for you. I just-I just suppressed them because of Terrell. But now I know I can go there with you."

"Charm I would leave my girlfriend of ten years to be with you," Denzel admitted. "Simply because I know I feel something special for you. Something that I've never felt for Gabrielle." Charm realized the intensity of what he just said.

"Answer me honestly Charm. You're angry and hurt right now. But think about down the line. Can you divorce him? Or will you just forgive him and try again?"

"I-I don't know what I'd do. But-" Denzel shook his head.

"That's how I know you can't go there with me Charm. I'm willing to leave my girlfriend because of how strange I feel around you. About how I know that I just don't feel the same for Gabrielle. You can't say that down the line you'd get a divorce to leave him for good to be with me." Charm realized what he was saying. She didn't want to use Denzel as the rebound. But she wanted him.

"I understand," She said. "But you shouldn't keep Gabrielle if you know another woman has your heart. It's not fair to you or to her." Denzel thought about that.

"If Terrell had just told me he'd rather leave me to be with another woman it would still hurt. But it wouldn't hurt as much as catching him having relations with her." Charm sighed then scooted over so she could lay down again resting her head on his lap. Denzel placed his hand in her hair and did his signature caresses.

****

Denzel wished he could have stayed with Charm for as much as possible, but in the end he had his own girlfriend that needed attending to. He stayed with Charm for the whole day but he made sure he communicated with Gabrielle. Once the sun was set and Charm was deep in sleep again, Denzel crept out of the bed and left the room. He waited until Jason was back home before he actually left the apartment. Instead of going home, he went straight to Gabrielle's house. He had a key to her place so he just let himself in.

"Gabby," He called out. She didn't answer but he heard the TV on in the living room. Upon entering, Gabrielle was just sitting on her couch. She turned and looked at him, her eyes red rimmed.

"What happened?" He asked her going to sit next to her.

"I'm losing you aren't I?" She asked. Denzel rubbed his eyes. That was a loaded question. But he knew that they didn't have a future.

"Things have changed Gabby," He admitted. "Ever since the marriage thing I've been doing a lot of thinking and it's just led me to certain conclusions."

"I told you Denzel. You're stuck with me. So whatever conclusions you think you made, you better rethink them."

"Gabby it's-"

"Now you've made me upset Denzel. So you know what you need to do. I'll be in the bedroom waiting. Give me 15 minutes to clean up before you come." Denzel threw his head back against the couch as she stood and left the living room. He knew that whenever he upset her he always had to spend the night in between her legs, feasting on her pink lips until she was shaking with satisfaction. But how could he even think about doing something like that right now when his heart was with Charm? Wondering if she was alright? But until he had balls enough to just end his relationship and stop letting Gabby suck him back in, then he had to do what a man was supposed to do for their woman. So like she said, after 15 minutes he went to her bedroom and he what she wanted him to do. Even if his head wasn't in the game, he forced himself to do what was necessary and when Gabrielle tapped out and fell asleep, he just laid next to her and forced himself to sleep as well.

In the morning, Denzel awoke to Gabrielle snoring heavily next to his ear. He pushed her to the side and sat up, rubbing the sleep from his eyes. He grabbed his phone to check his messages in the group chat. It was silent. The chat was never silent. Denzel didn't know if he should be constantly around Charm to make sure she was okay, or if he should be giving her space. It was weird for him because he didn't want to give her space. He wanted to be there at her side ready for when she needed him. But then he looked over at his sleeping girlfriend. She was pretty beyond reason. That was something he always knew. But sometimes it just didn't matter about being pretty on the outside. And Charm wasn't just beautiful outwards. She was beautiful inwards, and that's what Denzel wanted. He knew it would hurt Gabby. But it would hurt her even more staying with her when he knew he just didn't want her like he used to.

CHAPTER TWENTY-FIVE

"I'm gonna need you to get up and get yourself together," Jason said entering the guest room where Charm was occupied. Her phone had been shut off because Terrell wouldn't stop calling her. But it had been a week since his betrayal and Charm hadn't left Jason's place. Not even to paint.

"Jase just leave me alone," She pouted. "I'm not bothering you."

"Well ya making my room musty, how about that?" Jase opened all the windows to get some air in. It was a nice day out in LA, and Charm shouldn't be missing this sunshine because of that dirt bag.

"I want you up before I leave for work. You need to get outside. It's been a week for Pete's sake."

"Can you make me some hot coco?" she asked.

"You finished up my damn coco! I'll bring you some later. But come on I really want you out of this bed. And in a shower, like right now."

"What sense does it make?" Charm asked. "Denzel hasn't even been here in two days." Denzel was diligent in coming to see her but for the past two days he hadn't shown up.

"Maybe because he does have a girlfriend. And maybe because she doesn't want to crowd you. And besides, he texted me earlier. He's coming over to see you today."

"Really?" Charm asked sitting up.

"Yes really. Your phone is off so you probably didn't get his message." Charm quickly grabbed for her phone. She turned it on and waited for it to get booted up. She immediately cleared the missed calls from Terrell and looked at the text messages Denzel was sending her. He was coming to see her. Charm hopped out of bed quickly. She needed to shower and brush her damn hair!

"Look at that huh," Jason said shaking his head. "You got is bad sis." Instead of entertaining him, Charm just kept quiet and went to freshen up.

Jason didn't leave his home for work until Denzel arrived. The man looked relieved to be seeing Charm, just like Charm was relieved to see him. Knowing Denzel was there, Jason was fine with leaving her alone. Denzel walked with large strides to the bedroom

Charm was staying in. After a knock she granted him entry.

"Hey baby girl," he greeted.

"Hi," She smiled at him. She was wearing a large t-shirt and sitting in the middle of the bed. She smelled fresh out of the shower but her skin was as vibrant as he was used to.

"When was the last time you were outside?" he asked her. She shrugged.

"You're letting him win this way," Denzel told her.

"What else am I supposed to do? Besides painting I don't know how else to get my feelings out, and I just don't feel like painting. And I don't want to be seen. So yeah…"

"Alright that's it. Come on, get dressed."

"Denzel I just-"

"Either you're going dressed like how you are Charm, or you get up and put some clothes on."

"But I don't want to have to dress up!" she exclaimed.

"I didn't ask you to get dressed up. Some put something on. That's it. Come on." He grabbed her by the ankle and dragged her off the bed. When she was close enough to him, he took her by the arm to help her stand up. They came face to face, invading each other's space at the motion. Not wanting to have to battle to kiss her again, he moved away from her.

"Get dressed," He ordered one more time before leaving the room the giver her some privacy. He waited in Jason's foyer for 15 minutes before Charm emerged from the room. She was wearing her overalls again with a tight crop top shirt underneath so she was showing a little bit of skin on the sides of her overalls. Denzel smiled when he saw her. He loved the way she could dress up but then dress down and have it be so natural to her.

"Lead the way," she said to him.

"Let's go," He smiled opening the front door and gesturing for her to leave first. Denzel didn't have any experience for what she was going through, but he had experience with tying to cope with emotions. But his emotions wasn't broken heartedness; it was anger. Brianna wasn't joking about his incredible hulk. So he used the place he was taking her as his sanctuary whenever he felt as if he was about to go green and rip someone to shreds.

"You aren't kidnapping me are you?" she questioned as he drove to a part of town she didn't recognize.

"I doubt you'd care if I was," He responded.

"Yes, that's true," She smiled. Honestly she didn't care where he took her. She could go anywhere with him. But when they finally pulled up to the building of their destination, Charm gasped.

"A gun range?" She exclaimed. "I don't shoot guns!"

"Relax baby girl. I know you don't. But trust me. It's not as terrible as you're thinking. I come at least every weekend." Charm was very much unsure about shooting a gun. Inside the building she jumped every time she heard a gun go off. But Denzel comforted her, keeping her at his side with a hand at her back. She let him take control of everything including choosing the gun for her. He paid for their rounds before they were led to a booth.

"You'll be okay," Denzel assured her. She stood looking at the white paper of the body outline down the corridor.

"I don't know," She said shivering at just looking at the gun in his hand.

"Hold it Charm," He ordered. He placed the gun in her hand and made her hold it properly. He set her in a proper stance and turned her to face her target.

"Look at it," He said pointing to it. "Now aim your gun at it." Charm aimed her gun at the sheet of paper.

"Everything that upsets you, makes you angry, or has hurt you is now on that sheet of paper. Here, you have the power to eliminate those things Charm. So I want you to shoot until you have nothing left to try and eliminate. Do you understand?" Charm nodded slowly. While she stayed in her stance, Denzel put the protective glasses on her face and slapped the ear muffs onto her ears. He stood behind her just in case she lost control of the weapon. Charm felt silly with the weapon in her hand, but once she envisioned what Denzel told her to, all she saw was Terrell on that sheet of baby. And once she saw his face, she couldn't stop shooting. The place was loud, shoots going off at every angle, so when Charm screamed as she fired the gun repeatedly no one realized it. And that scream signified the release of all her pent up anger, all her pent up sadness. When her the bullet chamber was empty, Charm was still clicking the trigger away trying to shoot some more. Realizing there were no more bullets, Charm looked at the gun. There was an emotional drain that filtered through her but when she turned and looked at Denzel there was something else that she felt. She didn't care why she was at the gun range. Only that she was there with a man who made her feel free. And for the first time in a week, Charm felt good.

"Thanks Denzel," She said to him. He smiled and kissed her forehead. Oh Charm wanted so much more but she didn't dare press that issue again. Not after the way he put her in her place the last time. She didn't want to feel that rejection even if he was right.

They spent two hours at the gun range, where Charm continued to shoot at Terrell's head until her arms were too weak to hold the gun up. But then she loved to watch Denzel shoot with such precision. How could something like that attract her too?

"So tell me Charm, how do you feel?" Denzel asked her as they walked back to his car after their session.

"I feel good!" She exclaimed. She hugged him tightly not even realizing that she was doing it until he cleared his throat. Charm backed off immediately.

"Let me break up with Gabby before you do that again okay?"

"So you're for sure going to break up with her?" Charm asked. Denzel only nodded. He seemed to retreat into his thoughts for a few minutes before he came to and looked back at Charm.

"What do you feel for now?" Denzel asked her. She shrugged. "Come on Charm. You must want something right now. Or to do something."

"Well. I kind of do feel for a milkshake," She said.

"What's you're favorite flavor?" he asked teasingly.

"Chocolate," She winked. She went around to the passenger side and got into his car.

"I'll give you chocolate alright," He mumbled before getting in the car himself.

● ● ●
179

CHAPTER TWENTY-SIX

Denzel stared at the text message he'd sent to Gabrielle. He wasn't going to break up with her through text, but he was planning on finally sitting down with her to talk about their future. But since spending so much more time with Charm Denzel realized that it wasn't fair to himself or to Gabrielle to be in a relationship where his heart wasn't in it. And ever since Gabby brought up the marriage thing he knew it would come back and create problems even if she was putting on a front at the moment. And then he realized that there were always things about Gabrielle he just put up with because he thought he had to. Or he was just doing it because he didn't want to end something that he'd been doing for so long. For a while it was always him and Gabrielle. There was no other woman in his life. And not to have her would definitely be strange. But it was what was right.

He finally planned to talk to her and call things off even if it was going to hurt the both of them. They had set up a date for later on in the night so Denzel could get some work done at the gallery. Ever since he took her to the gun range Charm started spending more time at the gallery instead of being cooped up at Jason's place. Her paintings were still a little sad, but not as sad as what she was trying to paint before. That was progress to him. And plus, they spent every day together no matter what they had to do.

His concentration was completely on the task he had in front of him but that was thrown off when the front door banged and rattled. Charm jumped as well trying to see who was at the door.

"If it's Terrell I don't want to see him," She rushed out. She'd been ignoring his calls and figured he would get the picture. But then she always thought that maybe he would show up to the gallery to confront her.

"Long as I'm here I got you baby girl. Trust me." Charm nodded feeling confident Denzel would take care of her. He went to the door and looked out.

"Well it's not your crazy husband. It's my crazy girlfriend." Denzel opened the door for Gabrielle who was fuming outside.

"The lounge?" She shouted at him. "You haven't been around me for how many days and you want to take me to a lounge instead of a nice restaurant? What is wrong with you Denzel?"

"You do realize this is my place of work right?" he asked her.

"Work?! This is not work! It's finger painting for Pete's sake!"

"Seriously Gabrielle? That's where you want to take this?"

"Where have you-" Gabrielle noticed Charm. "Are you fucking her?" She asked bluntly.

"No." Denzel answered.

"Liar," She snapped. "Where were you all those nights when I texted you and you said you were busy? Was it because of her?"

"She was going through something Gabrielle. And like any other friend would be, I was there for her."

"As in what? Fucked her problems away?" Denzel took a deep breath. In a minute he was about to blow up on her. She knew anger was a problem for him but yet she provoked him. When he reached his boiling point he wasn't someone you wanted to be around.

"Well since you want to do this now Gabrielle then let's do it now. I was bringing you to the lounge tonight because I want to call it quits. You know I could have just texted it to you. But no, I thought we'd go to a laid back spot and I'll talk with you about why I think it's best we don't continue on. But then you show up here, where I work mind you, and have total disregard for the art I do and I really don't have to take it or to answer to your accusations."

"Wait? Call it quits? Who do you think you are breaking up with me? We're supposed to get married Denzel." Gabrielle's panic mode began to filter in. Denzel was the only man she'd had for ten years. And he was ready to just up and leave her? No, she didn't want that.

"I already told you I don't have the desire to marry you. Nothing has changed about that."

"You know what-" She balled her hands up into fists and began pacing. "Is it because of her?"

"Why does it matter Gabrielle? Me and you just don't work as a couple anymore. And I'm not willing to stay in something that's leading nowhere." Gabrielle looked at Charm with eyes filled with hate.

"Think you'd just take him away from me?"

"I'm not doing anything," Charm answered quietly. Gabrielle screamed and tried to rush up on Charm but Denzel grabbed her and pushed her back.

"I don't think so," He said. "Not that one." Gabrielle slapped him in the face. He just had to stand there and take it.

"You know Brianna will beat your ass if I tell her you did that," Denzel gritted. Charm balled her hands into fists not even realizing she was doing it until she looked down. She found out that she didn't like other women slapping Denzel. And she wanted to do something about it. Only the moment she stood Denzel pointed at her.

"Don't stoop to her level baby girl," He ordered.

"Baby girl?" Gabrielle shouted. "Seriously?!" She began pacing again. "I knew some bullshit like this was gonna happen. You were gonna stand in my face and not propose to me after I gave you ten years of my fucking life. And now you're fucking around on me behind my back." She shook her head hard.

"I'm happy as fuck I didn't keep it," She whispered to herself. Even though she mumbled Denzel heard part of what she said.

"Excuse me?" He asked.

"What?!"

"What did you just say?" Gabrielle rolled her eyes.

"I don't have to tell you shit," She spat. She turned to leave but Denzel jumped in front of her and blocked the door.

"I'm not playing with you Gabrielle. Repeat what you said!"

"I said I'm happy as fuck I didn't keep it!" She snapped at him.

"Keep what?" Denzel asked shakily.

"That night I wanted you to propose to me at that restaurant was because I found out I was pregnant. After ten years I thought to myself, you know what if I'm going to sacrifice my body and give you a baby then you're going to have to do something for me. And that was marry me, and support me. But what'd you do Denzel? You didn't want to get married. And I realized that I wasn't going to carry a baby for a man that wouldn't marry me. Simply put I wanted to have babies with my husband Denzel."

"What in the hell did you do?!"

"When I was gone those few weeks it was because I got an abortion. I needed the recovery time because I knew you'd want to have sex with me so I stayed away." She shrugged.

"So you killed my fucking baby because I wouldn't marry

you? Without even telling me you were carrying my seed in the first place?" Denzel gritted. Gabrielle backed up seeing the heat in Denzel's eyes.

"That's the price you pay for not willing to commit," She sputtered.

"Commit? You can't even spend the night with me in my loft cause it's not luxurious enough for you. You can't be natural faced around me because you think you're fucking Kim Kardashian or some shit. You don't even respect my fucking art and you want me to put a ring on your finger? You want me to give you my last name?" Gabrielle continued to back up until Denzel grabbed her wrists and held onto her.

"Remember in college? When we had that pregnancy scare?" Gabrielle nodded rapidly.

"And I specifically told you Gabrielle that no matter what we were going through, no matter what our relationship was like, abortion was never going to be an option to me. Don't you remember that?!"

"Yes I remember."

"So why in the fuck would you kill my seed and not tell me?" Charm was startled at Denzel's tone. Everything in his demeanor had changed and he wasn't that easy going guy she loved to be around. He was angry and looked ready to smack fire out of Gabrielle. Charm could understand his emotion. She knew how it felt to lose a baby, and here this woman was willingly aborting something her body naturally conceived.

Gabrielle was sorry she opened her big mouth in her frustration and told him something she vowed she was never going to reveal. There was no coming back from this. Denzel was never going to forgive her.

"You're hurting me Denzel," She squealed. Denzel squeezed her wrist tighter. Charm decided she couldn't sit there and watch him hurt a female. She rushed over to them and tried to split them apart.

"Denzel let her go," Charm ordered pulling at his hands. As if snapping out of a trance he looked directly at Charm. The hurt in his eyes was a mirror image of the way she felt inside.

"It's okay baby boy," She said to him. She smiled in an attempt to further relax him and it worked. He let go of Gabrielle immediately.

"You need to get out," Charm said turning to Gabrielle.

"Now."

"I'm not leaving until me and Denzel figure out what we need to do so we can be together." Denzel gasped and went to yell at her but Charm beat him to the punch.

"Honey you aborted his damn kid! And you think he'd ever going to trust you to be with you again? Are you for real?"

"You know nothing about us!"

"I know hurt Gabrielle. And the way you just hurt him, he's not willing to talk to you about any type of relationship. And that's just facts. So you have two options," Charm said. "Get out or I call the cops and get you kicked off my property. You choose." Gabrielle looked at Denzel. He couldn't even make eye contact with her anymore.

"Just think. If you'd only proposed to me that night, you'd have a wife to be and a baby on the way." Denzel snapped. He shouted in anger and balled his hand into a fist and charged at her ready to knock her teeth from her mouth.

"Denzel no!" Charm yelled jumping in front of him. Of course that stopped all his momentum. He wasn't going to put his hands on Charm. He couldn't.

"Are you a woman beater?" She asked him.

"No! But she knows I can't control my fucking anger when I'm pissed off!"

"Look at me," Charm snapped. "Control yourself baby boy. Because even if she's an inconsiderate bitch, I can't allow you to hit her. Or do you want me to call the cops on your ass too?" Denzel gasped at her. She waved a finger at him before looking at Gabrielle.

"You still here?" She asked. Gabrielle rushed passed them and left the gallery. But just because she was leaning now didn't mean she had completely given up. She was going to get her man.

Denzel watched her leave, the urge to snatch her up still deeply embedded in his soul. It was taking a great deal to try and control him. He started to pace.

"I could have been a dad," He said looking at Charm. Charm sighed.

"And I could have been a mom remember? And who was there to comfort me and tell me that everything was going to be okay? Wasn't it you?" He nodded. "Some things happen for a reason Denzel. I'm not in no way supporting what she did, but it happened and hurting her won't undo it."

"You're right," He said. "And I didn't mean to get that angry in front of you." Charm smiled at him.

"I um, I can't work anymore. Not after this. I think I'm gonna go home," Denzel said.

"Oh." Charm understood his mood was shot but she didn't want to be alone.

"Do you think you'd want to come with me?" He asked her.

"To your place?" She asked.

"Yeah, to my place."

"Okay yes, I'll come with you. I don't want to be alone anyway and Jason is still at work."

"Don't tell Brianna about what happened," He said. "You were able to stop her from going after Terrell, but if I told her this then there's no stopping her from whopping Gabrielle's ass."

"Oh I believe you completely."

"Good," He smiled.

Denzel took Charm's hand and left the gallery with her. He didn't know why he was bringing her to his place but the urge just overcame him. And he couldn't stop himself from asking her to come with him. When they arrived at his loft, she actually stood in the doorway looking in with her mouth open.

"Wow this place is amazing," She said. "I love the openness and the view."

"Thanks a lot," He replied. She entered the house fully and began looking at all his artwork hung up on the walls.

"You're amazing," She gawked. "Just purely talented."

"Look at that one," He said pointing to the canvas of the portrait he did of her.

"No," she gasped. "No you didn't paint me and hang me up."

"I display all my work," He said. "And you're part of my work."

"How much would you sell me for?" she asked.

"No price tag," He answered. "I'm not so lousy in the kitchen why don't I make you something to eat?" he asked her.

"Or I could cook for you," Charm countered. "I don't mind it and cooking is therapeutic."

"Okay sure." While Denzel sat on a stool around the counter, Charm made herself comfortable in his kitchen. She searched through his fridge and cabinets until she found something quick and easy to make. While the pasta boiled, Charm found a bottle of champagne. She popped it open and poured them both a glass.

"Terrell doesn't really like my painting either," She said. "He doesn't bother me over it but he'd never been to my gallery."

"And you were okay with that? Enough to marry him?"

"He didn't display his displeasure until we were already married. And I thought it was petty to get a divorce because he doesn't think painting pays the bills. But you realized that Gabrielle wasn't going to respect your work and I'm happy you didn't just settle and marry her anyway." Denzel just shrugged.

"I've never seen you that angry before. Kind of scared me."

"I'm sorry," He said. "There's just some things that are genetic I suppose."

"I don't understand."

"My father had a short fuse. The littlest thing could get him riled up. And then there was the fact that he was always drunk. So for my childhood I had an angry drunken father who liked the beat the crap out of me for no reason it seems. As I grew up I realized my temper was just as short. When I got mad, man I got mad. I realized that I didn't want to be like my father. So even if I had a temper I was going to make sure I didn't make it worse by ever being drunk. Now that I'm older I can control my anger. I don't get angry so quick anymore. But once I do get pissed off, it's hard for me to turn it off. And if you weren't there Charm, I would have put my hands on Gabrielle. And I promise you that's not the type of man I am."

"I know it's not," she said softly.

"That's the fastest I've ever come down from being pissed off," He said. "When you stepped in front of me and I saw your face all my anger just died out and I could actually hear myself think.

"Then I'm so happy I was there to help you. Especially after hearing the news you heard." Denzel shook his head just thinking about it.

"No matter how I feel about her Charm, I'd never deny my kid. I'd never tell her to abort and I'd never not want to be a part of her life if she was carrying my baby." Charm went up to him and stood between his legs. She caressed his face to try and keep him relaxed.

"What hurt me the most about Terrell cheating is the fact that she's pregnant. So I lost the baby I was carrying for him, and now his mistress gets the have his baby. It may sound evil but…I hate her so much for it."

"Don't taint your heart with hate baby girl. Not over that. Karma is a bitch you remember."

"And you, you have so much more chances to have a baby again. Gabrielle will regret doing this to you." Charm wrapped her arms around his neck.

"Please don't stop me this time," She whispered. She inched in and thankfully he didn't stop her as she kissed him softly. Denzel imagined what her lips would taste like the moment he met her. And that didn't compare to actually feeling them. They fit together so perfectly it was like they didn't need to tell each other how they wanted to kiss. They were just able to follow the rhythm. When she opened her mouth, Denzel invaded her with his tongue and allowed her to do the same. The kiss had gotten to deep, it almost began sloppy. He was hard a granite in his pants and yearning for so much more than a kiss.

Charm was weeping from her womanly core. Her counterpart was begging and pleading for some attention. She was moaning and shifting on her feet repeatedly and Denzel noticed.

"You want more?" he asked her against her lips. Charm's only answer was a high pitched squeal. That's all he needed. He unbuttoned her jeans and delved his hand inside. Her core was hot and slippery with her arousal. When he slipped his finger inside he nearly fell off the stool. She threw her head back and moaned as he caressed her clit. Since she was throwing her head back, Denzel continued to kiss her sweet neck, nipping at her flesh. He carefully inserted his finger into her channel. He didn't want to just caress her clit. He wanted to find her g-spot and rock her world with just his finger. And that's what he did. Digging deep he found the rough spot then added a second finger to her tight sheath. Her nails dug into his shoulders.

"Oh my god," She gasped. She straightened her head and looked directly at him, with her mouth parted in ecstasy as he was about to make her orgasm. Fuck! If only he had his dick inside her at that moment. Just feeling her walls tighten and flutter around his fingers made him yearn for their bodies to be connected. Denzel stood and held her around the waist as she came and nearly fell over. She took a moment to catch her breath. Denzel pulled his hands from her pants. She watched with wide eyed as he licked his fingers. She tasted so damn good.

"The-the food," Charm stumbled. She tripped over her own

feet as she rushed to the stove to cut the fire off. She looked back at Denzel who was licking his lips as if he was satisfied at what he'd just tasted on his fingers. Charm didn't know what the hell to do. She start fumbling around the kitchen to finish cooking but what she wanted was to get on top of Denzel's lap and ride him into bliss. She didn't know what to do.

"Are you okay?" He asked her? Besides her soaked panties and trembling pussy lips. Oh she was perfectly fine.

"I'm okay," She squeaked out. "Dinner should be ready soon. It's spaghetti doesn't take that long." Denzel nodded and just sat there as he watched her finished cooking. She would keep looking back at him and he didn't know what that meant. Was he wrong for going there with her? Or was he terribly right? But still she didn't say anything to him. She finished preparing the spaghetti and shared it out in a plate for both of them with some more champagne. He gave her props for making a good meal when he hardly had anything to cook in the first place.

They ate in silence and sipped in silence, but their stares, they were never able to break it. He couldn't stop looking at her, and she couldn't stop looking at him. At one point he even sat forward and licked the sauce off her lips for her. It made her jump but she accepted what he did and smiled at him. Once they were finished eating, he washed up for her since she did all the cooking. When he was done he jerked his head in a motion telling her to follow him. They went down the hall and entered his bedroom.

"Get comfortable," He said. "I know I'm about to. Especially after what just happened." He pointed to his bed and Charm reluctantly got in. He sat in his lounge chair after taking off his jeans and changing into basketball shorts. He rested his head back and closed his eyes.

"Can I use your sketchbook?" Charm asked seeing it on his night table stand.

"Go for it." She took his sketchbook and taking the initiative she turned on his speakers and connected her phone to it so she could play music. She had a list called her heartbreak list and that's all she was ever listening to. When Leona Lewis's 'Better in Time' started playing Denzel groaned and picked his head up.

"You and this sad ass music," He said.

"What? I can't help it."

"Well it's gonna put me in my feelings too now. With what

just went down with Gabrielle. But we were just making out in the kitchen and for that moment we were actually happy. Why revert back to this sad shit?"

"I'm sorry," she said.

"Don't apologize. Just play something else." Charm paused the song. They stayed in silence for a moment.

"Okay MC, why don't you pick a song then?" Denzel tossed his phone to her.

"Just hook it up and let whatever song comes first play. I guarantee it's better than that song you just had on."

"Fine." Charm sat up as she connected his phone. She opened his music app and without looking at what song was queued up she just hit play. 'Nobody' by Keith Sweat blasted through the speakers. The shock of it made her drop his phone from her hands.

"You did that on purpose," He stated.

"I didn't, I swear." Denzel swallowed and looked away from her. The last thing the both of them needed to hear was a damn love making song. An old school one at that. Or maybe it was exactly what they needed to hear. He was still confused on whether he should try to make another move on her or not. And Charm knew she should change the song but she couldn't. She just sat there like an idiot trying to refrain from looking at Denzel as he was trying to refrain from looking at her. She picked up the sketchbook and quickly started doodling because she just needed something to do. But then her eyes began to stray and low and behold she was looking at him again. His hair was pulled back from his face like it always was and his chocolate skin was glistening in the natural light coming inside the room. Feeling her eyes on him, Denzel slowly looked at Charm. The lust was written all over her face. It was so blatant it was as if she wanted him know exactly what she was thinking. In his head he kept telling himself he couldn't do it. That they shouldn't do it. The both of them were two hurt ass people that would only make shit worse for themselves if they actually did it. But what about what just happened in the kitchen? She'd wanted to kiss him and she'd wanted him to do more to her. So she wanted to have more. Just like Denzel did.

The song was ending soon and he knew as long as the song ended, they'd be safe. All of this feeling would go away. And then Denzel could think straight. But then Charm picked up his phone and put the song on repeat. It started again and Denzel just lost it. It was clear what they both wanted.

"Fuck it," He breathed getting up from his chair. She crawled backyard on the bed as he got in the bed and crawled between her thighs. The first connection of their lips were magical but this was even more so. Denzel felt the pleasure senses of his brain going off rapidly as he tasted her strawberry flavored mouth. She kissed ever so delicately, thrusting her tongue in and out of his mouth rhythmically. When she tried to wrap her legs around his waist, Denzel realized she was still wearing her pants.

He broke away from the kiss and sat up so he could take her pants off. After he did that, he pulled her shirt off to leave her in her underwear only.

"You're overdressed," She breathed. She didn't have to say more. Denzel pulled his shorts down, tore off his t-shirt then yanked his underwear down. Her eyes went wide at his erection but she didn't say anything.

Charm was right to call him Tall and Chocolate when she first met him. His penis was the perfect reflection of that sentiment. But his girth was something she didn't expect. After all Brianna had told her it wasn't that impressive. And here she thought Brianna always kept it real.

Moving back in between her legs, Denzel grabbed at her underwear and slowly pulled it down. Since he was doing that already she snapped her bra off and pulled it off her chest. He stayed where he was kneeling in between her open legs and just looking at her naked flesh. When she tried to cover up because his stare was getting too much, he smacked her hands away.

Finally, he grabbed her legs and pushed them as far back as they could go and held them there. Charm looked between her legs and watched as he leaned over and swiped his tongue up her womanly lips slowly. Her body naturally trembled but he held her down in a way that meant she wasn't going anywhere. As if teasing her, he used the tip of his tongue and played around with her clit before finally sucking it into his mouth. Charm let out a suffocated moan as he began to relentlessly suckle on her clit, alternating being using the tip of his tongue, the flat of his tongue, and then his lips when he sucked. She tried to move her legs forward so he wasn't pinning her down, but his grip didn't loosen. So she sat there being assaulted by his mouth and could do nothing about it, but scream out in pleasure.

He stuck his tongue inside her channel and she exploded around his tongue. Her body jerked so hard, her ass came up off the bed even as he held her down. He made one last pass over her clit, sucking up all her juices before he let her legs down and sat back up. He licked his lips in satisfaction. He held her hips and yanked her down closer to him. He hooked one of her legs over the crook of his elbow as he lined his erection up with her opening. Charm couldn't help but close her eyes as he stretched her deliciously. Inch by inch, he slowly entered her. Denzel tossed his head back as he continued to enter her. She was slick with her juices and his entry was easy. She had tasted so fucking delicious and she felt the same damn way. He was completely inside her and it was like he couldn't even move. He just sat there inside of her savoring the way her walls pulsed around him. Being inside her just felt…right. And for Charm she hadn't felt another man's penis in ten years and it should have been strange to her. But where Terrell's penis had fit inside her comfortably, Denzel's was fitting inside her perfectly. She felt him everywhere. Even though his girth had scared her a little it was the exact thing she needed to fill her completely.

Charm began moving her hips to try and get him to start moving. Denzel got the point and pulled out of her, stroking her slowly. She gasped and tilted her head back as he continued pumping inside her at a slow steady pace.

"Denzel," She gasped, clawing at his arms. Terrell had always satisfied her in bed. She never had to worry about that. But it was so strange for her body to be experiencing the feel of another man inside her. It was strange yes, but it was different. And it felt incredible. Denzel looked down between their bodies loving the way their flesh tones looked against one another, loving the way it looked as he made love to her body. Her muscles began to flutter around him so he hooked her other leg over his other arm and opened her legs wider as he began swinging his hips freely. He kissed her sweat pebbled forehead as she began to orgasm around him. Curse words left his mouth at the tightening of her insides as her orgasm rocked through her. He wanted to last long, man he wanted to but she felt too damn good. He maneuvered both her legs until he could brace himself on the back of her thighs. With the change of position her eyes popped open.

Charm tried to push at his abdomen but that didn't stop him from continuing to pump inside her. He kissed her sloppily, sharing breaths with her as their bodies shared pleasure with each other. She dug her nails into his sweat ridden back. Her moans lifted to the high ceiling and beyond.

"It feels so good," She screamed. Her insides began to gush and the softness became too much for him to resist. She clenched him inside her and Denzel lost his control.

"Charm!" He bellowed as he had a back breaking orgasm. He pulled out of her but orgasmed all around her small core. Her body shook as she had reached her climax and was riding the waves. None of them moved. Denzel kept his eyes closed until his tremors left him. Still leaning over her, the both of them fought to catch their breaths when they finally looked at each other. Denzel wiped the sweat from her face before leaning down to kiss her deeply. When he pulled away she drew at his bottom lip.

"Shit just got real," Charm giggled.

"Hell yeah it did," Denzel smiled. He kissed her on the forehead. He flopped down next to her and looked at his limp penis. When he looked at Charm she was looking at him with a heated look. And that was all it took for his penis to be waking up again.

"You're so beautiful Charm," He admitted. "You're soul, your features, just everything about you." Charm gazed into his eyes. She began shaking her head.

"What?" he asked.

"I've known Terrell for a long time. We dated for five years and then he proposed and we've been married for five years. But in all that time Denzel, I swear to you that Terrell has never looked at me the way you're looking at me right now. And those chocolate eyes, that's what captivated me in the first place. That's what let me know something was different about you. I can get lost in them all day Denzel." She didn't break eye contact as she slithered her way on top of him. Denzel helped her align herself with his erection before she could slide down. And when she did, she seated herself perfectly on him. He could still feel the flutters from her previous orgasm.

She began to ride him, and no matter how much pleasure overcame her, she forced herself to keep her eyes open so she could retain eye contract with him. And that only enhanced her pleasure more. Staring into his smoldering chocolate eyes, and feeling his girth tunnel through her was all she needed. Denzel looked at the perfection riding him and he just knew that no matter what happened between them, he wanted to have her to himself. Terrell fucked up big time. And this was the chance Denzel needed.

Charm fell on top of him getting too weak to ride him. Denzel took control, holding her around his waist and grabbing a handful of her ass. He began to thrust up into her, still without breaking his eye contact with her. She was trying hard not to close her eyes as she began to come again.

"It's okay baby," He breathed. "I'll still be here with you." Her moans began to sound like cries as he continued thrusting up into her. Her eyes finally closed and she came apart. This time he pulled out a second to late, but none of them cared.

"Fuck!" He shouted coming hard again. His tip was so sensitive when he put it back inside her to complete his release he couldn't even handle it. His body began to tremble. Charm held him tightly, feeling like she could fall asleep in this exact position.

"What does this mean for us?" Charm whispered to him. "I want to divorce Terrell but I can't move too fast."

"It's fine Charm I get it. And I'm not asking you for anything right now. I'm just going to tell you that I won't ever break your heart like he did." Charm looked down at him before kissing him deeply. She didn't think Denzel could ever break her heart like Terrell did. He just wasn't that kind of man.

CHAPTER TWENTY-SEVEN

In the morning when Denzel awoke, he couldn't believe he was lying next to Charm. He couldn't believe they'd made love either. Sitting up slowly didn't do him any good. Charm's eyes popped open and she smiled at him.

"Morning," She greeted. Denzel kissed her lightly in response.

"How'd you sleep?" he asked her.

"Really, really good," She groaned. "Jason's probably worried about me. I didn't come home to his place last night."

"Jason will be fine. He knows that you're with me." Charm sat up, letting the sheet fall away from her body, revealing her bare breasts. The quakes of her orgasms from the night before were still in her body. She couldn't believe she'd went there with Denzel but she didn't regret it. In fact, she was questioning if she should reach over and get some more. She wanted more.

"If you want some Charm. All you gotta do is take it," Denzel told her, seeing the way she was looking at him.

"I've got morning breath," She said covering her mouth. "I can't just hop on your chocolate stick, even if I wanted to."

"You're too cute," He laughed. "I don't care about that," He said. He pulled down the sheets to show her his erection. Charm licked her lips. She just loved how the veins on his shaft popped out and trailed pathways down his wood.

"Come here," He said lowly pulling her towards him. Charm inched over, and swung her legs over his lips ready to sit on his erection.

The sound of the door opening made her halt. There was a loud gasp and Charm's heart fell. Please don't let that be Gabrielle, she begged silently. Charm couldn't be caught like this with a man that was fresh out of a relationship by his Ex.

"What in the hell!" Charm felt relief at hearing Brianna's voice. But then she realized the position she was in. She slid off Denzel's lap and tried to cover her naked body with the sheets.

"Brie, why didn't you tell me you were coming?!" Denzel asked. Brianna had a key to his place just like he had a key to hers, but she always announced when she was coming over. Instead of answering him she looked just back and forth between the two naked people in the bed.

"You're not cheating on Gabby are you?" She asked. "You'd allow him to cheat on his girlfriend Charm after what your husband did to you?"

"No, no!" Denzel spoke up for her. "Me and Gabby we're finished."

"You know what I'll just go. You two can continue whatever it is the hell you're doing." She shook her head, as disappointment blended into her features. She loved Charm and they were so cool, but the last thing Brianna wanted for her best friend was the become to rebound. She knew that Charm and Denzel would eventually fall for each other, but she worried that it was still to soon. After a heartbreak like what Charm suffered it wasn't an idea to be with any man. And Brianna just didn't want to see her best friend get hurt.

Charm jumped from the bed after Brianna left. She felt so embarrassed for being caught how they were, but she knew what Brianna was probably thinking.

"Can you take me back to Jason's?" Charm asked Denzel grabbing her clothes and shoving them on. She didn't care about showering. She just had to leave.

"Charm, it's ok-"

"Better yet, I'll get an Uber. I don't want to take you out of your bed anyways." Charm quickly set herself up for an Uber that was already three minutes away.

"Thanks so much for opening your home to me," She told him. She went to his side and kissed him on the cheek before she was hurrying out of the room. She needed to get out of there, and fast. She'd deal with the repercussions for that they did later.

****

Jason already knew what Charm and Denzel had done via Brianna. But when Charm got back to his place she just smiled and went straight to take a shower. Jason cooked breakfast and waited for her to come back into the kitchen. when she did, she was wearing a fresh T-shirt and shorts. She began eating as if nothing was up.

"So you ain't gonna tell your bestie you was riding a chocolate dick?" Jason asked. Charm groaned.

"I feel so stupid," She said. "Brianna caught us."

"Don't feel like that. Hell I think you needed to get fucked by the right man anyways." Charm sighed hard.

"By the way, Terrell showed up earlier. Thankfully he didn't cause any problems just wanted to see if you were here. I told him no, he checked all the rooms then he left. Honey, you'd better serve him divorce papers and I mean soon."

"I know," Charm mumbled. She hadn't even thought about going to a lawyer to get their divorce started. She'd just been all over the place mentally.

Having sex with Denzel didn't make things better. Maybe for her body but not for her mind. After eating, she stayed in her room all day just doodling in her sketch book. By late afternoon, Jason came into her room smiling at her. She didn't know why until he opened the door completely and saw he had a large bouquet of flowers and edible arrangements in his hands.

"Guess what just came and for who," He sang. Charm sat up and took the flowers. She read the card and smiled at Denzel's words. She took the edible arrangements and popped a fruit into her mouth.

I'll never forget, or regret what we did. Enjoy the arrangements baby girl.

Charm felt gooey inside from those simple words. In all the things that Denzel was, he was just perfect for her. And it felt so strange meeting someone who you matched heart for heart, and soul for soul. Her feelings for him were deep. She picked up her phone and dialed his number. And when they began talking they didn't stop until the late hours of the night.

CHAPTER TWENTY-EIGHT

Terrell waited in front of Charm's gallery. He knew she'd be there soon so all he had to do was wait, and then he'd be able to talk to her. It had been 3 and a half weeks since she left home and he missed her. He figured giving her time was the only way he was going to be able to approach her and she actually talk to him. It was so weird not having her around, and Destiny was all over him. He wasn't interested in carrying out any type of relationship with her. Maybe the sex was good but he didn't want to be with Destiny. Not when his mind was on Charm 24/7. But with the baby in Destiny's belly she was going to have a place in his life. After losing other babies there was no way Terrell was going to let his one go. He just needed to find a way for Charm to be okay with it.

He knew she was staying at Jason's and after a failed attempt of talking to her, he chilled out for a couple more days. But he was tired of waiting now. If he did so any longer she would have thought he didn't care enough to come and talk to her. But he cared. And he was going to bring her home with him.

After waiting by the gallery for a couple hours he finally spotted Charm's car. She pulled up to the gallery and parked before getting out with a canvas in her hand. He expected to see her saddened and a hot mess but it was quite the contrary. She was wearing those overalls again but her skin was glowing and she had a smile on her face as she was talking on her phone.

Terrell hopped out of his vehicle and decided it was time to make his move. He needed to get his wife back. She ended her phone call and opened the door to the gallery. Terrell ran up on her to stop her from closing herself inside.

"Hi Mrs. Robinson," He greeted. Her body froze for a moment before she turned around and sighed. Early this morning Denzel had taken her to breakfast, filling up her stomach will pancakes, bacon, sausages, and muffins before taking her back to Jason's place. He didn't have to take her out to eat or worry about her, but Denzel just did. And it made Charm continue to slowly want him more and more.

"It's Ms. Bradley. How can I help you?"

"Not legally it's not," He smiled. "We're still married." Terrell looked her up and down. Something was different about her.

He leaned forward and sniffed her. She gave him a look.

"What the hell are you doing?" she asked.

"Cologne. You smell like that cologne but it's heavy this time. Instead of your perfume." Charm just shrugged.

"So?"

"Are you fucking someone else?" He asked. Charm didn't answer. "Alright fine. I deserved for you to fuck another man. But we need to work out our shit and move on. Seriously. Destiny means nothing to me. I'm still in love with you."

"You don't love me. Not if you were willing to have sex with another woman. And I'm done talking about this. Leave me alone."

He seriously needed to go away because Denzel was going to show up any minute. They were all supposed to meet at the gallery to get some work done. Ever since Denzel and Charm made love a week ago, they hadn't done it again, but she would never forget it. It was engrained in her brain. And though they both wanted to keep fucking each other's brains out, they refrained from it. which made it all the more special when Denzel did all these nice things for her and wasn't asking for sex in return. After getting treatment like that, Terrell was the last person she wanted to see. When she tried to turn away, Terrell held her arm.

"Can you seriously act like you don't miss me too?" he questioned. "I know what I did was fucked up, but you just don't stop loving someone like that. And you know what I'm saying is true."

"Terrell-" He put a finger to her mouth to silence her. "Let me prove that deep down you still want me. That you can come back to me." He cupped her face in his hands and kissed her lightly. It was such a stark contrast from the way Denzel kissed her that Charm just knew something wasn't right. She suddenly didn't like Terrell's kisses. Not when she'd been receiving something deeper and more sensual under the ministrations of Denzel.

"Charm." Charm jumped and pushed Terrell away from her when she heard Denzel's voice.

"Denzel," She breathed. He stood there with his arms crossed. The hurt was in his expression but he didn't say anything.

"Terrell was just leaving," Charm said. Denzel shook his head. He knew it was going to be hard for Charm to pull away from her marriage but he didn't expect to find her kissing on the very man that cheated on her.

"We can talk about this when you're ready," Denzel said. "But excuse me so I can go inside. You can finish up with your husband out here."

"No! You know I'm getting a divorce. Don't push me away. Not like he did." Denzel took a deep breath.

"Sorry baby girl. You know I'm not trying to hurt you. But what you want me to say?" Denzel asked.

"Look man," Terrell cut in. "No hard feelings and shit. But she's still my wife. She's always going to be mine. And we're not getting a divorce no matter what the hell she thinks."

"Terrell don't say that you know-" The sound of a gunshot broke off her next words. The people walking along the street all screamed and ducked for cover. Charm hit the ground as Denzel rushed to cover her as another shot rang out. Who was possibly shooting in the daytime like this? But Denzel had her secured and safe under him. She wondered who was hit.

"Denzel are you okay?" she rushed out. "Did you get hurt?"

"I'm fine baby girl, are you alright?"

"Yes." Charm peeked out from under Denzel's cover.

"TERRELL!" Charm screamed. She pushed out from under Denzel and rushed to Terrell who was kneeling on the pavement with blood dripping from his mouth. He fell back before Charm could catch him. She pressed her hand to his wound.

"Someone call an ambulance!" She shouted. Denzel pulled his phone out and called for help as he watched the woman he thought he was finally going to have lean over her husband crying.

"Ambulance is coming," Denzel said lowly.

"Don't you dare die," Charm cried. Even if she hated Terrell for cheating, death wasn't something she'd wish on anyone. Especially not someone she had shared ten years of her life with.

"You're about to be a father for Pete's sake. Stay with me." Terrell grabbed hold of her hand and tried to hold on for as long as he could.

****

Fear filled Gabrielle's body as she ran away. She knew the moment Denzel ended their relationship she was going to go after the woman who took him away from her. If not for their argument he would have never known Gabrielle aborted. And she would have been able to woo him enough to get him to propose. She was such an idiot to abort in the first place. She wasn't even thinking when she'd done it, and now all that anger and hurt she needed to cast out onto someone. If Denzel wasn't going to have her, then he wasn't going to have anyone else. But this had gone terribly wrong. Her bullet was intended for Charm's heart, but instead it struck a man Gabrielle didn't even have a clue who he was. And then when he fell to the ground bleeding from the wound, she felt her stomach collapse. What in the world had she done?

To be continued...

CPSIA information can be obtained
at www.ICGtesting.com
Printed in the USA
LVHW02s1846280518
578746LV00002BA/383/P